# Dark's Dominion

## Book of the Huntress, Volume Two

## Joshua David Bellin

Dark's Dominion

ISBN (paperback): 978-1-7348315-2-8
ISBN (e-book): 978-1-7348315-3-5

Cover design by Valued Creations

for M.C. and V.R., who came a long way

Neither fear nor demons can be regarded by psychology as "earliest" things, impervious to any attempt at discovering their antecedents. It would be another matter if demons really existed. But we know that, like gods, they are creations of the human mind: they were made by something and out of something.

—Sigmund Freud, *Totem and Taboo*

# Prologue

The Skaldi floated in darkness.

Even if it had been able to open its eyes, there would have been nothing to see. Even if it had strained its ears to the utmost, there would have been nothing to hear. It resided in an environment that was total void, with no light, no sound, no motion. The only thing it felt was a warmth that surrounded it on all sides as it hung suspended in the black. Though it couldn't put the feeling into words or conscious thought, it sensed that it was safe, that nothing was required of it except to linger here in blissful unawareness.

The Skaldi stretched and rolled, feeling its body move, testing its limbs. This was new: it hadn't known it had any such thing as body or limbs until these parts slowly unfolded from the central core of its being. It pleased the creature in a way it couldn't express to experience these sensations, how its individual features formed a single whole, how its unity was divided into separate forms with their own functions. Its mouth stretched wide, and in that movement, it discovered that it had a mouth; it couldn't name its mouth or understand what a mouth was for, but it knew that this was another un- tried part of it, with a purpose that would reveal itself in time. Its slender fingers flexed, then curled inward to touch its palms, and it became aware that fingers and palms were entirely different parts, though once again, their ultimate reason for existence was hidden for the time being. One of its skeletal arms jerked—it had two, and they seemed to function in the same way, though not always at the same time—and one of its fingers, somewhat larger than the rest, found its way into the cavity of its mouth. This was another new thing, to feel one part of itself enfolded by another, and it stayed like that for a long while, pleasuring in how it was made.

After a time, however, its finger fell from the orifice of its mouth, and it discovered to its frustration that it had no control over which of its parts moved when or where. Frustration was itself a new discovery, and it produced yet another something new.

The Skaldi opened its mouth and moaned.

The sound of its voice shocked it. The atmosphere in which it floated seemed to be agitated by the sound, which returned to its ears again and again like waves beating against the shore of self. It wanted to stop the sound, but it discovered that, as with its fingers and arms and hands, it had no ability to control its voice. The moaning continued of its own volition; if anything, the harder the Skaldi tried to quell the noise, the louder and more insistent it became. The Skaldi had discovered pain, and longing, and want, and it did not like those sensations at all. They made it feel empty, and the emptiness made it hunger for fulfillment.

The Skaldi flailed in the darkness, but there was nothing to find. Every so often, its fingers brushed against a part of its own body, and it felt momentarily appeased, but the relief didn't last long. There was something missing, a space inside that it could not fill on its own.

A space, it gradually dawned on the creature, that must be filled by another.

The Skaldi raged at this discovery. It seemed the cruelest of tricks to be trapped here, in this formless place, while the thing it needed was withheld from its grasp. Baffled anger made it frantic, and the moans it had hoped to smother mounted higher and higher. It wanted to force itself free of this place, to track down the one it sought and make their flesh its own. But there was no way out, no way to command its uncoordinated limbs to work together to achieve its purpose, and so all it could do was wail.

Then, amidst its wretched moans, the Skaldi heard another sound.

It was completely unlike the sound of its own voice. This second sound was steady, and soft, and as regular as the Skaldi's movements were spastic. The sound had a soothing effect on the Skaldi, making its whimpers subside. A finger found its way to its mouth once more, and this time, it stayed put. Even if the Skaldi had possessed words, it couldn't have said what the new sound was, why it affected the squirming creature so. The most it could think was that this was what it had been longing for, the thing that had been promised to fulfill its lack. If it could hold on a little longer, the darkness would recede, and the answer it so desperately craved would be revealed at last.

The Skaldi turned, groping in the dark, and waited to emerge.

# Chapter 1

Michelle squinted into a blood-red sun.

The western desert stretched before her, unbroken by trees or structures of any kind. Heat lay heavy on the land, a distorting wave that hung inches above the scorched ground. That shimmering band tricked the eye into seeing things that weren't there: pools of water, ridges of earth. In truth, there was nothing but red-brown dust that reached to the far horizon, a landscape as bleak and forbidding as the valleys of Mars.

Michelle turned to her commanding officer. "You're sure about this?"

"I'm sure we're where you wanted me to take us," Arachne said. "Are *you* sure?"

"It was a long time ago. I'm not sure about anything."

"Well, unless I'm going blind, they're not there."

"Maybe farther west?"

Arachne lifted binoculars to her eyes, then lowered them and shook her head. "We'd be able to see them. Mountains don't just disappear."

"A lot of things have just disappeared," Michelle said.

She took a step forward, shielding her eyes from the glare. Her face had tanned over the six months they'd been walking beneath the unrelenting sun, while her blond hair had whitened. She wore it short, just past her ears, refusing to adopt the shaved-to-the-scalp look that Arachne favored. Her camouflage uniform was filthy, as was everyone else's. When was the last time they'd had a chance to wash their clothes, much less themselves? Then she remembered: about a month ago, they'd come across a river, muddy brown and shockingly cold. Everyone had stripped down to their underwear and plunged into the sluggish current, Tyris shrieking and even Nausikaa and Aristodeme cracking smiles. It was Arachne who noticed that every handful of water they poured over their heads left black streaks down their necks. That ended their bathing party, and convinced some of the others to take their leader up on her offer of a trim.

*Ashes,* Arachne said to Michelle after she'd used her knife to snip Tyris's curls and sent the little girl scurrying off to find the twins. *From bombed cities.*

*From burned bodies*, Michelle thought, and shuddered despite the heat.

She took another step toward the desert basin, but the woman in the black jacket that matched her nighttime eyes put out an arm to bar her way. Though she was much smaller than Michelle, who had the long legs of a runner, Arachne's compact body was solid with muscle. "Where do you think you're going?"

"West. Where else would I be going?"

Arachne snorted. "Like hell. You're staying put while I scout ahead."

"You can't be serious."

"I can be a lot more than that," Arachne said in a voice too soft to be trusted. "Care to try me?"

11

Michelle let out a hard breath. This was the kind of treatment she'd come to expect from the foul-tempered woman who'd assumed command of their colony. "I already have a mother," she said under her breath.

"Not anymore," Arachne responded, before twisting the knife deeper. "If you did, what would she think about her little angel now?"

Instinctively, Michelle placed a hand on her bulging abdomen. It had gotten to the point where her top didn't fit anymore without unfastening the last two buttons, while her pants were so tight she'd stopped wearing her web belt. She'd been carrying this burden for six months, which meant that before she turned eighteen, she'd be a mother. A single mother, since the father had died only days after their baby was conceived.

*Kareem.*

The boy she'd lost her virginity to. The dark-haired boy she'd shared a night of terror and pain and love with. The mysterious boy whose secrets she'd never had a chance to learn: his family, his history, his dreams. Not even his last name. And now, she worried that she'd never know the answers, because he was gone.

And she was the one who'd killed him.

*I had to,* she said to herself for the hundredth time. *I promised him I wouldn't let him live that way. Wouldn't let anyone or anything steal the soul of the gentle boy I knew.*

Except me.

Arachne stared at her for a long moment, her eyes as hard and black as bullets. Then she held up a hand and signaled for the twins. The two approached, with five-year-old Tyris clinging to Nausikaa's leg.

"You're sticking with the girls," Arachne said to Michelle. "Maybe they can talk some sense into you."

Michelle made a face for show. "Fine."

She took Tyris's hand in one of hers and Nausikaa's in the other. There was no danger of the twins talking sense into her, since the only thing that came out of the twelve-year-old orphans' mouths was the occasional word of Russian they exchanged with each other. Tyris, by contrast, jabbered incessantly, but very little of what she said counted as sensible; instead, she poured into Michelle's ear all the discoveries and trivialities she would have shared with her mother if Helene had survived. Michelle knew why Arachne had assigned the three of them to watch over her: the camp leader was trying to guilt her into good behavior, to make sure she didn't do anything to put the little girl or the pre-teens at risk.

*And I won't,* Michelle said to herself. *So you can stop worrying.*

She started down the hillside. Arachne scowled at Michelle as she and the girls trooped past, but by the time they reached the basin, the commander had pushed her way to the front again.

The four adults in their colony brought up the rear. There was one woman, Calypso—whose real name, Michelle had discovered, was Bridget, far too cutesy for the hulking Amazon—and three men: Acastus, Nestor, and Polydeuces, heroic pseudonyms for the painfully pedestrian Charlie, Norman, and Dave. Along with Arachne, the four were the only adults who remained of the Argo, the camp their former commander, Jason, had founded in the Pennsylvania woodlands. Jason had been killed on the same day as Kareem and Helene—it was his jacket Arachne wore, the gold-banded cuffs rolled back to fit her smaller frame—and now there were only these nine survivors. Or, Michelle reminded herself, ten, counting the life that was growing inside her.

She tried to focus on that single bright spot as she took her first steps across the desert. A new life, a piece of Kareem that had been saved despite all the pain and death. Someone who would be hers for years, not merely days. Someone to share the world with, to teach, to love, to keep.

When she looked around and was reminded of what had become of her world, it was hard to hold onto that dream.

The heat of the sun-drenched plain bled straight through her boots, as if the ground had soaked up the past six months of sunlight and was spitting it back with a vengeance. The horizon seemed impossibly distant, a flat line that receded as fast as they approached, with nothing to show that they were moving at all. Arachne's words returned to haunt her: *mountains don't just disappear.* The cities that might once have stood here were gone, she'd accepted that, but was it possible that even the mighty peaks she remembered from her childhood had been leveled along with the works of human hands? And if so, if there was nothing but desert all the way from here to the coast, how long would it be before their bones joined the ashes of the millions who'd died when the bombs fell?

She looked at the sunburned skin of Arachne's neck and head, the two or three days' growth of black hair doing little to protect her from the sun's rays. Arachne was a former sentry, and surely she wouldn't have agreed to push ahead if there was nothing to find. Surely, she must have believed there was a possibility that something lay ahead.

But even as Michelle told herself that, she knew that heat and hunger and exhaustion weren't the only threats her colony had to face in this desolate landscape. They weren't even the worst threats, and they weren't why Arachne was moving even more silently than usual and scanning the empty plain with the superhuman focus only she could command.

The Skaldi were.

That was what Kareem called them. Monsters bred in the city back east by Jason's father, a military scientist whose son had assisted him in his project for years before vowing to stop it. He'd been unable to fulfill his vow, and the Skaldi had been released when bombs destroyed the lab. The creatures had consumed all of the children who'd been the subjects of Jason's father's experiments, and in the end, they'd taken Kareem, too. What had happened to the scientists, whether they'd succumbed to their own creations or not, no one knew. But if the bodysnatching monsters had spread this far west, they could be lying in wait beneath the desert, camouflaged as ripples of sand and dust. No one would know they were there until they emerged, their inhuman grip as strong and cold as steel and their sole object being to scavenge the living to replace their empty frames.

Michelle let go of Nausikaa's hand just long enough to finger the bow slung over her shoulder. This had become a habitual gesture, even though the weapon that had given her her camp nickname—Diana the Huntress, the name everyone now knew her by—was useless against Skaldi, who could be destroyed only by fire. Arachne had been able to salvage no more than four flamethrowers from the supplies in Jason's camp, and those were carried by Bridget and the three men. Michelle wasn't complaining about that; the bulky fuel tank and ignition assembly would have been torture to carry day in and day out, even without her additional burden. She was keenly aware, though, that if a Skaldi attack occurred, she and the "girls" would have to count on the others to defend them.

*I swore I'd never be a victim again,* she said silently as they toiled across the desert. *Never let anyone make me feel as helpless as Jason did.* Her fingers briefly stroked the feathers of an arrow before she gripped Nausikaa's hand again.

They walked for several hours without rest, creeping forward while Arachne tested the ground with her foot for quicksand or worse. When the afternoon heat mounted to its highest point, they took a break, covering their heads with coarse blankets from their packs. The sun had started its downward course by the time they resumed their journey, but Michelle found herself panting, sweat streaming into her eyes. She wished they could travel at night when the temperature dropped a few degrees, but Arachne would never risk it; the woman was convinced that Skaldi had better night vision than human beings. Michelle counted the seconds before the bloody ball met the horizon, looking forward to the moment she could give her legs a break and her weary mind a respite. As if the baby shared her feelings, she felt it wriggle inside her, making one of the periodic rolls she'd come to interpret as it settling down for sleep.

Arachne had stopped, her figure silhouetted against the sun, her hand held aloft in the familiar gesture for caution. Michelle blinked sweat from her eyes and tried to peer into the blinding light. Hushing Tyris and transferring the child's hand to Nausikaa's, she stepped to Arachne's side.

"What is it?" she asked.

"It's the reason I'm in charge of this colony, not you," Arachne answered in a tight whisper. "With Tyris making enough noise to wake the dead and you stomping around like an elephant—"

"We're quiet now," Michelle said. "What do you hear?"

"I don't *hear* anything. I *feel* something wrong."

"*What*, though?"

"If I knew that, I wouldn't have said *something*," Arachne replied. "Now shut up and let me—"

She stopped, her eyes narrowing on a patch of desert sand fifty yards in front of them. If Arachne hadn't been staring at the spot so intently, Michelle would have dismissed it as another heat mirage. Now, though, she saw that its color wasn't quite the same as the prevailing red-brown. It looked like something shiny that lay on the sand, a roughly rectangular shape reflecting the sun's dazzling light.

Arachne had freed her modified AR-15 from its strap. She brought the scope to her eye and edged forward, feet planted squarely and breath silent. For her part, it seemed to Michelle that her own breath had become as loud as the trumpeting of the pachyderm the camp leader accused her of being.

"Arachne," she said as the woman closed in on her target. "Guns don't work against—"

A cry came from behind them. Michelle spun to see Aristodeme in the clutches of a grimy figure that had appeared out of nowhere. It had the shape of a man and was wearing a camouflage uniform like theirs, but she was sure it was Skaldi that had materialized from the sand. Then she saw the shallow pit that had been dug into the ground, a flame-retardant tarp thrown back to expose the hole. The shape up ahead must have been another pit covered with a tarp, its reflective surface showing through the sand. The tarp from which the man had emerged had been camouflaged so well, even Arachne hadn't spotted it when they walked past.

The camp leader raised her rifle to her shoulder, lining up a shot at the man who held Aristodeme. He'd anticipated Arachne's move and was using the girl as a shield, so that not even a sharpshooter like Arachne could risk a burst from her rifle.

"Who are you?" she called at Aristodeme's captor. "What do you want?"

"Whatever you've got," the man shouted back in a voice as cracked and dry as the desert air. Michelle saw that he held a switchblade to the girl's throat, exposing only enough of himself that if Arachne fired at his hand, her bullet would rip through Aristodeme too. "Food, weapons, anything."

"We don't have much," Arachne said. "But we're willing to share."

Michelle glanced sidelong at the sentry. The day they'd set out from Jason's camp, Arachne had made clear that they didn't share with anyone. *You start giving things away to strangers,* she'd said, *you end up with your own knife in your back.*

The man who held Aristodeme must have lived by the same mantra. He smiled, showing a mouth more full of gaps than teeth.

"You think you're the only one who learned how to smooth-talk like that?" he asked. "I had two deployments in Iraq and Afghanistan. Now throw your gun down or the girl's dead."

"You can't fight us all," Arachne responded. "And if she dies, you've got nothing left to bargain with."

"I've had nothing left to bargain with for months," the man said. "I'll take my chances."

Arachne didn't answer, but she didn't lower her gun either. Out of the corner of her eye, Michelle saw more figures emerging from tarps that lay in a circle around them. Ten figures at least, some in ragged uniforms and others in equally threadbare civilian clothes, none armed with anything more than a knife or a baseball bat with a nail driven through the barrel. Michelle knew that Bridget and the men wouldn't use their flamethrowers without Arachne's signal, and while the camp leader hesitated, the desert scavengers drew closer. In a matter of seconds, they'd be able to swarm Arachne before she could take any of them down.

"Last chance," the man who held Aristodeme said. He pressed the point of his blade against the girl's pale throat, drawing a bright bead of blood.

Then he emitted a shriek, his hand flying from his victim and his knees crumpling beneath him. With his attention focused on Arachne, he hadn't seen Michelle step silently to the side and release the arrow that now protruded from his thigh. The man looked up at the teen as if pleading for mercy, but Arachne's single shot punched a hole in his forehead, and he sprawled on his back with blood spouting from him to stain the ground an even deeper shade of red.

The other vagrants attacked at the sight of their leader down. Arachne raised her rifle, not wasting ammunition but firing single shots with pinpoint accuracy until all but three of the scavengers lay bleeding and lifeless on the dusty ground. One of the remaining men swung his bat at Michelle, but she ducked and drove upward with an arrow, piercing his groin. When he staggered, she aimed a kick at his head that jarred teeth loose and spun him from his feet. He tried to regain his footing, but by that time, Arachne had reached him, bringing the butt of her rifle down on his head. He fell into one of the holes he and his companions had dug, the tarp ballooning upward before settling over him like a shroud.

The two remaining attackers had been taken care of single-handedly by Bridget, who'd downed them both and stood pointing her flamethrower at them. Arachne quickly checked the victims of her rifle, then, satisfied that they were dead, she approached the prostrate scavengers. One was a man, the other a woman. Both looked up at the black-garbed sentry as if she were the approaching messenger of death.

"Well, well, well," Arachne said, a nasty smile curling her lips. "What are we going to do with you?"

Their eyes glared in dust-caked faces, but they remained silent.

"Wait," Michelle said.

Arachne's gun didn't swerve an inch from its target. "For what?"

Michelle gazed at the two gaunt figures lying spread-eagled like children ineptly trying to make snow angels in the red-brown dust. Her eyes turned to the men and women Arachne had killed, including the first attacker, her own arrow protruding from the circle of blood that stained his uniformed pantleg. Her adrenaline rush fled so suddenly the world seemed to tilt before her vision. Nausea took hold of her, and she doubled over, her face twisting. "Oh, God … "

"Diana!" Arachne cried as Michelle crumpled to the ground, clutching her stomach.

Michelle moaned in answer. Arachne leaned over her, her rifle discarded, her normally expressionless face alight with panic.

"Are you all right?" she asked. "Are you hit?"

"It's coming," Michelle said. "Arachne, the baby's coming."

"Christ, Diana! It's not due for—"

"Three months," Michelle said, breathing hard. "It's—"

Her words were cut off as her body contorted in pain.

"Diana!" Arachne called, before spinning to face the twins. "Tell me what to do," she snapped at Nausikaa. "You've watched Helene. What do we do?"

Nausikaa's eyes widened. Her hands fluttered in a sign Michelle couldn't interpret, though she got the gist: the twins had helped the former camp doctor in the infirmary, but they'd never delivered a premature baby before.

"Give her room!" Arachne spat orders. "Boil some water! And get cloth. Tear strips of cloth!"

She scooped Michelle into her arms and laid her carefully on an edge of the tarp under which the first attacker had hidden. Bridget and the three men rushed around, fetching what Arachne had asked for. In the confusion, the prisoners leaped to their feet and ran off, no one making any attempt to stop them. Even the man Michelle had kicked crawled from the hole where he'd fallen and followed his companions. Michelle's last glimpse of them was of three shadowy figures vanishing into the red light of the sun before Arachne's body blocked them from view.

The camp leader brandished a knife before Michelle's fearful eyes. Blood smeared the metal, or maybe that was the reflected light of the sun. Michelle realized it was the switchblade the dead man had used. "What's that for?"

"To cut the cord," Arachne said. "Now lay down. You two," she said to the twins, "give her your hands to hold. Tyris, get the hell out of the way!"

The little girl skipped back, her eyes teary and her lip trembling.

"How close are the contractions?" Arachne asked.

"They're ... they're ... " Michelle's eyes squeezed shut, and her teeth clamped tightly together. "They're ... "

"Come on, Diana," Arachne said sharply. "Stay with me!"

Michelle opened her eyes to see Arachne kneeling before her, holding the knife in one hand and a strip of cloth in the other, looking about as much like an obstetrician as Tyris did. The teen shook free from the twins' hands and sat up. "Actually, I think they're gone."

Arachne fell back on the ground, looking stunned. Michelle rose, brushed her dusty hands on her camo pants, and calmly walked over to retrieve her discarded bow and quiver. Arachne's face went through every emotion it was capable of: incredulity, fury, disgust. "You actually faked ... "

Michelle met her look without apology. "I had to do something. You were going to kill those people."

"They were going to kill us."

"Not anymore."

Arachne shook her head, drawing a deep breath. Finally, her expression settled on something like grudging respect.

"Diana the Huntress," she said. "Haven't you heard about the girl who cried wolf?"

Michelle shrugged. "It was a boy. And he lived."

"So they say," Arachne replied, her gaze falling on Tyris, who stood clutching Aristodeme and sobbing into the older girl's shirt. "But his sheep got eaten."

Michelle flushed. While Arachne and the other adults checked under the tarps for surviving scavengers and whatever supplies they might have left behind, she went to comfort the little girl, who hugged her even more tightly than she'd been holding Aristodeme. Michelle stroked Tyris's shorn curls, murmuring softly in her ear. Within a minute, she'd calmed Tyris enough for the little girl to ask where babies came from. Michelle told her they came from love, and that seemed to satisfy Tyris for now.

Arachne threw the tarps down roughly beside them. Michelle flinched, but the commander's voice had returned to its usual flat, businesslike tone. "They had nothing."

"Not even food or—"

"Nothing." She shook her head. "In a way, I give them credit. A lot of people would have turned on their own long before they got to that point."

She shot Michelle a meaningful look and strode away.

The twins spread out the tarps while Arachne and the other adults conducted perfunctory burials, pitching the dead into one of the holes and shoveling dust over the mass grave. Michelle kept one eye on them while she helped Tyris get ready for the night. She wasn't entirely sure what had come over her when she'd faked labor; she'd told herself it was only to stop Arachne from needless killing, but now she questioned her own motivations. For some reason, she'd *wanted* to scare Arachne—to get back at her for treating Michelle like a child, or to assert her own independence, she couldn't say which. Either way, she hoped Arachne would be more forgiving than she'd been in the past.

They slept on the tarps, which provided some protection from the hot sand. Michelle pulled Tyris to her and read from the child's favorite—and only—book, *The Runaway Bunny*. The spine had cracked so that the board pages fanned out in a complete circle, but Tyris happily drank in every word. When the child fell asleep cuddled against her protector's side and Michelle was sure that everyone except the watchful Arachne had settled down for the night, she reached deeper into her pack and pulled out the two objects no one knew she was carrying. Turning from the sentry, she inspected her treasures to make sure they had survived today's adventure intact.

The first was a photograph, and though she couldn't see it clearly in the dark, she'd memorized every line: a black-and-white portrait of Kareem and the other children posing with the scientists who'd experimented on them, including the bearded titan Kareem had called the Tall Man, the head of the Skaldi trials whom she'd later learned was Jason's father. Ignoring the adults who stood possessively behind their experimental subjects, she ran her finger over Kareem's face, the face of the child he'd been when the trials started, not the lover who'd touched her with such gentle hands that fateful night. Returning the picture to her bag, she picked up the second object, a gift that tugged at her heart even more strongly and painfully than the first.

It was a jar made of translucent green glass, somewhat smaller than the jars in which the scientists had housed the immature Skaldi. Its outsides were scuffed, though six months of careful handling had smoothed the scratch-marks to shiny blots. Inside, the jar was filled to the midpoint with what looked like soot. Michelle had gathered these remains from the field where Kareem fell, his Skaldi-form burned to smoke and ash by the flamethrower she herself had wielded. Her cheeks and hands still bore the scars of that cleansing fire, ripples on her skin that made her look much older than she was. She spoke to all that was left of him in a whisper, repeating the promise she'd made to him on that day and every day since.

"Kareem," she said. "It's me. It's your Chelle."

Tears came to her eyes as she invoked the secret name he'd given her on the night their baby was conceived.

"We're getting closer," she told him. "We're almost there. Soon we'll find the mountains, and you can finally be at peace."

She kissed the glass softly, then tucked the jar into the bottom of her pack beside the photograph. Curling her ungainly body around Tyris, she closed her eyes to sleep.

# Chapter 2

It was on the day they left Jason's camp that Michelle first started wondering what had happened to her period.

That was at the very end of May, and she'd been a member of the Argo for a little over a month by then. Prior to that point, she'd been almost freakishly regular, something her best friend Janine used to gripe about. The absence of Michelle's monthly visitor wasn't exactly unwelcome—the Argo's feminine hygiene products were limited to bulky, utilitarian pads—but it was certainly unusual.

*Malnutrition*, she told herself at the time. *And anxiety. The last thing I need is to start worrying about this.*

Her biggest concern when they left camp was returning to the city that lay to the east of the Argo, and in particular to the underground bunker that had been Kareem's home—his prison—for most of his life. It was the same place where they'd made love, and it was where she hoped to find clues about his past. Everything else could wait until that task was accomplished.

Unlike her first attempted visit to the city, when she and Kareem had hiked across a scorched landscape only to be attacked by Skaldi before they arrived, getting there was easy this time. They had two vehicles from Jason's camp, stripped-down ATVs he referred to as moon buggies, with just enough room for all nine of them to pile aboard. That was lucky, since Arachne was hobbling on a broken ankle at the time and had agreed to visit the city only after Michelle convinced her they might find needed supplies there. They'd bounced through the forest in these jalopies, Michelle telling herself she couldn't possibly be pregnant if a ride this bumpy didn't make her lose her lunch. Leaving the vehicles outside the camouflaged entrance to the bunker, they'd descended into the subterranean tunnel and—Arachne's ankle notwithstanding—walked for an entire day, squeezing through debris that had fallen from the ceiling until they reached the door to the intersecting tunnel where she and Kareem had fought the fully grown Skaldi. Arachne held her flamethrower at the ready, but the tunnel was empty, with nothing but piles of some chalky substance on the floor. Michelle guessed that these were the remains of the Skaldi, their empty shells having fallen to pieces after days trapped in the underground lair with no living body to replace theirs. She gazed at the residue, fingered the jar in her backpack, and thought about the last time she'd seen Kareem alive. She remembered vividly the pain of the Skaldi's icy touch, and she had no wish to relive the day when she'd almost succumbed to it.

They started down this new tunnel in the direction the scientists' quarters were located, only to discover that the explosion of the bomb Michelle herself had planted a week ago had blocked the way. The farthest they could go was the lab where she and Kareem had battled the immature Skaldi. The barracks at the opposite end of the complex were still accessible, but everything else was sealed off, the facility's secrets buried along with the monsters it had contained.

While Arachne fumed and the others rested, Michelle entered the barracks. She stared at the bed, imagining Kareem's body beneath the rumpled sheets, his arms wrapped around her. She could still hear his voice pronouncing her secret name. On the floor where it had fallen, she discovered the photograph of him and the other children, but she knew from her previous time here that she would find nothing else of either sentimental or practical value. She tucked the picture into her bag along with the collection jar and left the room to face Arachne.

"It's empty," Michelle told her.

Arachne stopped pacing long enough to sneer at her. "You think?"

They had no choice but to retrace their steps. When they did, exiting the tunnel a day later, the moon buggies were gone.

Arachne spent another ten minutes cursing her young lieutenant, then another hour limping along the trail the carjackers had left. She returned in a particularly foul mood even by her standards, reporting that though the tracks were clear enough, the thieves had too much of a head start for her or anyone else to catch up to them on foot. She speculated that members of Jason's disbanded camp were to blame, since it seemed unlikely that anyone else would be in the area or know how to operate the vehicles. However true that theory was, all it did was make her angrier. To watch her dragging her injured ankle through the woods, swearing at everything and nothing while Michelle tried in vain to shield Tyris from the worst of the woman's profanity, you'd have thought she suspected members of her own nascent colony of betraying her.

They hiked through the woods until the trees yielded to the desert Michelle and Kareem had crossed partway, the same desert she'd traveled with Jason and the bomb he'd forced her to carry into the city. When she and Arachne tried to locate the bunker from that direction, they found that the destruction from the bomb was as bad on the surface as it had been in the tunnels, and every trace of a doorway was obliterated by shattered brick and crumpled steel. She spent an hour or two searching, but it was like trying to put together a thousand-piece jigsaw puzzle where every piece looked exactly the same. Finally, bitterly, she was forced to admit to the others that they were never going to find a way back in. Arachne treated her to a final volley of expletives before calming down.

"So," she said, "any other bright ideas?"

"We head west," Michelle answered automatically.

Arachne narrowed her eyes. "West where?"

"Anywhere," Michelle said, trying to cover her slip-up. "Jason said he'd lost communication with sites farther afield, so it's possible we'll find fellow survivors in the west."

"Fellow survivors aren't exactly what I'm eager to find," Arachne said. "You saw what our former companions did to our only means of transportation."

It was then that Michelle realized Arachne never let go of a theory. Or a grudge.

"But you're right," the woman said before Michelle had a chance to try to convince her. "Our best bet is to search for someplace that escaped the bombing, and west is as good as anywhere."

That settled it. What Michelle didn't tell Arachne—what she planned never to tell anyone—was that west was where she'd seen mountains when she was a little girl, and it was the only place she could think of that might still be beautiful enough to lay Kareem's ashes and his memory to rest.

They took a couple of hours to recover their strength, dreading the cross-country trek that was about to begin. Then Nausikaa and Aristodeme pointed excitedly at a parking garage that had slid to the ground like so much slag. There, miraculously untouched by the destruction surrounding it, sat a dust-covered delivery truck, the word *Tastykake* printed on its side. Even more miraculously, the engine started when Arachne jumped in and turned the key. It took a long time to negotiate around fallen buildings and then drive across the deep desert sand, but once Arachne found a four-lane highway northwest of the desert, they continued their journey in relative comfort. Arachne was even in something like a playful mood, honking her horn as she swerved around the burned hulks of cars and trucks, letting out a child-friendly oath every time she had to push in the heavy clutch. For Michelle, sitting in the passenger seat with Tyris on her lap, it felt almost like the old days, when she'd played games of I Spy and Count the Cows with her little sister Rosie. Except there were no cows to count, and very little to spy in the barren countryside that stretched on either side of the scarred and pitted road.

Still, there was plenty of junk food in the rear storage compartment where the others were sitting, and they made good progress for an entire day, with Arachne driving tirelessly through the dark while Michelle and Tyris slept, the little girl sucking her thumb and resting her cheek against Michelle's chest. Then the truck ran out of gas, and with no filling station in sight, much less in operation, they were forced to abandon ship. Michelle was reminded of how she'd come to Jason's camp on the night of her seventeenth birthday, when she hit a deer on the highway with her brand-new Mustang convertible and broke down in the middle of nowhere. That accident had saved her from the bombs, and joining the Argo had eventually led her to Kareem, which had led to … But no, she wouldn't think about that, wouldn't think about the fact that another week had passed without any sign of bleeding or cramps. While Arachne and the other adults collected weapons and the twins gathered what was left of their food from the Argo, she jumped out of the truck with Tyris, stuffed cupcakes and snowballs around the secret treasures at the bottom of her backpack, and started off with the others in the direction of the setting sun.

"Well, at least we proved one thing," Arachne said as she limp-walked in her cumbersome air cast at the front of their caravan.

"What's that?" Michelle asked.

The sentry threw the cellophane-and-cardboard wrapper of an apple pie on the buckled blacktop. "This crap really will survive a war."

Michelle smiled to herself. For Arachne, this counted as a very good mood.

But it didn't last. The sugar-laden treats soon ran out, and though they found other vehicles in varying degrees of disrepair along the westbound highway—not a single one, disturbingly, with even the remains of a driver behind the wheel—none of them would start, no matter how much Arachne tinkered under the hood or beneath the steering column. After a time, she stopped trying, and after a couple of weeks on the road, they stopped finding anything that resembled a vehicle. Arachne had no explanation for this, other than to suggest that out here, far from any urban area, there'd been fewer cars for the bombs to destroy.

In the case of everything else, the destruction was total. Gaping holes cratered the blacktop, transmission towers were singed to blackened skeletons, toothpick barns looked as if they'd died from the tobacco products faintly advertised on their sides. Arachne had filled Michelle in on the geography of the area, announcing, first of all, that Jason's camp had been near Johnstown, which made Michelle blush with the realization that she'd been lost only a few hours from her Laurel Highlands home. But out here, she felt completely disoriented, far from any place she might have visited. Highway signs, water towers with the names of cities painted on them, manmade landmarks like airports and public parks—all had vanished into the general dust. They must have passed Pittsburgh somewhere along the way; at least, they'd walked across a dangerously decrepit bridge while a sludge-brown river snaked below. And yet, there'd been no hint of its stadiums and skyscrapers. Even more surprisingly—though to Arachne's thinking, fortunately—they'd met exactly zero people on their journey so far; the one time a distant figure shambled into view, it proved to be a sickly deer, ribs showing and dark eyes dulled as if coated with dust. Michelle's arrow pierced the animal's heart, but when Arachne went to investigate, she announced that it wasn't safe to eat. Michelle tried not to look at the carcass as the colony marched past, but she caught a whiff of rotten flesh that reminded her all too much of the Skaldi.

Possibly the most disturbing thing about their surroundings was the condition of the natural world. Given how late in the spring it was when they'd left Jason's camp, they should have seen trees refulgent with foliage, roadside wild-flowers growing in a profusion of bright colors, blue skies adorning themselves with creamy dollops of cloud or darkening with the coming of storm. Instead, the season was autumnal in every way except the oppressive heat: leaves had withered and fallen from the few trees they found standing, while grasses stood rusty and sere beneath a parchment sky. Michelle guessed that they were in Ohio by now, but whereas she remembered driving through endless rows of tall green cornstalks on family vacations, they were hiking between flat, empty fields where nothing grew. On the day they left camp, Arachne had insisted on loading down everyone, Tyris included, with as much water as they could carry, but she'd already announced a regimen for rationing what was left. After nearly a month on the road and no sign of the heatwave abating, Michelle wondered if west was the wrong direction to go; maybe they should turn around and hope for a more hospitable climate on the shores of the Delaware, or angle north toward the Great Lakes. But every time she considered broaching the subject with Arachne, her pledge to Kareem returned to sting her, and she kept plodding mechanically westward, as if the only thing drawing her that way was the gravitational pull of the sun itself.

After two months on the road, she had another reason to worry, as well as another reason to go on: she had finally admitted to herself that she wasn't traveling alone.

In all that time, her period had yet to make an appearance. Instead, she'd developed another symptom: the violent inability to hold down anything more flavorful than a saltine cracker. Granted, after the Tastykake banquet ended, their diet was enough to make anyone sick: leftover pemmican bars from camp, wormy apples scrounged from beneath leafless trees, moldy potatoes torn from hard, dry ground. But no one else was puking every morning, and she was; the moment she stood up from whatever uncomfortable bed they'd chosen for the night—tall grass, a rocky quarry, the remains of a deserted parking lot—her legs would feel weak, her stomach woozy. She'd cup her hands over her mouth and run for cover, usually finding it, sometimes befouling her uniform in her haste. Tossing her cookies became as much a routine as the morning ritual of triple-checking her bag. You could set your watch by it, as her father used to say.

The nausea subsided after the first month, but it was replaced by a new symptom in roughly the same region: drumtight skin over her midsection, as if her undernourished belly was swelling outward. Along with that uncomfortable sensation came the constant need to pee, which made no sense given how little she was drinking. In rapid succession, other symptoms she'd probably been ignoring for weeks announced themselves. Migraines? Check. Sore breasts? Check. Mood swings? Double-check; she'd nearly bitten Tyris's head off for wiping her hands on Michelle's already filthy uniform, then sobbed and begged the bewildered child to forgive her. She could have attributed all of these physical and emotional changes to the situation they were in, but she'd taken sex ed in school, and she knew better. More than that, her *body* knew: there was another life inhabiting the space inside her. She was going to be a teen mom, the one thing everybody from her own mom to her teachers to her track coach had told her not to be. The one thing *she* had told herself she'd never be. Sleepless nights, colic, diarrhea, and all the rest of the things she'd been warned about lay in her not so distant future.

But at least the average teen mom didn't have to worry about raising her child in a world filled with monsters. At least they didn't have to worry about their child *being* a monster, the offspring of a fully human mother and a half-Skaldi father. That was the thing that ate at her mind and her heart the most: the possibility that the father of her baby, the boy she'd lost her virginity to and had been willing to give her life for, was the one who'd tricked her into bearing the Skaldi's spawn.

Like so many of her secrets—her name, her hidden treasures, her destination—she wished she could keep this one to herself. But the farther they walked, the more she realized she'd have to come clean soon, and to Arachne no less. Ever since Michelle's morning sickness started, the camp leader had been throwing sidelong glances at her, eyebrows lowered and lips parted as if about to ask a question or issue a reprimand that never came. It would have been hard enough to tell a close friend—Janine, or one of the girls from the track team—that she'd had unprotected sex with a virtual stranger and was carrying his baby. To admit the truth to Arachne, a woman she could no more imagine having sex than she could picture her own mother engaged in the act, was nothing short of impossible. It seemed Arachne knew it, too, and was punishing Michelle for her indiscretion by making her sweat out the older woman's judgment.

Finally, almost four months into their journey, when she'd started untucking her uniform top to hide the growing bump in her abdomen, Michelle couldn't take it any longer. She settled Tyris for the night beside an abandoned combine and approached Arachne privately. The camp leader always took the first watch at night and never awakened Michelle to serve a shift, which made Michelle wonder if, like the spider from which she'd earned her code name, Arachne went without human sleep altogether.

Arachne's dark eyes were alert in the night, flicking in Michelle's direction the moment she left Tyris's side. Michelle considered an ice-breaker or some other pleasantry—she actually had a greeting prepared on the tip of her tongue—but ended up blurting out, "I'm pregnant."

"And I'm crushed," Arachne said. "Because I've been waiting to see you pull a rabbit out from under your shirt."

Michelle's heart skipped a beat. "Do the others know?"

"They're too busy worrying about their own safety to notice your stomach. Was it Jason?"

"What?"

"Jason. You know, our dauntless skipper? Was he the one who ran off with the booty prize?"

The thought of having sex with the murderous leader of the Argo nearly made Michelle lose her meager dinner. "Why would you think it was him?"

"No reason," Arachne said. "So it was that boy, then? That Kareem?"

Michelle nodded.

"Which explains why you were in such a lather to get back into the lab. Looking for mementos of him, I assume? Selfies you took on the boardwalk?"

Michelle couldn't deny it, so she said nothing.

"He was your first, I take it?" Arachne continued, not bothering to hide her contempt. "The one you couldn't say *no* to when he dropped his jock? Or was it his dreamy eyes?"

Michelle was thankful for the cover of darkness to hide her blush. She couldn't believe Arachne was talking so snidely about this—couldn't believe the woman thought it was her right to talk about it at all. It was as if, having held off on voicing her opinion for four months, she felt entitled to say anything she pleased.

"It wasn't like that," Michelle said. "He never—"

"Save it for confessional," Arachne said. "I don't particularly care *how* he got inside your pants. But did it ever occur to you that it might be a bit inconvenient to lug a baby around the set of *Hell, Part Two: This Time It's Personal?*"

Michelle's embarrassment flared into a hot wave of anger. "It *occurred* to me. But—"

"But you were a typical teenager, thinking with your hormones instead of your head. And now you've become nothing but a major pain in the ass for those of us who were hoping to survive this trip."

Michelle steamed in silence. Arachne couldn't understand what she'd felt that night in the Skaldi lab, couldn't know what she and Kareem had been through together. What they'd meant to each other. A person like her couldn't possibly understand that, more than anything, Michelle had *needed* to be held by him, to feel his arms anchoring her to sanity while the world around her sank deeper and deeper into nightmare. And then, when being held by him wasn't enough, she'd needed more, some way to escape the demons that threatened to devour her soul. She'd found what she craved in his touch, his kisses, the way their bodies moved together toward a final explosion of light and joy. During those moments, the thought that *he* might be one of the demons she was fleeing couldn't have entered her mind. And now, she knew that if she allowed that thought to take hold, it would break her.

But she couldn't say anything like that to the woman who studied her with cold disdain written on her face. "What do you want me to do about it now? I can't … there's no way for me to … "

"There are plenty of ways," Arachne responded. "But you wouldn't try any of them, not if I handed you the means and showed you how they work. I'd have to force you, and if you resisted, then I'd have to kill you."

Genuine fear spiked through Michelle's chest, but she decided her best approach was not to back down. "Wouldn't the others be a bit suspicious if I suddenly disappeared?"

"You're not hearing a word I'm saying," Arachne answered. "Tyris and the twins might be your special friends, but Bridget and the Three Stooges want one thing only, and that's to live. They don't give a damn about you and your monster baby love child. If they thought that getting rid of you bettered their odds, they'd be only too happy to hold you down while I put a bullet between your eyes."

She held Michelle's gaze, her own eyes as piercing as the promised bullet. For some reason, hearing Arachne describe an act of cold-blooded murder in such stark terms, Michelle knew the sentry wouldn't do it. She *could* do it—maybe she even *wanted* to—but she wouldn't. And she would make sure nobody else did, either.

"What do you need from me?" Michelle asked.

Arachne nodded as if acknowledging this acceptance of her terms. "I need you to follow my orders. To stick close, and not let your guard down. More than that, I need you to stop hiding things from me. I know there's more to where we're headed than you're letting on. I need to know every-thing you know."

Michelle took a deep breath. Even with the potential loss of Arachne's protection hanging over her, she found that she couldn't tell her *everything*. "There are mountains to the west," she said. "I camped there with my family when I was a little girl, about Tyris's age."

"The Rockies?"

"The southernmost tip. The campground where we stayed was in the Jemez Mountains, in New Mexico. If there's any place that's safe from the Skaldi, that's the place."

Arachne looked skeptical. "There are plenty of mountains, Diana. And the ones near Johnstown didn't do us much good."

"These were special," Michelle insisted, hoping she didn't sound like the preschooler she'd been when she vacationed there. "They were much taller than the ones in Pennsylvania, much wilder. They were so remote, so isolated—even though we were close to Santa Fe, it felt like we were a million miles from anywhere else. If we could get there, we'd at least have a chance."

"A chance at what?"

"To *live*," Michelle said. "To be free of all this … all this death. And if my baby … if there's anything wrong with my baby … "

Arachne waited, cocking an eyebrow.

"I'll leave camp," Michelle finished. "I'll go off by myself, somewhere you'll never find me."

"Give me a little credit, Diana."

"All right, then, somewhere *I* can't find *you*. I'll go off alone with my baby, and if I die—if we both die—then we die. No danger to anyone, no regrets or remorse. No looking back. Either way, you live."

Arachne studied Michelle for a long moment, her expression unreadable. Michelle was convinced she'd reject the proposal as a little girl's fairy tale, either that or ask more prying questions. When Arachne finally responded, Michelle froze, the camp leader's words fading while something far more important rooted her to the spot.

" … Diana? Hello? Earth to Diana? We were, you know, talking?" Arachne's face floated before her, anger changing to something like concern. "What is up with you?"

"I think … I think I just felt the baby move."

She closed her eyes, tuning out the world. There it was again: a tiny flutter at the core of her being. She remembered her aunt telling her that when she first felt Michelle's cousin Dana move, she thought it was gas. But this didn't feel like gas. It felt like a moth, a hummingbird, a candle flame gently wavering. *The quickening*, people used to call it, and that was the perfect word: a coming to life, a binding in the flesh. Michelle's eyes filled with tears, and she wished it were anyone else in the whole world she could share this moment with.

"This is real, Arachne," she said. "This is really real."

"If you're trying to play on my sympathies," Arachne said, "you're barking up the wrong tree." But her face had relaxed and—almost—broken into a smile. When Michelle saw that, she relaxed too, and felt the flame inside her flicker one more time.

"So we head for the mountains," Arachne said. "Just remember, this was your brilliant idea. If you start getting tired or bloated or whatever you get when that Chicken McNugget grows, I don't want to hear a single word of complaint out of you."

"You won't," Michelle said, and they sealed their compact with another nod.

Michelle thought about that conversation now, as she rose from her makeshift bed and felt her baby perform one of its seemingly weightless backflips. During the two months since then, Arachne had been as good as her word, pursuing the westward course she'd agreed on and making sure that nobody in camp questioned Michelle, much less threatened her, when the bulge in her belly became too large to ignore. Arachne never said a word about it to Bridget and the boys, but the sheer force of her will was enough to keep them quiet. She did tell everyone where they were going, and why; at least, she offered the explanation that Michelle had provided her. The things Michelle hadn't said—that her own mother was pregnant with Rosie when they'd traveled out west, that she'd promised Kareem she'd see him safely to the mountains—weighed on her conscience. And now that Arachne had actually killed for her, or for everyone, it felt even harder to withhold the truth. She'd rewarded the woman for her constancy by pretending to go into labor. Didn't she at least owe Arachne an admission?

But no. No matter how hard she tried to bring the words to her lips, she found that she couldn't. It would be too much of a betrayal—of Kareem, of their night together, of her own heart. Having admitted as much as she had to Arachne, she was able to admit the rest to herself: that this pregnancy was what she'd hoped for all along. The hope hadn't started with the first missed period, the first bout of morning sickness. It had started on that terrible day when, facing the Skaldi her lover had become, she'd felt a strange twinge in her gut that was something greater than fear, even if it was considerably less than fetal movement. At the time, it was probably no more than a bodily response born of a wish: *what if?* What if, for all she'd lost, she'd gained something in return? And now that the vagrant wish had blossomed into a solid presence, she knew what it required of her: that she keep Kareem's secret safe and secure until they reached the mountains, as safe and secure as the new life that nested inside her body.

And yet, as they packed up the scavengers' tarp and started across the desert for a second day, Michelle began to wonder if her vivid memory of the mountains was nothing but a childhood dream after all. She'd done her best to describe the spot to Arachne, but it had been so long ago, her sense of geography so muddled at the time, she couldn't be sure she had the right place or even the right name. They had no map; Jason hadn't allowed anyone in camp except his lieutenant Argus—Tyris's father, killed along with Helene—to have access to maps, which was one of the many ways he'd cut his recruits off from the outside world. For the same reason, they had no radio, no cell phone, no GPS, not that any of those would have worked anymore. Arachne had a compass, and she claimed to know the geography of the west well enough to find her way, but now that they'd reached this seemingly endless expanse of desert, Michelle was wracked with new doubts. For all she knew, they'd overshot their target and ended up in Death Valley, or veered too far north and were heading toward the Grand Canyon. If Arachne felt the same doubts, she remained as tight-lipped about them as she did about everything else. She just kept trudging across the desert, putting one foot in front of the other, as if she shared

Michelle's hope that the mountains would rise up out of no-where and they'd both be able to lay their burdens down at last.

The second night, all they were able to lay down was their parched and exhausted bodies. For the first time since they'd left Jason's camp six months ago, Arachne immediately slumped over, her hand on her rifle but her eyes too fatigued to stay open. Michelle had never been able to guess the wom-an's age—she could have been anywhere from thirty to fif-ty—but with her face pinched and wary even in sleep, she looked older than ever before.

Michelle watched Arachne even more closely on the third day of their march. What she saw was frightening: the colony's leader was definitely slowing down, her steps becom-ing less straight and sure. By now, it had become obvious to everyone, except possibly Tyris, that they were in grave dan-ger of dehydration. Water mirages danced at every moment on the horizon, but actual water was confined to the few sips left in their canteens. Despite that, Michelle's bladder kept insisting on being emptied, even when she could only squeeze out a few drops. When she lifted her canteen to cracked lips and felt how light the container had become, she sensed that if they kept going for even one more day, they wouldn't have enough water left to return to the eastern margin of the de-sert and search for a water source they'd missed on their way west.

And yet Arachne kept plowing ahead, not even glancing at the troops behind her. Eyeing the back of the sentry's freshly shaved scalp, Michelle couldn't help wondering when she would call a halt and turn them around. Was this some bizarre way of disciplining her lieutenant for the performance of two days ago? Was it meant to be punishment for suggesting their western wild goose chase to begin with? Michelle couldn't believe Arachne was so angry at her that she was willing to make her responsible for everyone's death, so maybe she was waiting for Michelle herself to give the order to stop. But even with the merciless sun blistering her face and the knowledge that she was risking the life of Tyris, the twins, and her own child—Kareem's child—with every step she took, Michelle couldn't bring herself to admit the failure of her dream.

It might have been because that dream was in her mind, or it might have been because she was so tired she was half-dreaming on her feet, but when the sky ahead of them turned the same red-brown color as the desert, her first thought was that they'd floated free of the earth and were flying toward the hidden mountains. Arachne, however, reacted with a quickness that belied her exhaustion.

"Sandstorm!" she shouted at the top of her lungs. Michelle could hardly hear the word against the rumbling that filled the air. Tyris screamed, or opened her mouth to scream; Michelle couldn't hear the little girl's voice at all.

"Cover your face!" Arachne called, her words thin and distant. "Diana, get ahold of Tyris! Find rope—we can't be separated! And the tarp—what happened to the tarp?"

Bridget and the men were wrestling to open their rudimentary shelter, but the wind snatched it from their hands. Michelle watched it fly off, flashing silver against the brown sky like a lost birthday balloon.

"How much time do we have?" she yelled back, her own words stripped away by the wind and hurled beyond her hearing.

"We don't—" Arachne managed to say, and then the storm hit.

Instantly, Michelle was swaddled in a brown blanket that erased the sun and made everything on planet earth disappear. She opened her mouth to scream Tyris's name, only to choke on a mouthful of desert. The storm threw sand against her face like bullets from Arachne's rifle, but the howling had reached such an intensity she wouldn't have heard an actual gun if it had been fired right next to her ear. She turned to search for Tyris, but her body was buffeted by the wind and knocked to the ground. Before she had a chance to push herself upward, she was buried beneath a blanket of sand, the way Rosie used to do to her on trips to the Outer Banks. Except this time, it wasn't just her chest and legs that had been covered; it was her back and neck and head, and she couldn't shake free of the weight the storm had deposited on her. She was trapped in a grave of sand, and she felt as if hands from beneath were clutching at her, pulling her deeper below.

She struggled, panic-stricken at the thought that it was the Skaldi trying to drag her and her baby down to join them in living death. Her head broke the surface; it was only a few inches above her after all. She tried to call again for help, only to inhale enough debris that her lungs seized and could draw no air. She was drowning, not in water but in sand. Flashes of light danced before her eyes, warning signs of asphyxiation. The wind rumbled like thunder, and the earth shook, opening its mouth as wide as the Skaldi's scar to swallow her. Her fingers scrabbled against sand, but she couldn't hold on, and she felt herself sinking below, never to rise again.

Then the darkness of her shroud was torn away, and she saw what she dreaded most: tall shadows standing around her, featureless and blank except for their brightly glowing yellow eyes. It was impossible to count their number through the flickering veil of sand that whipped around them. One of them, however, loomed much taller than the rest, standing in the rear of the group like a mountain forming a backdrop to low rolling hills. She thought she heard the deep rumble of its voice, but that had to be the sound of the storm flooding her ears.

Two of the figures lowered themselves before her. She couldn't see their faces, only their eerily glowing eyes, but she felt their hands on her arms. She would have struggled against their grip, but she had no strength left. The two lifted her from the ground, holding her between them and letting her take her first breath in minutes that wasn't filled with suffocating sand. When she drew in that life-saving breath, she realized that the smell of their bodies was clean and human, nothing like the rotten stench of the Skaldi's decaying flesh. She relaxed into their arms, feeling a living warmth that could never flow through the creatures' bloodless bodies.

Her eyes fell on the figure to her right. She could see enough to tell that it had a thick mop of dark hair, but the rest of its face was obscured by the gleaming circles of its eyes—or no, not eyes but night vision goggles, shining bright yellow-green against the swirling air. She drew another unobstructed breath, and realized that something had been placed over her nose and mouth: a plastic mask, through which she sucked oxygen so pure it made her swoon. Her vision blurred, and she had the confused thought, at once terrifying and tantalizing, that she was about to die. But not before the desert granted her this one last, impossible reunion.

"Kareem?" she whispered.

Then nighttime fell, and she sank into the shelter of his arms.

# Chapter 3

Michelle wasn't sure whether to be thankful or not when her eyes opened again.

She was lying on a soft bed, much softer than any she'd known since she joined Jason's camp. Her head no longer pounded from dehydration, though she did feel a bit groggy, as if she'd slept for days. Still, she was alive, which was a lot more than she'd expected after the sandstorm.

But being alive meant that her dream from the desert was over. Even though she knew that it couldn't have been Kareem who saved her, even though she knew that he was gone and that she was the one who'd destroyed him, it felt for a moment as if the past six months had never happened and she'd watched him die in a fiery maelstrom just moments ago.

She closed her eyes to trap the tears, took a deep breath to stifle a sob. When she did that, the baby in her womb rolled like an otter, announcing that it was alive, too. That was all it took for her to decide in favor of thankfulness.

The sound of someone clearing their throat came from the room. Michelle opened her eyes to find herself being stared at by a teenage boy in jeans and a black T-shirt who lounged in a chair beside the door. He was pale and scrawny, with a prominent Adam's apple, spotty strands of facial hair covering pimples galore, and long jet-black locks that made him look like he either wanted to be a rock star or was trying to hide his acne-scarred face from the world. All he needed to complete the picture were braces—probably in some neon green or puke purple color. When he saw her looking at him, he nodded nonchalantly, lifting his chin in a *what's up?* gesture.

"Are you the one who brought me in?" she asked him, and was surprised at how scratchy her voice sounded.

The skinny boy nodded again.

"And everyone else? There was a little girl with me, and two other girls—twins. Are they all right?"

"Everyone's fine. But you were put in a separate room because … "

She waited for him to complete the sentence, then decided he wasn't going to. "Because?"

"Because you're … " His hands waved randomly in her direction.

"Pregnant," Michelle said. "The word is *pregnant*."

At that, his cool pose utterly deserted him, and he blushed to the roots of his greasy hair. The mortifying thought struck Michelle that he'd seen her with her clothes off, but when she checked beneath the covers, she found that she was wearing a blue gown, the papery kind with string ties in the back. Her uniform, cleaned and folded, sat on a second chair in the small room, which had a hospital feel to it: plain white walls and tiled floor, glowing light panels in the ceiling, and an antiseptic smell that reminded her of Helene's clinic at Jason's camp. A clear plastic pitcher of water sat on a nightstand, but there was no other furniture or equipment in the room.

The boy watched her as she examined her surroundings. There was something else he obviously wanted to say; he chewed his lip, then took a deep breath. "We noticed you didn't have ... that you weren't wearing ... "

Michelle registered the *we*, storing it for future questioning. "Yes?"

Instead of speaking, the boy closed the thumb and forefinger of his right hand over the ring finger of his left, twisting his hand back and forth as if he were turning something invisible. It took Michelle a second to realize what he meant, and when she did, she was the one to flush, not with embarrassment but with anger.

"I appreciate your helping me," she said. "But whether I'm married or not is none of your business."

The boy visibly shrank from her, as if he could merge his body with the brushed metal chair. Michelle softened at the sight of his discomfort. She remembered how awkward her first conversation with Kareem had been, when he was the patient and she was the interrogator, dispatched by Jason to his bedside to gather information. Maybe this boy was acting on behalf of someone else, just as she'd been. Someone in charge of this camp, whatever and wherever it was.

"I'm sorry," she said. "I'm just tired, and a little disoriented. But I do want to thank you, um ... "

"Laman," he said. "Laman Genn. And you must be Diana."

"How ...?"

"Your uniform has your name inside. Only your first name, though."

The word *inside* made Michelle's heart flutter. Yes, a patch bearing the code name *Diana* was stitched into the waistband of her uniform pants and the collar of her jacket; everyone in Jason's camp had those patches to make laundry sorting easier with so many otherwise identical uniforms. But what exactly was this teenage boy doing looking inside her jacket and pants? More importantly, had he been poking around *before* the clothing came off her body, or after? She decided it was best not to think about that too much.

"Where I'm from, we only use first names," she said.

"Well, that's really normal," he muttered. Then, in a more conversational tone, he asked: "Where was your camp, anyway? We know that most sites didn't survive when … "

The fog was lifting from Michelle's mind, and the wariness that Jason and then Arachne had instilled in her rose up as a reflex action. When Jason had sent her to question Kareem, it was because the survivalist leader feared strangers, because—though he didn't tell her this at the time—he suspected Kareem of being linked to the Skaldi lab. This boy, this Laman Genn, could be using the cover of shyness and hesitancy to probe her past, to find out what she knew. She didn't trust him, and so she decided to be as vague as possible. Hopefully, if the other members of her colony were being questioned, they would opt for a similar strategy. "It was back east. We've been walking for six months."

"Where back east?"

She met his look with a level smile. "A long way from here."

"Another place with no name?" She bristled at the sarcasm, but he quickly changed the subject. "What brought you out west? Six months is a long time to walk."

"Our camp was one of the places that was destroyed in the … the wars," Michelle said, not knowing what else to call

51

them. "And we lost our commander. We were looking for other survivors."

"Well, you found them. We lived in the east for a while, too, before we decided to relocate. That was before the *wars*, though." He said the word with an archness that made her sure he doubted her account. "We've been out here for five years."

"And where is *here*?"

"Texas. About fifty miles from San Antonio." With his next words, the note of mockery returned to his voice. "You know, someplace with a name."

Michelle was silent. Whoever this Laman Genn was, she'd been right not to reveal too much; he might come across like a bashful innocent, but he'd seen through her ploy in a minute, and now he was doing no more than playing along. Even more troubling, to learn that her colony had ended up in southern Texas, far off course from their destination in northern New Mexico, made Michelle wonder how Arachne had miscalculated so badly. Laman's people had taken her and the others in when they needed help—but would they let the colony go when Michelle decided it was time to move on?

It was too much to think about all at once, so she called on the strategy Kareem had perfected during their first interview. Stifling a yawn, she said, "I think I need to get some sleep. I'm really tired from being out there in the desert."

"I don't blame you," he said. "Sandstorms can be deadly around here. Do you need anything?"

"An extra pillow would be nice." Then, to see if she could crack through his mask, she added: "Would you mind telling me where the bathroom is? I have to pee a lot these days because of the baby sitting on my bladder."

He'd risen to get the pillow, but when he heard those words, he froze, the tops of his ears turning red where they peeked through his tangled hair. No one could fake the physical signs of embarrassment like that, so he must actually be uncomfortable around her body. *Let's keep it that way*, she thought. She was convinced by now that whoever the *we* was that Laman kept referring to, they had sent him on this little visit against his wishes. And that made her certain that the people who had saved her colony—Laman's people—hadn't done it solely out of the goodness of their hearts.

Laman handed her the pillow, holding it as if her fingers might clutch his and not let go. "The bathroom's down the hall," he said. He was on his way out when he paused with his hand on the doorknob and looked back at Michelle.

"Who's Kareem?" he asked.

Her heart stuttered. "I'm sorry?"

"Kareem. You said that name when we brought you in."

"Nobody," Michelle said. "Just a friend. You reminded me of him."

"Oh." He stood motionless, his hand on the door, his face struggling as if there was something more he wanted to say. When he slipped out of the room, he lifted his eyes for just a second and looked at her with an expression she hadn't seen from him before.

She knew what the expression was, though. She'd encountered it more and more frequently in the seven months since her nightmare began.

It was fear.

MICHELLE REALLY DID have to go to the bathroom, so she waited until she couldn't hear Laman's footsteps anymore and then rose from bed. She shed the hospital gown and pulled on her underpants and uniform, which smelled much cleaner than it ever had. There was no sign of the sports bra she'd worn for seven solid months—probably a good thing, since the frayed material chafed against her tender boobs. She searched for the boots she'd worn since joining Jason's camp, but they weren't there, so she had to content herself with the soft white slipper socks that sat beside the bed—again, something of a relief after the discomfort of hiking all day every day in the stiff, heavy boots.

She tried the doorknob, half expecting it to be locked. It opened, and she peeked out into the hallway, which was identical to her room with its ceiling lights, bare white walls, and tiled floor. She looked up and down the hall, but there was no one there. There were no windows, either, which struck her as strange and worrisome. A faint hum filled the hallway, possibly from a hidden ventilation system. The temperature was slightly chilly but not cold, and the sterile aroma tickled her nostrils as it had in her bedroom. A single door halfway down the corridor to her right must have been the bathroom, so she headed in that direction, the slipper socks rustling softly across the tiles. When she reached the bathroom door, she saw that there was a recess beyond it, with another door at the end of a short hallway. That must have been where Laman had exited. She considered following him, but she *really* had to go now, so she entered the bathroom first.

Ceiling squares flickered on. The room was tiny, just large enough for a toilet. There wasn't even a sink, though there was a dispenser with hand sanitizer on the wall. The toilet was oddly shaped, without any water in the bowl; it must have been the kind that worked by composting. There was no unusual smell, and a roll of toilet paper hung beside it, so Michelle sat and let her bladder empty. She stood once to check her pee for the dark yellow color of dehydration, but it had returned to its normal pale gold, which meant that Laman's people must have given her fluids while she was asleep. When she was done, she stood, feeling awkward not to flush. Then again, she'd been doing her business in bushes and open fields for months, crouching low to stay out of sight and using grass and leaves to wipe, so having an actual toilet was definitely a treat.

Michelle exited the bathroom and, after checking to make sure she was alone, headed toward the second door. When she got there, she found that it had no knob or handle; instead, a glowing square was embedded in the wall at waist level, obviously some kind of sensor. She knew it was a waste of time to try to beat the system, but she did anyway, first testing the scanner—which made no response to her hand or voice or eye—then attempting to wedge her fingers around the door. She wished Arachne were here with a knife or one of the tools she always seemed to carry, tweezers or needle-nose pliers or something like that. When she patted her own jacket and pants pockets, she found that she had nothing, nothing at all …

Michelle froze, realizing that when she'd woken, her thoughts had been too fuzzy to check what had become of her belongings. Not that anything in her bag would help with her current dilemma. But there were two items she owned that were even more precious than her freedom, and she'd completely forgotten about them until now.

She ran back to the bedroom, all thoughts of escape gone. She rushed to the chair where her uniform had been, checked beneath and behind it, then did the same with the nightstand and the bed. It took only seconds to confirm her fears, but she kept searching fruitlessly, running her fingers between the mattress and the bed frame, checking corners of the room that her eyes told her were empty. The backpack was gone, taken by Laman's people, or possibly by Laman himself. They might have no idea what its contents were, what they meant, yet somehow she knew that they wouldn't return the items to her, not if she asked, not even if she begged. The loss of the photograph she might have been able to bear; she knew it by heart, and the boy in the picture wasn't the Kareem she'd fallen in love with anyway. But she couldn't stand the thought that she would never touch the memory jar again, and that Kareem's spirit would remain forever trapped inside its cold green glass.

Michelle fell to the floor, the tears she'd held inside for six long months flowing from her in an endless, bitter stream. Nothing was worse than this. Not the fact that she was trapped in this strange place, not the disappearance of Arachne and Tyris and the twins, who she suspected were being detained in their own small rooms on similar hallways with no way out. Not the danger to herself and her baby, not the end of the world. She'd failed him, breaking the one promise she'd made to the one boy who'd held her through the night and told her he loved her. If *this* was her punishment for the things she'd done, it was too cruel by far. It would kill her, not at once but slowly, the hurt and recrimination consuming her every day for the rest of her life.

A muffled voice in the hall made her head snap up. It sounded like Laman's, but she couldn't make out the words. She wiped her teary cheeks with the back of her hand, stood and glided silently to the door. With an ear against the metal, she listened.

" … only let her out to use the bathroom," the voice was saying. It was definitely Laman's, though it carried a whining tone she hadn't heard previously.

He was answered by a deep rumble, indistinct even with her ear pressed against the door. It went on for a few seconds, then Laman's voice returned, higher-pitched than before and almost pleading.

"I did everything you told me to," the boy said. "If you didn't think I could handle it, why didn't you ask … "

The next words were drowned out by a loud thump against the wall that made Michelle jerk back. But the door didn't open, and after a moment, she shakily laid her ear against it once more.

" … so sick of this," Laman's voice resumed. "I don't see why we have to—"

This time, the boy's words were cut off by the rumble— the voice of the person Laman was talking to, Michelle realized. It didn't sound like a human voice, though. It sounded like some kind of machine, the growl of an eighteen wheeler or the roar of an airplane taking off. Something powerful, something that wouldn't stop or even slow down no matter what stood in its way.

" … must be back by now," Laman picked up after the rumble ended. There was a sulky quality to the boy's voice, which was complemented by his next words. "Or did you expect me to go to the bathroom with her?"

Michelle waited for the rumble again, but there was nothing but silence. She flattened her ear against the door, hoping to pick up more of the one-sided conversation. Instead, she felt vibrations in the metal as the doorknob was turned, and she barely jumped back in time before the door swung open.

Laman was there, his expression matching the peevish tone she'd heard. When she looked up at the person behind him, she understood why Laman seemed so scared. The man filled the corridor, his shoulders more than twice as wide as Laman's, the top of his head nearly touching the hallway ceiling. His eyes were as black as his crew-cut hair, his severe brows a parallel to the unyielding line of his mouth. Where Laman was dressed in the black T-shirt and ratty jeans from earlier, this giant wore an immaculate dark blue uniform with a high collar, gold buttons and cuffs, and rows of multicolored squares—medals, they must have been—across the left side of his impossibly broad chest. It was when Michelle's eyes fell on the red letters stitched above the pocket on the right side that she gasped and retreated from the man's stormy gaze.

*S K L D I*

The uniformed man placed a massive hand on Laman's shoulder. Laman winced as if it hurt, but he cleared his throat and spoke in a tightly controlled voice.

"Dad," he said, "this is Diana."

# Chapter 4

Michelle backed toward the bed as the Tall Man entered her room.

Her mind reeled at the import of Laman's words, or of his single word. *Dad.* If the titan who stood with his head inches from the glowing squares of the ceiling truly was the Tall Man of her stolen photograph—and beard or no beard, who else could he be?—then not only was he the chief scientist of the Skaldi lab, but Laman was Jason's younger brother.

Did Laman know what had happened to his older sibling? Did their father know that Jason had sworn to destroy his experiments, only to die trying?

The already small room shrank to dollhouse size as the man advanced. In the photograph, his height had been partially disguised by the way he'd stood hunched over, leaning on a metal forearm crutch. She'd assumed his disability had to do with his unnatural stature; maybe mere muscle and bone couldn't support a body that big. Now, though, he stood military erect, shoulders squared, chest out. Michelle sat on the bed, the farthest she could get from him. Even so, she felt as trapped as a laboratory animal in a wire mesh cage.

The Tall Man turned to his younger son, who had the appearance of a child on his first day of kindergarten—not just his puny size but the look of utter dread on his face. The only thing missing was for his father to hold his hand. Michelle had the feeling that if the man did that, he'd mash the boy's bones to putty.

"Laman," the giant rumbled, "you can go."

Laman looked guiltily at Michelle. "Maybe I should—"

"Laman." From that grim mouth, the word fell like an anvil. "I said you can go."

The stricken look in Laman's eyes deepened. Though she knew he could offer her no protection from his father, she felt absolutely alone when the boy ducked his head and slouched from the room.

Michelle watched warily as the Tall Man lowered himself into a chair that had been built for a body half his size. The metal squealed under his weight; she could picture it bending, if not snapping. The man placed his hands neatly on his knees, his posture never deviating from the vertical, his dark eyes never leaving hers.

"Well," he began. His face formed the approximation of a smile, but it was a smile without warmth, the kind your coach would give you right before telling you you'd been cut from the team. "It seems introductions are in order. My name is Udain Genn, and you go by the name of Diana?"

"That's right."

He leaned forward slightly, but even that small movement made Michelle feel as if a wall of darkness were crowding her into a corner. "Just Diana?"

Under the pressure of his penetrating gaze, she was tempted to tell him the truth, the same way she'd felt compelled under the influence of his son Jason's wolf-blue eyes. She decided, though, that she had no choice but to stand up to him. She couldn't win a fight against the merciless man who'd experimented on Kareem and the other children in the Skaldi lab, but she wasn't going to give him the satisfaction of watching her quail before him like Laman had.

"I lived in a camp back east all my life," she said, which felt close enough to the truth. "Like I told Laman, we only used first names."

"Hm." He frowned, maybe at the reminder of his younger son. "Well, I must inform you that this camp of yours provided you with very poor prenatal care. Dr. Melan, our chief of medicine—"

"Is this a hospital?"

"In part." Again, the mirthless smile. "As I was saying, Dr. Melan examined you when you arrived at this facility. He performed an ultrasound and other tests, and he has assured me that your unborn child is developing normally. That's little short of a miracle, considering—"

"He did an ultrasound?" It struck her how much had changed in her life, that such a basic procedure seemed like a lost art, as miraculous as all the other technologies she'd lived without for over half a year.

The man who called himself Udain Genn straightened in his chair, which whined in protest. His eyes flashed a warning that he wouldn't tolerate another interruption. "We have the results prepared for you. Would you like to see an image of your baby?"

Michelle's heart leaped at the prospect, and her lips opened to respond with an enthusiastic *yes.* Then she reconsidered. She didn't want to be indebted to this man in any way, no matter how slight. And she wasn't sure she wanted to know about her baby yet. Whether it was a boy or a girl.

Whether it had ten fingers and toes or the awful chest scar of the creatures she'd fought in the Skaldi lab.

"No, thank you," she said. "I want it to be a surprise."

He nodded curtly, as if he was bound to respect her wishes even if they displeased him. "In any event, it's fortunate for both your health and that of your unborn child that we found you. Given the lack of prenatal care—"

"I got checkups."

"From two preadolescent mutes, if I understand correctly. You've taken no multivitamin, nothing with folic acid to prevent neural tube defects. So far as we can tell, you've pursued no exercise or diet regimen—"

"I walked a lot."

"Self-evidently." It seemed that he'd accepted her interruptions the way he'd accepted her refusal to view the ultrasound: as the behavior of a typical teenager very much like his truculent younger son. "Pregnancy places significant stress on the human body, and Dr. Melan has informed me that you're drastically malnourished, with much lower bone density than expected for a healthy female of your age, and with signs of the possible onset of gestational diabetes—"

"But my baby's healthy?"

"So far as we can determine. It's likely you can thank your youth for that. An eighteen-year-old—"

"I'm seventeen."

"I beg your pardon. Dr. Melan made an educated guess based on the factors he observed."

Michelle was silent, wondering what those factors might have been. What did he do, count tree rings?

"The good news is, we can address all of those issues now," Udain Genn continued. "The malnutrition, the glucose abnormalities. We have a top-notch obstetrics and gynecology team on site, and they'll work diligently to ensure that you bring a healthy baby to term."

Once again, the humorless smile flickered across the giant's face. There was something odd about the way he delivered that speech, something that sounded like the PSAs she'd been forced to endure in Health class. It made Michelle think he'd said the same thing to other girls, and it increased her distrust of this man who'd headed the Skaldi experiments back east. Nausikaa and Aristodeme had fled from those experiments with most of their memories and identities stripped away, though thankfully, based on how Udain Genn referred to them, it seemed he didn't remember who they were. Still, why would such a man be so solicitous about a complete stranger? Did he honestly expect her to believe that he'd gone from breeding monsters to opening a halfway house for knocked-up teens? The only advantage she had over him, she decided, was that she knew who *he* was, but he—apparently—didn't know that she knew. Unless, that is, this Dr. Melan character had scanned her mind, recording her thoughts along with her low bone density and possible gestational diabetes.

"Thank you," she said, and hoped she didn't sound too out of character for the churlish teen he supposed her to be. "Can you tell me more about this place? Or even show me around?"

"Of course," he said. "You'll find you're in good hands."

*With All-State,* Michelle said to herself. When the man made no move to rise from his chair, she asked, "Could we go now? I want to see how my friends are doing, especially Tyris and the twins."

Udain Genn hesitated just long enough for Michelle to notice it. "Of course," he said, with that strained smile on his thin lips. "Right this way."

He stood. Having grown accustomed to his size while he was seated, she found herself shocked once again by how he filled the room now that he was back on his feet. She hunted on the floor beside the bed before she remembered. "I don't have my boots."

"We run a sterile facility," he said. "We were able to clean your uniform, but I'm afraid even our autoclave wasn't equal to your footwear. I think you'll find our replacement completely satisfactory."

She wiggled her toes in the slipper socks. The unwelcome thought flashed through her mind that Udain Genn might have recognized her uniform as having belonged to his son's camp, but she pushed the thought down. The truth was, she was unclear how much the senior Genn knew about his son's activities after Jason stopped working in his father's lab. "I guess I'm ready," she said, and the hulking man led her from the room.

He strode down the hall, his legs swinging as sharply as if he were marching to a tune in his head. Michelle had to scurry to catch up. When they reached the door she'd found in the alcove, Udain Genn laid neither a hand nor an eye on the sensor. Instead, he held out his arm, and a metal wristband that had been covered by his sleeve flashed a green pinpoint of light. The door slid into the wall, revealing that what lay behind wasn't a room or another hallway but an elevator.

"We're currently on the second level of this facility," he said. "The maternity ward, you might call it. The general infirmary is one level above."

"How many levels are there?"

"Quite a few," he sort of-answered. He held out a hand double the size of hers, gesturing for her to enter the elevator. "If you please."

Michelle stepped inside, and the man followed. The roof of the elevator was just high enough that he didn't have to duck. She wondered if he was the one who'd designed this place, or if, at least, it had been built with someone of his dimensions in mind. She had so many questions that she felt in desperate need to have answered. For example, if they were on the second floor, why were there no windows? She kept silent, sensing that she had to choose her questions carefully, knowing that even then, Udain Genn would supply only a fraction of the answers she craved.

The elevator had no buttons for floors, only a sensor like the one outside. That didn't present a problem for the man with the wrist cuff. He simply tapped the cuff with a huge, blunt finger, and the door slid closed and the elevator started upward. Thankfully, the ride was short; being trapped in this box with a man whose medal-decorated chest stood well above her head level would have been unendurable for more than a few seconds. When the elevator glided to a stop and the door opened, she was about to step out, but Udain Genn caught her by the elbow and held her, gently yet with enough contained force that she knew she could never free herself if he didn't want her to.

"I need to make one thing clear before we begin our tour," he said in a voice that might have been conversational if he didn't have control of her arm. "We follow very strict procedures here for the wellbeing of all our residents. There are some three hundred people who live and work in this facility, and I'll not allow the actions of any one resident to jeopardize the safety of the others. Is that understood?"

Michelle didn't answer at once. Through the open door, she could see another sterile white hallway, this one filled with people wearing black, white, or blue military uniforms who'd paused whatever they were doing to watch the new arrivals. Obviously, Udain Genn had waited to deliver his lecture so others could witness it. But what did he expect her to do that might disrupt the routines of this citadel? Was his warning the kind he gave to every new resident of his base, or was there something about her in particular he was worried about?

She answered him as truthfully as she could. "I just want my baby to be safe."

His hand loosened, and his craggy features relaxed into a smile that conveyed something like genuine warmth. "That's what we all want, Diana. That's why we're glad you're here."

As they exited the elevator, a small man with a dark complexion and black hair combed neatly across his brow hurried down the hall to meet them. He wore a blue uniform similar to Udain Genn's, but he looked like a child beside his commanding officer.

"General," he said, saluting smartly. "It is a pleasure to see you this morning, sir." In his voice, Michelle heard the precise cadences of a native of India or Pakistan.

Udain Genn casually returned the salute. "You should be even more pleased to see your patient on her feet. Diana," he continued, indicating the little man, "this is Dr. Praneet Melan."

Dr. Melan reached out to take Michelle's hand. His grip was delicate, his skin dry. "You are feeling better?"

"Much."

The man stared at her, smiling eagerly, to the point where she was actually thankful when Udain Genn broke the spell.

"Let's be on our way," he said. "Dr. Melan, I'll see you this afternoon. Please let me know if you need anything before then."

"Fourteen hundred hours sharp, sir," the man said, snapping another salute before he ran off. Michelle craned her neck to see Udain Genn's face, and found that it bore an uncharacteristically amused look.

"Dr. Melan and I will be meeting with his medical team later today," he said by way of explanation.

"Oh." She was dying to ask what exactly this medical team did, but she had a strong feeling that was one of the questions she wouldn't get an answer to.

Udain Genn strode down the hall with Michelle taking two steps for every one of his. The other men and women had gone back to their work, passing in and out of doors, consulting computer monitors on carts, clustering at what looked like a nurses' station, a kidney-shaped island with brightly colored monitors hanging above. No one was dressed like a doctor or nurse, all of them wearing military uniforms. Though there was no shortage of doors, there were no windows, which Michelle couldn't understand. It made the hallway seem more like a prison than a hospital ward, and finally, the feeling of claustrophobia got to be too much for her. "Why aren't there any windows?"

Udain Genn answered without looking at her or pausing in his stride. "The entire facility is built belowground. For purposes of security."

*For purposes of insanity*, Michelle thought. "So it's like an office building? Underground?"

"Something like that. Originally, the installation was designed for military use—as a research facility, as well as a shelter for top-level officials in times of national crisis. Needless to say, that's been a blessing for us in light of present circumstances. We're fully self-sustaining, capable of generating power and supplying our own needs for as long as is necessary to complete our work."

"What kind of research are you doing?" she asked, though she doubted she'd get an answer to that one.

"I'm not at liberty to disclose the specifics," he confirmed her hunch. "You must understand, Diana, that some of the nation's top-priority national security projects were conducted right here, with the very highest clearances required to so much as set foot inside. Though we've repurposed operations to adapt to changed conditions on the surface, we're still functioning under strict classification protocols. No one here, not even myself as commander of this facility, can discuss our business openly with civilians."

"But if everything's changed so much," she asked, "is there even a government anymore? Does it even matter?"

He stopped abruptly. She was taking so many steps to keep up with him, she nearly collided with his back. When he pivoted to look down at her, the expression of disapproval from their original interview had returned.

"There's *my* government," he said. "And it matters very much to me."

Michelle hated herself for this, but she quavered before the man's gaze, just as Dr. Melan had seemed nervous and oh-so-eager to please in his superior's presence. She had the sudden, sinking feeling that she could spend the rest of her life in this cold underground chamber, could raise her child in a room like the one where she'd woken up, live in relative comfort, even know some moments of pleasure, but never get answers to the most basic of questions, such as what the purpose of this place was or what had happened to the green jar that held the ashes of her baby's father. If Udain Genn wanted to keep those things secret, he would. And if he'd taken the jar for some mysterious reason of his own, then it was gone forever.

She'd no sooner had that thought than the giant's face softened like a parent's who regretted having to discipline a wayward child. "Well," he said. "We're here."

Michelle looked at the door they'd reached, which stood at the very end of the long infirmary hallway. It was no different from the others, a plain metal door with a regular doorknob, but on the dry erase board beside the door three names were scribbled in green ink:

*TYRIS*

*NAUSIKA*

*ARISTODAME*

"We had no more luck with their last names than with yours," Udain Genn said. "So I suppose there's something to this camp story after all."

Michelle was too relieved to react to the dryness in his voice, or to point out that they'd misspelled the twins' names despite the tags on their uniform pockets. When Udain Genn pushed open the door and she heard a familiar shriek of joy, tears pricked her eyes.

Tyris threw herself at Michelle, squeezing her waist with all the strength her five-year-old arms could muster. The twins were more reserved, but they came over to Michelle with shy smiles while Tyris dragged her into the room, which was more the size of a suite. The little girl was eager to show Michelle all the new toys she'd gotten: a doll—something she'd never had before, since it was far too frivolous for Jason's camp—along with a coloring book and crayons, a miniature tea set, and, most magical of all, a computer tablet loaded with games. She made Michelle sit on one of the room's three beds while she exhibited all the qualities of each new possession, and though Michelle couldn't help wondering whose toys these had been before, Tyris's excitement helped loosen the knot that shared space with the baby in her stomach. Udain Genn didn't interfere with their reunion, though he did hover in the hallway just outside the door while Tyris caught Michelle up on the thousands of words she hadn't had a chance to tell her caregiver since they'd parted in the desert.

Those words had finally slowed to a trickle when Tyris jumped up with another exclamation of delight, and Michelle turned to see an African-American girl about Tyris's age, squat and moon-faced, peeking in at the doorway. Tyris grabbed the girl's hands and drew her into the room, though it seemed that the new child resisted somewhat. When the two stood in front of Michelle, however, the newcomer met her eyes with a mischievous twinkle.

"Diana, this is Petra!" Tyris announced. "Petra, Diana's going to have a baby!"

Petra's eyes widened as she reached out boldly to lay a hand on Michelle's stomach. Her mouth fell partway open, then she leaned close as if to hear the baby's heartbeat. Seemingly satisfied with her inspection, she grinned and slipped her arm through Tyris's, and the girls retreated to play with their toys. Michelle felt her heart melting as she watched the two. She wished Helene could have lived to see her daughter make her first friend.

It was just at that moment that Udain Genn leaned in the door, clearing his throat in an authoritative way his younger son had obviously tried, and failed, to emulate. "I need to be getting along to my meeting. And I think a break might do you good as well."

Michelle would have objected, but this obviously wasn't a suggestion. She said goodbye to Tyris and the twins, and followed Udain Genn down the hall to the elevator.

"Petra is one of many refugees we've taken in over the past months," he explained to Michelle's unasked question. "Her mother and father almost certainly perished in the desert, but she was able to find her way here on her own."

"And she's how old?"

"She won't say. Dr. Melan estimates she's no more than five, but she already has the makings of a first-class scout."

His words reminded Michelle of the woman who had led her colony here. "Is there any time for me to see the rest of my friends before your meeting? Especially Arachne?"

He frowned. "I beg your pardon?"

"The leader of our camp. Is she on this floor, too?"

For the first time since they'd met, Udain Genn seemed disconcerted, as if words weren't ready at his command. "I'd have to check with Dr. Melan to see—"

"Could you do it now, please?"

He frowned more severely, but touched his cuff with a finger. In no time, the small figure of Dr. Melan came hurrying down the hallway. He stopped in front of his commanding officer and gave a breathless salute that the general didn't bother to return.

"There seems to be some confusion about our patient list," Udain Genn said to his chief of medicine. "Our young guest has inquired after a woman named—"

"Arachne," Michelle cut in. "She was dressed in a black jacket with gold cuffs, and she has her hair shaved all the way down."

Dr. Melan glanced nervously at his commander, then unclipped a small computer tablet from his belt and scrolled through the screen. With each second that passed, Michelle's anxiety grew. When the doctor returned the tablet to his belt and faced her with a look she'd have called more grieved than apologetic, she knew.

"It is my unfortunate obligation to inform you," he said, "that no one matching that name and description was recovered from the desert."

# Chapter 5

Michelle sat on her bed, staring at the blank white wall, trying to forget.

She'd been there for hours, ever since Udain Genn guided her to the room with a huge hand on her shoulder. She could barely remember the trip back, though it covered the same short walk and elevator ride they'd taken to get to the infirmary floor. When she tried to reconstruct her steps, it felt as if the hallways had been obscured by fog, or maybe by the ghosts of all the people who had vanished from her life.

Kareem. Helene. Everyone from home, her parents and sister and friends. And now, Arachne. All of them, she couldn't help feeling, might be alive today if not for her.

In some part of her mind, she knew that was crazy. She couldn't have stopped the bombs from falling. Couldn't have halted the Skaldi experiments. Couldn't have prevented the final confrontation at Jason's camp that had claimed her baby's father.

But she *could* have kept her finger from pulling the flamethrower's trigger. She could have told Arachne the truth about where they were going, rather than keeping secret a dream she'd forced on everyone else. For the six months of their westward march, Arachne had warned her repeatedly of the dangers that surrounded them, insisting that she be watchful and smart. Only days ago, the sentry had tried to tell her again, to remind her that it wasn't just her life at stake but the lives of the most vulnerable members of their colony. But she hadn't listened, not really. She'd been too eager to fulfill her personal quest, to satisfy the promise she'd made to a boy who would never even know what she'd done. And now, with the walls of Udain Genn's stronghold rising even taller than the Tall Man himself, she'd walked her colony straight into a trap from which none of them could escape.

*You did this to them,* she said to herself. *You could have let your own life end that day in Jason's camp, but you chose to kill the boy you loved instead. And now, you've killed Arachne, the one person who might have been able to get us out of this place. Who will be next, Michelle? If Tyris becomes the Tall Man's latest experimental subject or he decides to finish the work he started on the twins, how will you justify the actions that delivered more innocent victims to his doorstep?*

She covered her face with her hands, but the tears she hoped might release some of the despair in her chest wouldn't come. When her baby, maybe sensing its mother's disquiet, tried one of its happy otter-rolls, it did nothing to quell the pain.

*I'm sorry,* she spoke to the unborn life inside her. *I've made too many promises I can't afford to keep. I won't let anyone else die because of me. Or even because of you.*

Michelle rose and padded the two steps across the room in her ridiculous slipper socks. She took the metal chair from the corner and laid it on its back beside the bed. Even as she prepared her plan, she knew it didn't amount to much— certainly nothing like the devious, ingenious strategy Arachne would have come up with. But Arachne was dead, and if there was to be any chance of freeing her friends, it all rested on her.

Removing the socks so she wouldn't slip, she climbed onto the bed and jumped, landing on one of the upper legs of the chair. She lost her balance, but the bed was there to catch her. When she investigated the chair, she saw that the force of her landing had bent the leg slightly, so she returned to the bed and jumped again. This time, the leg bent enough that she could see the strain in the metal. She half-smiled, thinking, *I guess there's some good to being a whale after all.* She worked the damaged leg back and forth until the stress on the metal was great enough for it to move without much resistance. Then she jumped on it a final time and was gratified when it snapped off. She hadn't anticipated this, but when she saw how jagged the metal was where the leg had broken loose, she nodded in grim satisfaction.

Armed with her inadequate weapon, she opened the door and slipped into the hall. She already knew what lay to the right-hand side of her room, so without much hope of discovering anything useful, she checked the hallway to the left. As expected, there was nothing there, not even another door. She scanned the ceiling and walls, looking for some sign of entry to the ventilation system that hummed audibly around her, but the place was sealed tight, everything hidden from prying eyes. The thought of disguised vents made her wonder if there were hidden cameras too, streaming an image of her acrobatics to Udain Genn the same way his older son had spied on members of the Argo. She remembered the Tall Man's words of warning from their brief tour: *I'll not allow the actions of any one resident to jeopardize the safety of the others.* But that seemed like ages ago, in a different time, a different life. Shaking her head to chase his voice away, she walked silently to the intersection where the main hallway met the elevator alcove and stood with her back pressed against the wall, waiting for whoever would come to visit her next. Something told her she wouldn't have to wait long.

She'd been there for no more than a dozen breathless minutes when the elevator door slid open and footsteps sounded hollowly in the corridor. In the second before the footsteps reached her, she told herself they were too light to belong to Udain Genn. She didn't let herself think too much about who else it might be as she threw herself at the person who was approaching the corner.

She collided with him, and the combination of her weight and the surprise attack was enough to bring him to the floor. She raised her weapon just as Laman Genn threw his arms in front of his face to defend himself.

"Are you crazy?" the boy sputtered, but by the time the final word left his mouth, Michelle had flipped him onto his stomach and braced her knee against his back, her free hand pressing his face to the floor.

"*I'm* crazy," she said, "and *you're* helping your father make monsters. Who's the crazier one?"

"I don't know what you're talking about," he said, his words slurred by contact with the floor tiles. "I—ow!"

He reached for his head where she'd clubbed him with the blunt end of the chair leg, but she cracked the metal rod against his hand too, and he withdrew it, wincing.

"That's for Arachne," she said, gripping his hair and raising his face an inch or two from the ground. "You want to try me again?"

"I told you I don't know—*OW!*"

When she lifted his face from the floor this time, blood smeared the tiles from his split forehead. He struggled to free himself, but with his scrawny frame and ineffective maneuvers, he was no match for someone who'd been training for months in the wilderness, pregnant or not. When he realized that, he went still, though his voice shook with the next words he spoke.

"I don't know what you're trying to accomplish, but I can guarantee you it won't work. This place is like a fortress. If you kill me—"

"Then there'll be one less Genn in my life to deal with."

"But I didn't *do* anything. I swear—"

She flipped him onto his back before he could finish and looked into his teary eyes. Blood streamed from his nose as well as his forehead. She pressed one hand under his chin, bringing the sharpened end of the chair leg to his throat.

"I don't want to kill you," she said, "but I will if that's the only choice you leave me. You're going to take me to my friends. And then you're going to help us gather our supplies and show us the way out of this madhouse, and if anyone tries to stop us, I'll cut your heart from your chest and leave you for Dr. Melan to put back together again."

The boy was actually crying now, tears mingling with blood and snot. "I told you, that'll never work. There are too many guards, too many things they can do to you. You don't *know*, Diana. We're probably being watched right now, and everyone's laughing at the idea that you think my dad cares enough about me to negotiate for my life."

Michelle hesitated for a moment, though she didn't loosen her grip on the boy's throat. If this wasn't a bluff, if there really were cameras as she'd feared and Udain Genn was sending an armed force to storm the maternity ward right now, then Laman was right: there was no chance of her plan working. Maybe she shouldn't have resorted to such drastic measures right away; maybe she should have tried talking to the head warden of this penal colony first. And yet, she was more certain now than ever that talking to the chief of the Skaldi experiments wouldn't get her anywhere. Or it would—but *anywhere* would be a locked unit with guards at the door and scientists probing her body with their microscopes and needles.

*No.* She'd made her choice. And she had to make Laman see that she meant it.

"Maybe he doesn't care about you," she said. "But you're as much a part of this as he is. You've been guarding me the whole time, doing his bidding. Telling me everyone was safe, when you could have been out searching for Arachne."

"I didn't know," he said. "How was I supposed to know how many people you had with you? If I'd known there was anyone else—"

"You're lying, Laman," she said. "You're a scared little daddy's boy, and it's time you grew up."

He cried out as she twisted her hand in his hair and yanked him to his feet. Quickly, she spun him around so that he was in front of her, his thin body fitting awkwardly against her protruding stomach. She jabbed the point of the chair leg against his jugular and whispered in his ear, feeling him tremble with every word.

"All I need to do is press hard, and you'll be dead by the time you hit the floor. Now take me to the infirmary. And for your sake, you'd better hope your father loves you more than you think he does."

He started to nod, then realized what a bad idea that was. With his hands held high, he headed for the elevator, Michelle matching him step for step. He had no wrist cuff like his father's, but he placed an unsteady finger against the sensor, and it brightened at his touch, the elevator door sliding open. When they entered, Michelle leaned forward to talk to him in a voice that reminded her so much of his dead older brother's, it frightened even her. "You need to understand something. If that door opens and we're anywhere other than where I told you to take me, you're dead."

She could tell he was fighting back tears, but he pressed a finger to the interior sensor and the elevator began to climb.

The most uncomfortable ten seconds of her life ensued. Being alone in an elevator with someone she barely knew had always ranked high on her list of least favorite scenarios; when that person was trying not to blubber and she was steeling herself to do what she'd threatened to if the door opened on Udain Genn's private headquarters, the weirdness quotient went way up. By the time the elevator stopped, she'd hardened her heart and was ready to slit his throat if she had to.

He must have realized it, because the door opened on the infirmary ward.

The men and women in the hallway froze when they saw Laman. Michelle shoved him out of the elevator, gripping his arm to keep him close, holding the lethal point of the weapon so securely against his throat she could feel his fearful pulse through the metal.

"On the floor!" she shouted to whoever could hear. "No one comes near an alarm!"

To Michelle's immense relief, they obeyed. Quickly, she pulled Laman against her and pressed her back to the wall so no one could sneak up on her. She had a clear view of the hallway, left and right; bodies in their black and white and blue uniforms lay on the tiles as far as she could see. She leaned close to Laman again and whispered in his ear.

"I want everyone where I can see them. If anyone's hiding and doesn't come out by the time I count to three, you know what happens next."

"But how will you know if everybody—"

"One."

"Diana … "

"Two," she said. "Now tell them! And make sure they know I'm not joking."

Laman raised his voice, though it shook badly. "Everyone, come out so she knows you're there. Please, she'll kill me if you don't."

"Dangerously close to three," Michelle reminded him.

"Right now!" he screamed. "*Please!*"

There was a silent moment, then several uniformed people walked out of bedrooms, hands raised. They were followed by a patient or two in hospital gowns, who looked utterly bewildered at the sudden crisis. Dr. Melan crept on his hands and knees from behind the nurses' station, the shock in his large bright eyes making it clear that he thought his newest patient had gone completely insane.

"Electronics out," Michelle called, remembering the doctor's tablet. "Put whatever you've got on the floor and slide it away from you. *Now!*"

Tablets, pagers, and phones dropped to the floor and went spinning down the corridor to collide with the walls.

"That's good enough," Michelle said. "Stay where you are and nobody gets hurt. Now, you, start moving!"

She didn't have to tell Laman twice. Keeping her back against the wall and her weapon at his throat, she sidestepped toward the room where she'd found Tyris and the twins. The people on the floor looked up at her with permutations of terror, astonishment, and outrage in their eyes. The girl Petra stood by one of the doors; in the brief moment that Michelle caught her gaze, Tyris's playmate seemed to stare at her not with fear but with admiration. Michelle had no time to wonder how such a young child could remain so calm in the face of death. Every muscle in Michelle's body was wound to its tightest point, and though she told herself it would be easy to plunge the blade deeply into the boy's yielding flesh, she was still praying that she wouldn't have to test his father's affection.

Moving quickly, almost as if they'd acclimated to each other in some sick three-legged race, she and Laman reached the girls' room at the end of the hallway. When she peeked inside over Laman's shoulder, she saw that Tyris was asleep, a complication she hadn't anticipated. The twins, though, were wide awake and on their feet, having obviously heard her voice and figured out what she was up to. Aristodeme held a mesh bag that contained a collection of plastic water bottles and packaged nutrition bars, which she must have gathered on the spot from the hospital room. Nausikaa scooped the sleeping Tyris into her arms, and with the three of them walking in front where they could remain in sight, Michelle nudged her hostage with the chair leg and reversed course down the hallway.

None of the infirmary staff had moved that she could tell. The phones and other devices remained where they'd been thrown, and Michelle was tempted to tell Aristodeme to grab one of them. It had been so long since she'd held—or even seen—a phone, her fingers itched to send a text, browse the web, *anything*. But even if she was able to connect to what was certain to be a secured network, who was there to receive her message? She put the phones out of her mind as she inched closer and closer to the elevator.

Petra was still there at the door to her room, looking earnestly at Michelle as the group passed by, and Michelle's heart—or maybe it was the baby's—tugged at her chest as the little girl's dark eyes beseeched her. At that moment, she felt that it would be far easier to kill Udain's son than to leave Petra to suffer at the hands of the father. She resisted the girl's silent entreaty, telling herself she couldn't afford to trust anyone in Udain Genn's facility, not even a child.

*I can't save her*, she told herself. *I don't even know where Bridget and the others are, and I'll be lucky enough to save the ones I have with me.*

The elevator came in sight. Laman's breathing had calmed; maybe he foresaw that his ordeal was almost over. She wondered whether she should take him with her when— if—they were free of this place, but immediately decided against it. Already, she was dreaming of the moment she could relax her grip on his arm and lower the stake from his throat, plus she supposed she owed him his freedom after breaking his nose and, unless her own nose deceived her, making him wet his pants. She was trying to decide on the right moment to let him go when the elevator door opened and a shadow fell into the hallway.

Michelle tightened her grip on Laman, but the person who emerged wasn't his father. Instead, it was a child no more than ten years old, with skin as pale as Laman's and wearing jeans and a red T-shirt. The child's long brown hair made Michelle think it was a girl until she got a closer look at the unnaturally lean, hardened face. She couldn't understand why, if one of the medical personnel had managed to send a distress signal, they'd called an unarmed boy even younger than the twins instead of the master of this compound. She quickened her pace, gesturing for the girls to duck behind her while she pushed Laman ahead. Hopefully, she could scare the child away and take the waiting elevator to freedom.

When she drew close enough to see his eyes, she felt a jolt of misgiving that nothing up to this point had produced. Maybe it was because, having terrorized Laman and practically everyone else for the past fifteen minutes, she was startled to see the boy confront her without a trace of fear, standing with his thumbs hooked in his belt loops like some street kid from *West Side Story*. Or maybe it was because, looking into the flat black eyes that flicked watchfully over her as she advanced, she felt as if she were being scrutinized by something reptilian, something that knew only calculation and intent, not compassion or pity or doubt.

"Nice going, Lame Man," the boy called out in a voice that hadn't yet deepened. "Looks like you're going to win the prize for base screw-up six months in a row."

Laman said nothing, but his body trembled in Michelle's grasp.

"I told Dad he should never have put you in charge," the child continued with a scornful laugh. "But I guess he keeps looking for ways to get rid of you."

Michelle paused in her approach, thinking, *Dad?*

"Sorry if this hurts," the boy said, directing his words at her. "On second thought, I hope it hurts like hell."

83

His finger hovered over his wrist, where Michelle saw the gleam of a cuff like Udain Genn's. Laman stiffened, and with a burst of strength that took her totally off guard, he tore himself from her grip. Before she had a chance to react, white-hot pain shot through her legs, slamming her backward against the wall, her weapon clattering to the floor. Without Laman's body to stop her, she fell face forward, her arms refusing to catch her before she hit the ground. She landed with enough force to knock the wind out of her, then rolled onto her back. The pain was gone, but her teeth had locked together and her eyes fluttered uncontrollably, showing her a strobe effect of black-uniformed bodies converging on the girls, bringing them to the floor beside her. The awakened Tyris screamed, but Michelle could neither see her nor reach out her arms to fend off the swarm.

Laman's blurry face appeared above her. His nose dripped blood as he spun toward his younger brother. "You idiot! Can't you see she's pregnant?"

"What's it to you?" the emotionless voice spoke out of Michelle's vision. "Just be happy you didn't get zapped."

Laman's face twisted with fury, but he throttled his reply and turned to check on her. "Diana! Are you all right? Diana! Answer me!"

Michelle's jaw loosened and a groan escaped her. She tried to say something in response to his urgent query, but pain buckled her middle, totally different from the electric shock. It felt like every muscle in her body was cramping all at once, and even before Dr. Melan's face replaced Laman's, she knew what that meant.

"Bring a gurney!" the doctor called to someone out of sight. There was a flurry of activity, but Michelle saw only the beginnings of it, her eyes squeezing closed as another contraction twisted her gut.

She felt a new presence nearby, like a wave of cold that cut through the pain in her body. She looked up to see the child leaning over her.

"How interesting," he said.

She would have cursed him, but the pain was so great she could only grind her teeth together to stifle a scream.

*The girl who cried wolf*, she thought as hands lifted her onto a hospital bed and raced with her down the corridor. *Only this time, she can't save her sheep.*

# Chapter 6

She passed in and out of consciousness for what seemed like days.

Her dreams were of blood and fire, Skaldi rising from the desert only to wither at the touch of the flamethrower in her hands. Then she saw that it wasn't Skaldi after all, it was Kareem, his eyes less accusatory than mournful as she tried in vain to turn the spout of the flamethrower from his body. When he was gone, leaving nothing but whirling clouds of ash that filled the sky and danced just beyond reach of her collection jar, she found herself in a hospital room with four figures hovering beside her bed, the giant commander of the Skaldi trials dwarfing his three dark-haired sons. The pain in her abdomen was so strong she felt as if she were being torn apart from the inside, becoming one of the monsters that fed on human flesh. When she looked down between her blood-streaked legs, she saw that the thing that had emerged from her had the hollow face and skeletal frame of the creatures she'd fought in the Skaldi lab. It opened its toothless mouth, and she screamed as its body split down the center to reveal the wet gray emptiness within.

She tore herself from delirium and lay as if shipwrecked, her body shaking and drenched in salty sweat. When at last she assured herself that the dreams were done and that *this* was reality, she discovered that a number of changes had taken place since she'd fallen in the infirmary hallway. First and most evident, the terrible vise-like clamping in her middle had ceased, and her muscles felt as quivery and weak as if she'd run a marathon. Did that mean the baby had come? But no, looking down at the stiff white hospital sheet that covered her, she saw that her belly was as big as ever. She was trying to convince herself it must be a vision or a hallucination when her resident life form executed a particularly intricate maneuver that would have made her laugh if not for the presence of the other objects her eyes took in around her.

She was on a hospital bed, true. But she wasn't in a room in the infirmary, or back in the bedroom they'd assigned her on the maternity ward. Instead, she was in a space that looked much more like a lab than a living area, with stainless steel cabinets and blinking lights from tall machines she couldn't identify. Directly overhead, blinding circles of light shone down on her, the kind she'd seen in operating rooms on TV. When she turned her head to avoid the glare, she found that another bed was on her left, not a comfortable bed like the one in the maternity ward but a simple metal slab with a stark white sheet stretched overtop of it. She looked to the other side, and received an even greater shock: the bed-slab to her right was much larger than the first, and it was occupied by a giant form lying on his back beneath a sheet the size of a tent. His head was turned in her direction, and his open eyes were fixed on her.

Michelle reacted instantly, trying to pull away from Udain Genn. She found that her wrists were restrained beneath the sheet, something cutting into her flesh as she tugged to free herself. When she attempted to move her legs, she discovered that they were tied down, too. She strained as hard as she could, but the bonds were too tight to give her any leverage, and she quickly gave up, gasping as fresh beads of sweat broke out on her forehead.

"Nice try," a voice spoke from behind her. "But it's not going to be as easy with me as it was with my pathetic excuse for a brother."

Cold fear shivered down her spine at the sound of that voice. She tried to twist her head to see him, but he remained out of sight, out of reach. He didn't laugh the way he had at Laman in the infirmary ward; he made no further sound, not even a breath to show he was there. Still, she felt his remorseless eyes roving over her body, and she could sense his pleasure at reducing her to complete helplessness before him.

"What are you going to do to me?" she asked.

"Nothing too drastic," he said. "We were worried you were going into preterm labor up there, though Melan thinks it was only Braxton Hicks contractions. We gave you a shot of terbutaline just in case. Given the unprecedented nature of this pregnancy, we can't be too careful."

Very little of this registered on Michelle, but she did catch the words *up there*. So they were in one of the facility's lower levels, maybe on its bottom floor? Farther from the ground-level exit, farther from escape. What was Udain Genn doing down here? And why had the colossus not stirred from his bed while his youngest son spoke, his dark eyes remaining open in an awful, unblinking stare?

"It was probably the shock that did it," the boy's voice continued. "Melan tells me that an electrical discharge can trigger uterine contractions. Wish I'd been aware of that particular side effect, but you know how it is—you learn as you go."

He didn't sound apologetic about nearly causing her to deliver a premature baby. He sounded like a doctor reporting on a uniquely challenging case to his colleagues, and the incongruity of his high-pitched, childish voice speaking so clinically about her pregnant body made her tremble as badly as Laman had in her grasp.

"In any event, you'll be here for a while," he went on. "And I'll be right here with you, monitoring you in case the contractions start again. Which means I should probably introduce myself." She heard movement, then his face appeared, black eyes staring down at her without blinking and a bland smile like a ventriloquist dummy's on his lips. "I'm Athan Genn, and I've heard a lot about you, Michelle."

Nothing he'd said so far scared her as much as the sound of her own name. "How do you know … "

His smile broadened without in any way seeming more sincere. "I know more about you than you can imagine. Like the fact that you spent a month in my big brother Jaden's camp, where I'm told you became quite the expert at premodern weaponry. Sort of an odd choice considering what we're up against, but hey, to each his own."

Michelle struggled to overcome the trembling that made words hard to form. "Jaden? Do you mean Jason?"

"Jaden, Jason, whatever you want to call him," the boy said. "I don't remember him—I was only a year old at the time—but word on the street is that he was quite the big shot in the early trials. Until he got cold feet and went rogue, and then ended up dead in an attack on his camp. Which just goes to show you, you can be too smart for your own good."

He laughed carelessly, then gestured at the giant form before him.

"But even Jaden was smarter than this big fella," he said. "Udain Genn the military genius, who was going to make the scary monsters do his bidding, then, *poof!* convince them all to go away when they refused to play his little tricks." He performed a lewd gesture right in front of his father's eyes, but the man didn't so much as flinch. "You can see how far *that* got him."

Michelle turned her head toward the supine giant, and saw to her disgust that his tongue was exposed. "Is he dead? Did you kill him?"

"That would hardly serve my purposes," the boy answered. "I need him around to keep things running. Right now, he's under general anesthesia while he receives his weekly dose of bug juice. Good for the body, though maybe not so much for the soul."

He laughed again, and Michelle felt imaginary spiders crawling up her neck. When she studied the motionless figure more closely, she saw a plastic tube snaking from one of the machines to disappear beneath the sheet that covered him. "He's getting … an injection?"

"More like an infusion," Athan Genn said. "The Skaldi genetic material breaks down quickly, but in the short term, it boosts cellular mitosis, which helps fortify his bones and musculature." His lips curled in an approximation of his father's humorless smile. "I do like the name *Skaldi*, by the way. It has a certain ring to it. Your boyfriend was some kind of street poet, wasn't he?"

Michelle closed her eyes to shut the boy's smug face from her sight, but she couldn't prevent his taunting words from burrowing into her heart. He knew so much about her, about her past, about Kareem—how was that possible? And the thought that he was filling his father's body with Skaldi genes made her shudder with revulsion. As if he derived immense satisfaction from the effect his speech was having on her, Athan Genn kept talking, a hollow voice in a darkness deeper than her closed eyes could either create or escape.

"I wasn't even born when the first Skaldi experiments started at another site out here in the Wild West," he said. "That's *S K L D I*, by the way, for *Strategic Kenos Living Defense Initiative*. Top-secret DOD stuff, with good old Dad at the helm. He and Melan were satisfied to stick with applications they understood from their military background: to build bombs and super-soldiers, use Skaldi genes to treat Dad's hereditary abnormality. Small-time stuff, in my opinion. They were afraid to push through to the next logical step. The *only* logical step, considering what happened when the trials moved east."

He laughed giddily, as if he were reciting the funniest joke he'd ever heard. Michelle wished she could cover her ears, but the restraints held her fast.

"Did you know that Skaldi are capable of absorbing all kinds of biological energy?" he asked once he settled down. "Not just from human beings but from any living organism? Trees, microbes, you name it. The process is complicated, but basically, they bleed the physical environment dry, then use the stored energy to bomb the hell out of anything that's left standing. Makes it kind of hard to mount a meaningful counterattack against them. Here, let me show you something."

A whirring noise came from overhead. Michelle opened her eyes fearfully to see a mechanical arm lowering something that flashed in the lights directly above her. Every muscle in her body tightened as she imagined what it could be: a surgical instrument, a probe, a torture device created by this soulless child to invade her body or assault her mind. As it came closer, she saw that it was nothing more menacing than a silver-coated rectangle the size of a computer screen. The arm stopped moving once the rectangle floated a couple of feet above her face, and a spark flickered in its center as if the screen were powering on.

"I call this little beauty a *protograph*," Athan Genn said. "In its earliest incarnation, it was nothing but a recording device, but I add a few new wrinkles with each update. You can communicate through it, use it to store and process data, that sort of thing. I've incorporated the protograph technology into all of the hallways around here, which is how I keep tabs on what's going on up above. And of course you've already learned that the floors are wired."

Michelle flinched when he touched his wrist cuff, but this time, all it did was make the room's theater lights dim. The silver rectangle brightened, the spark suffusing it until it appeared almost transparent, a window instead of a screen. She could easily believe that the hallways were coated with these things, invisible to the naked eye but streaming images of everyone in the facility to Athan Genn in his basement lab. The boy must have enjoyed a good laugh at his brother's desperate tears and Michelle's futile escape plan.

"You might want to grab hold of something," he said as an image formed on the screen. "This stuff is not for the faint of heart."

Michelle watched with horrified fascination as the image grew, sharpened, solidified. It seemed to be a panoramic shot of the desert she'd walked through to reach this place, with its endless sand dunes and heat-mirages distorting the air. The only difference was that there was no color, like an old movie except with startlingly crisp picture quality. A silent movie, too: no sound reached her ears, not even the wailing of the wind as dust swirls were lifted from the ground and sent spiraling away into the screen's flat distance. The camera—she guessed that was what to call it—panned over the dunes, showing how extensive the desert was. The thought passed through her mind that if Udain Genn's forces hadn't found them when they did, every member of her colony would have died as surely as Arachne. Maybe, she thought, it would have been better if they had.

"This is streaming live," Athan Genn's voice broke the stillness. "Or anyway, *my* device is." He flourished his wrist cuff, and she saw a miniature screen embedded in the metal. "The image you're seeing is on a slight delay in case … "

"In case what?"

"In case there's anything I don't want you to see," he snapped, sounding like the petulant child he was.

Michelle returned her attention to the larger screen, where the sunlight reflecting off the sand was so bright it made her squint. "Is this near the base?"

"You can't see it from the surface," Athan Genn answered. "But the protograph's showing the area a quarter mile away from us right … now."

The camera stopped at his command. Michelle stared, but even with the protograph motionless, nothing disturbed the monotony of the dunes. The protograph zoomed close to a dune that was as nondescript as all the others, then came to a stop so sudden Michelle caught an involuntary breath.

"Like I said, batten down the hatches," the cool voice of the boy murmured from the darkness beyond the glowing square.

The dune shifted, and something crawled to the surface: a human figure caked in the desert's red-brown sand, which appeared gray on the screen. The protograph zoomed even closer, and she saw that the body of the desert inhabitant was naked and riddled with holes, as if its flesh had been eaten away in numerous places. It took a single step before it staggered and fell, one of its arms breaking free from its shoulder on impact. It tried to regain its feet, but its legs failed next, the weight of its torso pulverizing them to dust. The top half of the creature twitched uselessly on the ground for a few seconds, then melted away entirely as if the heat of the sun had burned it to vapor.

Michelle glanced at the boy who stood watching his own miniature protograph with an expression as rapt as if he were playing a video game. When he saw her looking at him, his eyebrows lifted.

"Not to worry," he said. "The ones in worst shape are always closest to the surface."

She turned back to the screen in time to see the top layer of the desert boil with motion. Arms emerged, then heads, hairless and gray. The first ten or fifteen humanoid figures to break through the sand suffered a fate similar to the lone pioneer, their bodies crumbling, their heads toppling from their necks as if lopped off by an axe. Some managed to open their chest scars before they succumbed; from these creatures, Michelle heard the first sound she'd detected in the protograph recording, a low and pitiful moan that ended abruptly as their bodies sloughed into nothingness. Once they were gone, there was no change in the scene to mark that they'd been there at all, not even noticeable piles of sand to add to the vast empty expanse of the desert.

The figures that followed this initial onslaught were different. They moved fluidly, without the halting, jerky motion of the first wave; they seemed comfortable in their bodies, even if those bodies weren't their own. Whereas the faces of the earlier creatures had been blurred like sand castles softened by an incoming tide, the newcomers' features were recognizably human, their eyes bright, their mouths opening to reveal teeth or lick their lips. The protograph's crystalline image enabled Michelle to see wrinkles and age spots on some of the taller ones. Others had the shape of children, and it was even harder to look at them, knowing they were parasites that had hollowed out children's bodies and donned their empty shells. Bile rose in her throat when she saw one tiny figure squirming on the sand like a newborn that had gestated in its underground womb before it was ready to show its false skin to the world.

And there were hundreds of the creatures, maybe thousands. As the protograph panned over the dunes, the pale things multiplied like maggots on a rotting carcass. It was as if the earth had been sliced open and bled their bodies. Michelle knew, though, that if any of those bodies were pierced by an arrow or bullet, no blood would flow from the dead gray cavity inside them.

"You get the picture," Athan Genn's voice interrupted her thoughts. "But maybe you could profit from a wider view of things."

The protograph screen went dark, then brightened again. This time, it didn't show the desert but the husk of a city, the girders of skyscrapers swaying like hanged criminals, rubble piled at the base of the scaffolds like entrails no scavenger had come to claim. The protograph drew closer, and Michelle saw movement among the ruins, human figures shuffling across the barren cityscape in numbers as great as she'd seen in the desert. The protograph switched scenes again, this time to the shreds of what might have been a forest, where closer inspection revealed human forms flitting like shadows be-tween the boles of leafless trees. Then a field rose before her filled with tall stalks of grass as dead as the last vestiges of her dreams, and though all of the grass waved in a restless wind, some of the blades seemed to have gained independence from the earth, wandering from place to place in search of new bodies to feed their hunger. Again and again, no matter where the eye of the protograph roved, it was the same: de-mons in human form walked the land, the chorus of their moans taking her back to the night in the Skaldi lab when she'd sought refuge in the arms of love. But the boy she loved was gone, and the one who'd replaced him was this child, human in form but as dead inside as the monsters on his screen.

The protograph went blank, though the screen remained illuminated. In its white light, Athan Genn nodded in satisfac-tion. Michelle found herself trembling as if her body had been immersed in freezing water. Much as she feared the boy's an-swer, she preferred the sound of any human voice to the deadly silence that had fallen.

"They're everywhere, aren't they?" she asked.

"Everywhere we managed to install the protograph tech-nology," he said in an offhand way. "So, statistically speaking, yes, they're everywhere. According to the models I ran, they shouldn't have been able to spread this fast this quickly, so there are obviously variables I wasn't able to factor into my calculations."

"But didn't we … " She wasn't sure how to ask this. "Didn't our government try to fight back, or …?"

She recoiled when he barked a laugh.

"If you mean by bombing our own cities, then yeah, I suppose they did," he said. "Oh, and someone had the bright idea of sending the whole flipping military against the Skaldi. Hundreds of thousands of soldiers. You can probably guess how that turned out."

Michelle tried to breathe evenly, but the horrors he was describing, the horrors she'd seen with her own eyes, nearly drained the will from her. It occurred to her why they'd seen no people until the very end of their long march west. "But there must be some places that are still safe," she said, hating herself for the pleading note in her voice. "You reached this base without being … taken, and so did we. How is that possible if there are so many of them?"

"The big guy moved us out here before the Skaldi were released," he answered. "In your case, I'd say you benefited from the odds. You were a small lifeboat of survivors in a raging sea of Skaldi. You had a good guide. Though from the look of it," he added with a cruel smile, "not good enough."

She ignored his mockery and grasped at the one thing she'd seen in the protograph that might contain a seed of hope. "But the creatures in the desert, the ones that came out first—they were dying, the same way the ones died in the desert back east."

"Seemingly so," he said. "If, that is, one assumes they were alive to begin with. We've learned that though Skaldi can leech immense amounts of biological energy from their surroundings, they lose it quickly, after which point their bodies pretty much eat themselves up from the inside. Dad has some wacked-out theory that they transmit the stolen energy somewhere or other, through a spacetime portal or something, but I've seen no evidence to substantiate that."

"But then couldn't we outlast them?" she asked. "In places like this? Wait until they've all died, or whatever you want to call it, and then return to the surface?"

He looked at her sourly. "You probably believe in Santa Claus too, right? And his little pal Rudolph? You think they're going to come rescue us, along with all the other misfit toys?"

She was silent.

"I've already run those numbers," he continued. "And they don't exactly come out in our favor. Suppose the creatures find a way into the base? Or we deplete our food supply before they disappear? What are you going to eat then, the little girl you came with? Skaldi fricassee? Trust me, their flesh tastes as rotten as it smells."

She couldn't answer. Though she'd expected no better from him, though she knew it was pointless to beseech him in the first place, she felt as if her tenuous hold on sanity was slipping farther and farther away from her with each unfeeling word he spoke.

"Here's what I think," he said. "I think we can sit on our cans and pray to our favorite nonexistent deity while the Skaldi continue the business of taking over the world, or we can get out there and take the world back. My dad insists we can do that by building more bombs, but I'm not the starry-eyed optimist he is. I've seen what happens to people who try to fight atypical problems with conventional solutions. So

don't get me wrong, I'm building his bombs—I wouldn't en-
joy the freedom I do around here if I didn't play the boss
man's game—but I'm keeping a little something in reserve at
the same time." He paused, and his pale face, which had
turned red with exertion or excitement during his speech, resumed its characteristic air of scientific detachment. "Which
is precisely where you come in."

She felt the baby jerk as if at Athan Genn's words.
"Me?"

"You got it," the boy said. "The human race as a whole
is doomed, but that doesn't mean some of us can't come out
on top. Evolution is all about taking advantage of opportuni-
ties, right? So what if, instead of exhausting our limited re-
sources fighting the Skaldi, we were to *join* with them—not
sign up for their team, but literally, physically, merge our genome with theirs? What if we were to create a new, improved
version of the human race, capable of absorbing energy like
the Skaldi, but without the unfortunate side effect of needing
to gobble up more and more energy to avoid crumbling into
dust? Human somatic cells die over time, but nowhere near as
fast as Skaldi cells. So it stands to reason that if we could find
a way to mate *our* cells' resilience with *their* cells' aggressive-
ness, we could invent a prototype capable not only of with-
standing the Skaldi but of supplanting them. Right?"

His voice had risen with eagerness, as if their roles had
been reversed and he expected—even needed—her to confirm his theory. Her head, though, spun too badly to try.
"You said your dad gets the genes every week. Because they
don't last."

"Not so far, they don't," he said. "But my dad is a terrible test subject: a man in his fifties, crippled by congenital

99

mutations, who's receiving artificial infusions of Skaldi genes. As it happens, I have at my disposal something much better: a part human, part Skaldi organism that hasn't seen the light of day yet, and that could hold the key to successful symbiosis between us and them."

He laid a small hand on her cheek. It was the first physical contact he'd made with her, and her stomach twisted as violently as if he were Skaldi and the process of draining her soul had begun. His flesh was cold, so cold. She struggled with her bonds, but he stayed as he was until her body was weak with exhaustion and her wrists raw from the leather straps. Then he removed his hand and spoke in a calm, cruel voice.

"That's the problem with most people. No vision. You're like fish in a barrel, you know that? Blindly floating around while the guy with the shotgun lines you up in his sights. The only difference is that fish have no choice in the matter. You do, and yet you prefer to be victims."

He stepped away from her, disappearing into a part of the lab she couldn't see. The mechanical arm that held the protograph retreated, and the room lights sprang back on. The trembling that had never left her limbs since she'd heard Athan Genn's voice was so powerful her teeth actually chattered, even when she tried to clamp them together. Though she'd dreaded all along what her baby might be, veered back and forth between convincing herself it couldn't be part Skaldi and it must be, even told herself she was prepared to face that horror when she saw it for herself, hearing it at last from the boy's bloodless lips made her feel as if her body had fallen into a pit without bottom, without light, without hope. To know that the child she carried was no different from the abominations she'd seen spilling from the sand in the proto-graph was worse, far worse, than losing the boy she loved. And to hear the euphoria in Athan Genn's voice when he anticipated extracting that monstrosity from her body after weeks or even months of holding her here, as if he were the proud father instead of the progenitor of evils she couldn't imagine … She wished she'd taken Arachne up on her initial offer and ended the life of the miserable creature inside her when she had the chance.

But the moment that thought entered her mind, she knew she could never have carried it out. Whatever her baby was, it was hers, and Kareem's—the first thing their love had made, and the last. Even now, she couldn't dream of taking its life before she saw its face. She would not be Athan Genn's victim. She would survive his taunts and his tortures to the end, and if her baby was what he said it was, she would find a way to rip it from his filthy grasp and end its life the only way she could: in her arms, and with her own life the next to follow.

She heard water running, the sound of him washing his hands vigorously for long minutes. When he came back, she smelled disinfectant soap and something else: the latex gloves he held in his hands. Carefully, taking as much time as he could, he pulled the gloves on, finger by finger, until the last digit snapped into place. Then he wheeled a metal tray over and picked through the instruments on it, finally selecting a syringe filled with clear fluid. He held it to the light, tapped it professionally, and moved closer to her while she strained with all her might to free herself.

"Be a visionary, Michelle," he said, holding the needle lovingly before her eyes. "The baby you're carrying has enormous potential, and you could be the mother of a whole new race of beings, a race with the power to reclaim the earth. To *rule* the earth. Ever since I heard about you and— what was your lover boy's name, Kareem?—I've been trying to bring you here, one way or another. And now ... " His smile spread as wide as the Skaldi's open scar. "Well, now I've got you."

He leaned close to swab her shoulder with alcohol. The tip of the needle touched her flesh. Before he could press the plunger, she twisted her head and caught his hand in her teeth, biting as hard as she could, tasting rubber and blood. He cried out, the syringe clattering onto the tray as he fell back.

Michelle spat the boy's blood from her mouth. He touched the torn glove, then stared at his red-tipped fingers. When he met her gaze, his face was crimson with rage. But then, to her surprise, he smiled.

"That's the spirit," he said. "Don't go down without a fight."

He removed himself from view once more, and she heard water running again. He winced, then cursed. The water stopped, and there was silence behind her. The next thing she knew, the theater lights had dimmed, and she heard his steps echoing loudly, as if he were stomping off in a tantrum. His voice returned to her.

"You stay right there," he sang. "I won't be long."

Then he was gone, and Michelle felt the baby performing blissful, unconscious pirouettes in the dark, as if it trusted her frail body alone to protect it.

# Chapter 7

She didn't know how long she waited before a distant door creaked open then closed without a sound.

It seemed that Athan Genn had been gone much longer than he should have been. She must have bitten him more deeply than she realized, so deeply he'd needed to visit the infirmary for stitches or a tetanus shot. Maybe he'd been delayed on the way there, or detained by Dr. Melan. With the extra time, she tried to untie the wrist restraints, and then, when that didn't work, to gnaw them off, but even if there'd been no baby to impede her flexibility, she was held too tightly for her mouth to reach them. So she lay there, each moment that passed in the darkened lab feeling like an eternity of torment. And now that he was back, she steeled herself for the real suffering that was about to begin.

Soft footsteps crossed the lab. The overhead lights stayed off, the unmoving figure of Udain Genn visible to her darkness-trained eyes like a mountain covered in snow. When a face finally emerged from the gloom, Michelle was startled to see who it was.

Dr. Melan placed a finger to his lips. Behind him, Laman Genn appeared out of the darkness, his nose and forehead bandaged, the bruises from her attack forming a black bandit's mask around his eyes. He met her gaze with a look not of anger but of compassion. He even smiled a little, ludicrous as the sight was on his mutilated face.

"What do *you* want?" she whispered.

"Shh," he said. "Give me a second."

His hands disappeared beneath the sheet, but before she had a chance to react or ask what he was doing, he'd unbuckled the restraints that held her. Blood flowed back into her wrists and ankles with a prickling sensation. When she sat up, she saw that she was clothed in nothing but the flimsy hospital gown. She hugged her arms across her breasts to hold it in place, only to realize that probably exposed her butt. Laman reached into a bag he'd set on the floor and removed her uniform, which bore a bloody blotch on the front, no doubt from his own nose.

"Put this on," he said. "We won't look."

Quickly, while the two of them turned their backs, she dressed in the uniform. Like typical men, they'd forgotten socks and underpants, but she'd just have to do without.

Michelle slid down from the table, her bare feet meeting the freezing cold floor. "I'm ready."

Laman glanced at her fleetingly, then the three of them departed the lab, leaving the giant leader of the base to dream his dreams alone in the darkness.

The corridor outside the lab was just as dark, and just as cold. Dr. Melan removed a phone from his pocket and shined its light in front of them, revealing the unfinished bowels of the building, concrete floor and exposed pipes and ventilation ducts. At the end of the hallway was a battered set of double doors that looked like they belonged to a service elevator. Laman swiped a plastic card, and the doors squeaked open.

"This is a restricted area," he explained as they entered the elevator. "Only my dad and Athan have access. Fortunately, Athan's never upgraded the technology, and it still works by key card."

"Where'd you get the card?"

"We took it from him," he said, and even in the bad light, she saw his face coloring. "I got worried when we couldn't find you, so when Athan showed up at the infirmary with a bite wound and claimed he'd cut himself, Dr. Melan put him under to stitch his hand."

"Didn't that make Athan suspicious?"

"Hardly. He totally freaks out at the thought of pain."

"Except when he's inflicting it on others."

"Yeah," Laman said, and lightly touched his bandaged nose. "But he's got nothing on you."

The inside of the elevator had another card reader and buttons running from *SB*—subbasement, she guessed—to *7*. Laman swiped his card again and pressed the button for the top floor, and the elevator started upward with a lurch. In the ghostly light of the doctor's phone, Michelle studied the boy's averted face, trying to come up with a way to tell him she was sorry.

"Why are you helping me?" she asked at last.

"Because you were right," he said. "You were right all along, and I knew it. But it was easier to pretend I didn't."

He let it go at that. Dr. Melan, however, picked up where he'd left off, speaking rapidly in a hushed tone. "None of us knew the full extent of Athan Genn's plans. Or perhaps, none of us fully believed. I have less of an excuse than our young friend here. I should have known, and yet I turned a blind eye to what was plain to be seen."

The little man took a deep breath before resuming.

"I am a geneticist by training. In this facility, I double as chief of medicine, but my background is in research and development. When the general took command of our base, I was assigned to work with his youngest son on priority weapons projects."

"Athan said you and his dad were the ones who started the Skaldi trials," Michelle said. "Before he was born."

Dr. Melan shook his head. "The boy's chronology is flawed. I knew of the general by name and reputation, but I did not work with him until he relocated with his two younger sons to this base."

Michelle eyed him suspiciously, noticing that Dr. Melan had avoided saying whether he knew about the Skaldi trials before he met Udain Genn. He gave her no chance to challenge his version of events, as he quickly returned to his tale.

"It was I who furthered the general's research into the devices he called *drones*—biological manufactures first engineered in the eastern facility that drew on the creatures' capacity for energy absorption and emission. Bombs, you might call them, but bombs powered by genetics, not mechanics."

Michelle suppressed a shiver that had nothing to do with her bare feet on the cold elevator floor. Was *that* what Laman's older brother had forced her to deliver to the Skaldi-infested city back east? "Athan never explained how the Skaldi can do that."

"It is rumored that their genetic material was harvested from alien specimens," Dr. Melan answered. "I cannot speak to the veracity of that intelligence."

Michelle was about to ask him to cut out the military gobbledygook, but he rushed on.

106

"At first, the drones were intended to be used against human adversaries. But during the past year, due to the creatures' spread, the drone technology has become integral to the general's strategy of counterattack. Athan Genn was only seven years old when his family arrived at this facility, but in recent months, he has taken the lead in advancing his father's project. The boy is, by any measure, a genius."

"And a psychopath," Michelle said.

"I cannot deny that his methods—"

"It's not only his *methods*. Why are you defending him?"

Dr. Melan pressed his lips together. The elevator rumbled and shook, its gears creaking as it crept upward. At last, the doctor sighed.

"I blame myself," he said. "As our work has neared its end, there have been signs of Athan's growing dissatisfaction. He has spoken to me of deploying the drones for another purpose: as a means of seeding human survivors with the creatures' genes, thereby giving birth to a race of supermen who would dominate the globe. I listened to his childish visions, and perhaps, in my unwillingness to place limits on his imagination, I encouraged them. I thought to myself, he's only a boy. A lonely boy, raised in almost complete isolation by a demanding father, and desperate to prove himself."

"Your mother?" Michelle asked Laman.

"Died of breast cancer six years ago," he replied. "Right before we left the eastern facility. She and Athan were pretty close, or as close as he gets to anyone."

"But then Athan told me of another plan," Dr. Melan continued in a hushed voice. "He spoke of a project to breed a new organism here in the laboratory, one that went far beyond his father's mandates. You must understand that, to this point, Athan and I had worked solely with the creatures' genetic material, never with human subjects. Yet he hinted that he was nearing a new phase in his investigations, and that he lacked only one component necessary to bring his project to its completion ... "

"Me," Michelle said. "And my baby. That's what we are to him. Components, not people."

The two were silent. In the light of Dr. Melan's phone, Michelle could see the man's drawn face and haunted eyes.

"Why didn't you tell Udain about this?" she asked. "After what happened back east, I'm sure he would have shut Athan down if he knew what his son was up to. Who's running this place, him or a ten-year-old?"

"Twelve," Laman chipped in.

Dr. Melan turned imploring eyes to Michelle. "Udain Genn is our commanding officer, but we fear ... you do not understand, Miss ... "

"Diana. Just call me Diana."

"Miss Diana. Athan is unpredictable, and his hold over his father has grown stronger with each passing day. For years, Udain Genn has used the boy's considerable talents to generate much of the technology that keeps this base secure, but it now seems that, in so doing, the general has unwittingly allowed his son to use *him*. The infusions he insists on receiving, for example ... there is some evidence that they have destabilized the general's mind. And yet, were we to breathe one word of our misgivings to him or to any other on this base, we might find ourselves ... "

"Where you found me," Michelle finished. "So Laman was right. It was much easier for you to pretend as long as it was somebody else's life at stake."

The little man actually hung his head. Thankful as Michelle was to him and Laman for what they'd risked, she couldn't help worrying that, once the magnitude of that risk sank in, they would fall back into the old pattern of silent obedience. In the doctor's case, she sensed kindly intentions, but also weakness—maybe brought on by a lifetime of following orders, maybe a simple result of who he was. In the case of Laman, she was less sure. He was, as Dr. Melan had said of Laman's younger brother, only a boy, and she couldn't divine what kind of man he might choose to become.

"So why should I trust you now?" she asked. "You know I'm carrying a child Athan's dying to get his hands on. Why should I believe you won't change your minds and turn me in?"

The two looked at each other. Dr. Melan was the first to answer. "Because I have learned my lesson. I swore an oath to preserve and protect life, and I do not wish to cover for Athan Genn's crimes any longer."

"And I don't want you to get hurt," Laman spoke up. "I never did. I just want to find a safe place for you until your baby's born."

"But there *is* no safe place inside this building," Michelle said. "Is there? Any place where the two of them won't be able to find me?"

The elevator had come to a stop, but the door stayed closed. The would-be rescuers looked at each other again, and Michelle knew immediately that they hadn't worked out this crucial part of their plan, probably because the answer to her question was *no*.

"I don't want to sound ungrateful," she said. "But you both know there's no way to hide me here. You can't keep

Athan and Udain asleep forever, and you can't stop them from searching for me when they wake up. They could torture you," she added, and the fear in their eyes told her that Dr. Melan had already considered the possibility, and that Laman hadn't. "I don't want you to suffer any more for me than you already have. If you want to help me, you have to let me go."

"Impossible," Dr. Melan said, shaking his head vigorously. "Your likelihood of preterm labor is unacceptably high at this point, and the grounds surrounding our base—"

"Are swarming with Skaldi," Michelle said. "I know. Athan showed me the protograph, and I know that the whole country, maybe the whole world, belongs to them now. But I'd rather take my chances out there than with Udain and Athan. The creatures can only kill me once. Those two can keep me alive for months while they dissect my body, along with my baby's."

"I must strongly object," Dr. Melan began, but Laman laid a hand on his arm before he could continue. The boy turned to her, and despite the fear in his black-ringed eyes, he found the courage to straighten from his usual slouch.

"I'll go with you," he said. "I know this area better than you do, plus I can gain access to some equipment that might help us out. It won't protect us from a thousand of those— what did you call them, Skaldi?—but it'll give us a better shot than if you headed off alone. And," he added when Dr. Melan lifted a finger to begin another cautionary harangue, "I can help you in case you go into labor."

"What do you know about delivering a baby?" Michelle asked, the corners of her mouth tugging against her desire to stay serious.

"Not much," he admitted. "But I'm a fast learner."

Hard as she tried to stop it, the smile finally won out. "You won't have to do it all by yourself. The twins can help. Even Tyris knows a few things. Her mother was a doctor."

Laman smiled back, a broad smile that made his face relax for the first time she could remember, without a trace of sullenness or fear. Dr. Melan broke the moment, shaking his head and his hands at once.

"This is madness," he said. "It would be difficult enough to spirit the two of you from this facility even if there were any hope of your surviving in the desert, much less of Miss Diana's baby being safely delivered. But her entire colony, including a five-year-old child? The general will not permit such an exodus, I can assure you. He will come after you in force, and I will be powerless to protect you."

"Then come with us," Laman said. "You can bring the supplies we need to help Diana out—medicine, whatever."

Michelle smiled again, privately. The boy's "whatever" showed how little he'd actually be able to assist her when her baby was born.

"And you can help us in other ways," Laman continued. "It's going to be a rough trip, and we could use a real doctor out there."

Dr. Melan hadn't stopped shaking his head from the moment Laman began talking. "You do not understand. I am a commissioned officer of the United States Air Force, and I cannot simply desert my post at the whim of two"—he pursed his lips as if trying to find a particularly trenchant put-down—"teenagers."

"Ooh, that hurt," Laman said, and he and Michelle shared a short laugh.

Dr. Melan stood blinking at the two of them, a hurt look on his face. Michelle stepped closer to him in the confined space of the elevator. She thought of laying a hand on his arm, but decided against it.

"It's all right," she said. "You've done so much already. But can you promise not to let anyone know which way we've gone? And maybe give us a little more time before you wake up Udain and Athan?"

She saw the struggle in his face, but at last, he expelled a startlingly loud breath and nodded.

"I will do what I can," he said.

For some reason, Michelle expected the elevator door to spring open at that moment, as if now that the decision was made, the plan would immediately go into effect. Instead, they stood there even more indecisively than before, each of them waiting for the others to act, or possibly for someone to come up with a better plan.

Then Laman slapped his forehead—not the best idea considering his injuries, but for once, he didn't even cringe. "Of course," he said, and Michelle laughed, the tension broken.

"Anything you'd like to share?"

"Just something I remembered." He swiped the key card once more, and the elevator door opened on a darkened hallway. "Come with me."

# Chapter 8

The supply truck rumbled across the desert, raising a cloud of dust behind it.

Bridget sat at the wheel, while Michelle occupied the passenger seat. Everyone else was crammed in the back, along with the supplies that Laman and the others had hurriedly assembled: flamethrowers with full tanks, ration packs and water jugs, tools, medical supplies, and, perhaps most important of all, fuel barrels to keep the truck running as long as possible. The rear compartment was nothing more than an open space covered by a canvas top, without so much as benches to sit on; every time the truck's wheels went over a bump, Michelle winced to think of how badly the passengers were being jostled around back there. But after every jolt, Laman would shout out, "We're okay!" and the others would laugh, particularly Tyris and her new companion, Petra.

As with just about everything they'd loaded into the back of the truck, the little girl had been a spur-of-the-moment decision. When Laman told Michelle he had something to show her, she'd jumped to the conclusion that he'd found Kareem's collection jar, and she'd eagerly followed him into the deserted hallway on the top level of the base. It turned out that all he meant was that he'd remembered the facility's trucks, and she'd tried not to show him how crushing her disappointment was. When they returned to the infirmary floor to gather the other members of her colony—and to find Michelle a fresh pair of socks and underpants—she had looked at the two orphaned children sitting on the bedroom floor playing with Tyris's doll, and the wide, dark eyes of the quiet Petra had made her think about what might happen to the girl if she grew up in this place, with no one to protect her from whatever the next phase of Athan Genn's experiments might be. She stooped to study the two more closely, noticing the alertness with which Petra took in everything around her. The child's watchfulness made it no less remarkable that she'd found her way to the base through a desert full of Skaldi, but it reminded her of what Udain Genn had said: the girl was a born scout. So when Michelle took Tyris's hand and stood, she held out her other hand to Petra, and the child accepted her touch as if a silent understanding had passed between them. None of the others objected, and Laman, who was busy overseeing the collection of medical supplies with Dr. Melan, nodded when Michelle approached with the two children by her side.

"Is there anyone else?" Michelle asked.

"No other parentless kids, if that's what you mean. I'm not sure we have room for any more grownups."

Michelle looked up and down the infirmary corridor, wondering who was tucked away in the other rooms, what lay in store for them. Selfishly, she considered asking Laman to help her search for the missing collection jar. But she knew that he was right: they couldn't start plucking random people from the hallway, and they couldn't waste any more time on her personal Easter egg hunt. She let what felt like her final dream go, and clung to the two children's hands all the more tightly.

Dr. Melan proved as good as his word. He told his staff that the new patients were being moved to a separate floor to prevent another disruption such as the one Michelle had caused, and though they watched her warily the whole time she was there, they accepted his explanation with military indifference. Once all the members of Michelle's colony, plus Petra, were hurried off the ward, he used his security clearances to get them into the weapons cache, the food dispensary, and finally the surface-level garage where the truck was waiting. They loaded everything quickly, and he handed Bridget the keys. Then he circled to the passenger side and leaned into the cab to buckle Michelle in, the seatbelt pressing uncomfortably against her belly.

"I wish I did not have to be the one to tell you this," he said. "But a newborn at the gestational age of less than thirty-four weeks has a minimal chance of survival without a first-rate neonatal intensive care unit. The cardiovascular system will be immature, as will the integumentary system—"

"The what?"

He grimaced. "The skin and other connective tissues. There will be a heightened risk of infection, and an underdeveloped immune system to fight disease. I have packed extra courses of steroids, which might help hasten fetal lung development, but there are limits to what the drug can achieve, as well as risks to you and your baby from repeated doses. Should uterine contractions resume, there is little you can do at this point to stop them. Your best chance is to avoid over-exerting yourself for the next several months, and hope that the pregnancy follows a normal course."

She looked into his anxious eyes. She almost laughed despite herself; how on earth was she supposed to avoid over-exerting herself while fleeing for her life across a desert filled with Skaldi? But she was touched by his concern for her and her unborn child, and though she couldn't find it in her heart to forgive him for what he'd done under Udain Genn's orders, she leaned over and kissed his cheek for what he was doing now.

"Thank you," she said, while tears gathered in the little man's dark eyes. "I promise I'll be careful."

From his belt, he took his computer tablet and handed it to her, along with a charger. "I have loaded information about labor and delivery on this device, as well as instructions for neonatal care." He tried to smile. "All may yet be well. You bear a remarkable child within you, Miss Diana—a being that to the best of our knowledge has never existed before. Who can say what awaits you?"

Laman leaned into the cab through the canvas flap that separated it from the back. "Time to go, Doc," he said. He reached out to shake the doctor's hand, then signaled to Bridget. Dr. Melan closed Michelle's door, and the truck's engine coughed to life. In the passenger side-view mirror, Michelle watched his small figure recede in a pool of light. Before he disappeared, he waved the way you would to someone you never expected to see again.

A long, straight ramp angled upward to an imposing set of doors that Michelle worried wouldn't open. But they did, and the truck rolled through the opening into a darkened hangar with another set of doors visible at the far end. The doors behind them began to close, momentarily making her fear they'd been betrayed, but as soon as the rear doors clanged shut, the second set opened, and they roared out into the desert night.

It was an oddly beautiful night. Maybe that was because she'd been trapped in Udain Genn's base for at least two days—she wasn't sure how long she'd been imprisoned in Athan's torture chamber—and it was a relief to roll down the window with its old-fashioned handle and breathe actual air, not the cloying disinfectant smell of the maternity ward, much less the stifling atmosphere of the lab. The desert wind was warm, and dust floated in through the open window, eventually forcing her to crank the glass closed so Bridget could see. There was a half-moon out, turning the hills and valleys to bronze ripples like frozen waves, and there was a feeling of peacefulness she hadn't known since … well, she couldn't remember since when. She knew the Skaldi were out there. She knew that Dr. Melan would be waking his patients soon, and then the pursuit would begin. She supposed there was nothing to do right now but let her body relax into the ride and her mind escape for a moment from the terror, the way she'd done on the night her baby had come to her.

She woke to daylight and an irresistible urge to pee. The driver—Charlie this time, Bridget having traded places with him while Michelle slept—pulled over, though "over" meant no more than wheeling the truck against the base of a dune. She was opening the door to climb out when a hand caught her arm.

Michelle reacted instinctively, lashing out with her other hand. She turned just in time to see her fist narrowly miss Laman's jaw as he jerked away.

"I'm not going to have many unbruised places left if you keep that up," he said.

"I ... " She was about to say *I'm sorry*, but she instantly reconsidered. "If you don't want to be hit, then don't touch me without my permission. I've had too many members of your family do that to me."

His pale face turned the color of the desert dawn. "I won't do it again. But I don't think it's a good idea for you to walk on your own. There might be Skaldi out there, and you heard what Dr. Melan said about taking it easy."

"He never said I can't *walk*."

"He said you shouldn't overexert yourself."

"I'm not planning to run a marathon," she said. "I'm just going outside to pee. Come join me if you like."

That had the expected result: the scarlet shade of his face deepened, bringing out the unsightly white spots of his pimples. She thought that settled the matter, but when she slid from the truck and set her feet on the desert sand—in sturdy new boots, thankfully—he scrambled out of the cab after her.

"What in the world are you doing?" she asked.

"Joining you." He wouldn't meet her eye, but he drew close without actually touching her. "Can I ... I mean, is it all right if I give you my arm? Just to help you walk. I won't look when you ... "

"Laman, for God's sake." This was like Arachne ten times over. "I'm not incapacitated. I'm *pregnant*. Along with not touching me goes not treating me like I'm a china doll." She glared at him until he backed off. "Now if you don't mind ... "

Her bladder was close to bursting by the time she ducked behind the dune. She smiled to herself as she let go, and hoped she was pissing directly on the heads of Skaldi. It was only when she was done that she realized she'd forgotten anything to wipe herself with. She debated going without, but given the high-risk status of her pregnancy, she decided this was no time to ignore Feminine Hygiene 101. "Laman ... "

"Are you okay?"

"I'm fine. Don't look. But I forgot ... " She hoped he'd take the hint, but that was giving him more credit for understanding basic female anatomy than he'd showed so far. "I need ... a piece of toilet paper, or something. Can you throw it to me?"

She was thankful she couldn't see his face. A moment elapsed, then a package of tissues sailed over the dune, landing at her feet with a soft *poof.* She finished up, wiggled back into her underpants and uniform bottoms, and returned to find her self-appointed bodyguard standing there. His expression was impossible to describe, something between protectiveness and abject terror.

"Didn't you ever take Health class?" she asked him, trying to tease.

"I never really went to school," he answered seriously. "Regular school, anyway. We were always moving, and my dad ... well, he didn't pay much attention to me, except ... "

*Except when you screwed up,* she finished for him. She wondered if Jason—Jaden—had ever stood up for his younger brother, or if Laman had been forced to confront the domineering Udain Genn all on his own. "Wasn't there anything you were good at?" she asked, then cringed at the way the words came out.

He laughed, easily and without bitterness. "Only at ticking Dad off. I was glad when we moved to the lab in Pennsylvania, because ... well, at that place, he was so busy I never saw him."

"Because he was working with Jaden."

"Plus he was an important man," he said defensively, though Michelle couldn't tell if he was defending his dad or himself. "We went to an amusement park once," he added.

"Idlewild?" she asked, remembering the days she'd gone to Storybook Forest with her parents and Rosie.

"Hershey," he said. "Except Dad had to make some calls at the last minute, so Jaden ended up taking me instead. Not that it mattered. Dad wouldn't have fit on any of the rides." He started to laugh again, but then the look of chagrin returned to his face. "I'm sorry. I know what happened to you in the eastern base. I didn't mean to treat it like a joke."

She took a step closer to him. "I think we should get back to the truck. I can play with the girls for a while, if you want to take a turn up front."

She held out her arm, and with extreme delicacy, as if he were balancing something more precious than his own life, he put his hand under hers as they walked the short distance back. Unsurprisingly, he ignored Michelle's offer to switch places with him and helped her into the front seat.

"The base wasn't all bad, Laman," she said to him before he climbed into the rear compartment. "It's where I learned to fight. And to love."

He ducked behind the canvas, but not before she saw the look—was it embarrassment, or something more?—on his bandaged face.

ANTICIPATING THAT DR. Melan would be interrogated as soon as he woke Udain and Athan Genn, they hadn't told the chief of medicine where they were going. But for once, that didn't mean they didn't know.

Along with instructions to Michelle on how to give birth, the doctor had loaded interactive maps onto his tablet. The GPS technology still worked, which Laman explained was because the satellites operated autonomously. "They'll need to be recalibrated after a while," he said. "But as long as there's no damage to the transmitters, we're good." After being subjected to Udain and Athan Genn's space-age military technology while she herself lacked the most basic things like blow-dryers and cell phones, Michelle found it almost miraculous to stare at a computer screen and watch the solid brown background scroll behind the shimmering blue caret that marked their position. There was some static and the occasional blip where they seemed to be floating in a shapeless void—probably produced by atmospheric interference, Laman said—but there was no doubt that the miles were ticking down and the virtual landscape changing to reflect the real.

When they left, Michelle told Laman about the Jemez Mountains, though she said nothing about her original reason for wanting to go there. Now that that reason had disappeared, she didn't object when he told her that was the wrong place to seek safety.

"Dad started the Skaldi experiments in New Mexico more than twenty years ago," he said. "I don't know if the installation's still there, but I'd rather not find out."

"Where to, then?" She pictured herself standing on a lonely peak, emptying the contents of her collection jar in a ceremonial goodbye, but as she watched the imaginary ashes drift out of sight on the wind, she let that dream go, too.

Laman's finger scrolled the map back and forth while Michelle peered over his shoulder. Whether he was looking for a particular place or just anyplace, she didn't know. When he reached a spot in northern Arizona, he stopped. "Well, this is interesting."

"What?" She looked more closely and saw that the map had come to rest near the blue line of the Little Colorado River, southeast of a large green blotch that represented the Grand Canyon.

"Right here," he said. "We can take Route 10 west to El Paso, then keep going until we hit Tucson. It's pretty much straight north from there."

"I can see that," she said. "But what exactly is *it*?"

He paused a moment before answering. "An old army base, just outside the borders of the Navajo Nation. When we left the lab back east, my dad was considering establishing himself there, but he found out that it's abandoned. Which means—"

"Which means it was probably one of the original Skaldi labs."

"It wasn't. He told me."

"And you believed him?"

"He had no reason to lie. But the point is, it's the last place my dad would expect us to go."

"For once, I think I agree with him."

Laman's eyes pleaded with her. "Our food won't last forever, Diana. We need a place that's well stocked with provisions, and we can't drive around blindly hoping to find one."

"We could go where Phoenix or Tucson used to be, and take our chances there."

"No," he said, more forcefully than she'd thought him capable of. "The Skaldi will concentrate in the cities once

122

their food supply runs low. This place is in the middle of no-where. If it's infested, we leave. But if it isn't … "

He lowered his eyes, and she cocked her head to see what he was hiding. "Yes?"

"Then we'll have a place to stay," he said. "A place of our own. You can have your baby, and then we can … "

He looked away from her, over the dunes. She wondered what sort of future he imagined for them in this abandoned base, what sitcom domestic paradise he seemed to have in mind. For herself, she'd given up on the belief that her world could ever return to any semblance of normalcy. Even if the baby wasn't what she feared, even if they managed to evade the Skaldi for days, months, years, what did they have to look forward to? For a moment, she understood what the young-est son of Udain Genn desired, why he was willing to sacri-fice other people's lives to get it. To defeat the Skaldi, no matter what the cost—was that a choice *she'd* make if it meant safety for herself and her baby?

"All right," she said. "We can try it out. But at the first sign of danger, we're out of there. I mean it."

He broke into one of his all too infrequent genuine smiles, without embarrassment or awkwardness. "I won't take chances with you or the girls. Or with your baby. I promise."

They drove along the route he had mapped, stopping on-ly to change drivers, refuel, and use the bathroom. Night turned to day as they gobbled the miles between Udain Genn's sanctuary and the mystery fortress to the northwest. The landscape remained more or less constant throughout the trip, with occasional spells of highway—most of them too battered to drive on—appearing without warning from be-neath the predominant red-brown of the desert. They avoided areas that the GPS told them had once been cities, but even when they passed close enough that they might have seen signs of human habitation, there was nothing to see. The desert rolled on in undisturbed emptiness, making Michelle wonder whether the entire western United States had been turned into a single sheet of sand that ended only with the sea.

After their route bent north past Phoenix, however, the landscape underwent a noticeable change, with massive red cliffs and boulders jutting from the ground, all the more impressive, Michelle supposed, now that nothing built by human hands remained to compete with their lofty shapes. The terrain didn't match her memory of the mountains—it was too stark and bare, with scrubby foliage and cactuses instead of the lush verdure she recalled from her childhood—but it had a monumental silence and beauty that took words away. She felt as if she'd stepped into prehistoric times, when the desert had been home to people who'd built their cities of baked brick on cliff faces and mesa tops. Thinking about them gave her a mixed feeling of hopefulness and fear. The cliff-dwellers had lived here, according to her history teacher, for hundreds of years, flourishing in hostile terrain, but eventually they'd vanished, and no one knew exactly why. Had they succumbed to enemies and natural disasters? Or had they left this unsparing land and found someplace better to spend the rest of their days?

The next time Bridget took a break so everyone could climb from the truck to stretch their legs, Michelle wandered away from the others to the base of one of the hills. She hadn't gone far when the stillness was broken by Laman calling her name.

He came up behind her, keeping a respectful distance. He'd shed the bandages, and his bruises were healing. But his uniform top was sweat-stained, his hair tangled and dirty. Michelle didn't want to tell him, but if his hygiene was this bad when he had daily showers at his disposal, she wasn't sure he was going to last out here. A slight breeze prickled hot on her skin, and she tried to stay upwind of him.

"You're not thinking of climbing that thing, are you?" he asked.

She peered at the red rock that towered above them. "It might be worth it for you to try. Take a look around."

"What's to see?"

"I mean in case anyone's following."

A frightened look passed over his face, departing quickly. "No one's following us, Diana. I'm a hundred percent sure of that."

"How can you be?"

"I just am." Without apparent pretext, he added, "You still don't trust me, do you?"

"I trust you," she said automatically, though she felt that, like her name and her future, *trust* no longer meant what it once had. "I don't trust *them*."

"The Skaldi? Or my family?"

"Either one." She wrapped her arms around herself as if an army of the creatures had risen from the plain before her. "How did we let this happen?"

"Let what happen?"

"This." She waved at the desert. "All of this. How could we have been so … careless?"

He looked out over the distance, shielding his eyes with a hand. "I don't know. I just know we can't afford to give up."

"I never said anything about giving up," she responded. "But I understand how some people might. How they might feel so sick they wouldn't want to go on."

He said nothing more, just stood looking at her until the grownups called them back to the truck. The shadows of the red rocks lengthened across their path as the vehicle rolled steadily north.

Toward dusk, they came to the banks of a river, or what counted as a river in this dry land, more like a trickle cutting its feeble way through sand and sheet rock. The label on the GPS said it was the Little Colorado, though even Laman had to admit he'd expected it to be more noteworthy than this. They took on extra water while they could, and followed the winding course of the river through land that was mostly barren, without the imposing monoliths farther south. Their headlights had gone on by the time the rocking motion of the truck settled Michelle to a fitful sleep.

She woke when they came to a stop. The headlights were off, and the darkness beyond was so deep she couldn't tell whether the river was still there or if the land had changed shape once again. She looked to the driver's seat and found it empty, which caused momentary panic to flare in her chest. Then she heard the low register of voices outside, and she climbed out to join Laman and the drivers, who stood in a huddle at the back of the truck, their faces illuminated by Dr. Melan's tablet.

"What's going on?" she asked in a whisper.

"I'm not sure," Laman answered. "The GPS says we should be close, but we're not seeing any signs of the base. So it could be—"

"Buried by the desert. Like everything else."

"Either that or the GPS is wrong." He frowned at the tablet, shaking it as if that might make it yield its secrets.

"Those things never get you right where you're going," she said with an attempt at levity. "Only a block or two away."

"This one's military grade, though," he said, immune to her joke. "If the satellites aren't out of whack, it should guide us to within millimeters of our target."

He monkeyed with the screen for a few more minutes before turning it off in disgust. As if in response to the sudden darkness, the sky flickered with a weird yellow light, heat lightning arcing across the land. In its brief glow, Michelle saw only emptiness, without even a single rock formation to break the ruler-straight horizon. Laman, though, gave an excited cry.

"Of course!" he said, and smacked his forehead, which seemed to be his go-to move. "I'm a complete idiot."

Michelle waited, wondering if he expected her to contradict him.

"We're here," he said. "But this base must have been built like the ones in Texas and Pennsylvania. See?"

He pointed, and Michelle followed his finger until the next flash of lightning revealed a series of razor-thin verticals standing against the brightened sky. The next instant, everything was plunged into darkness again, until Laman turned the screen on to show his battle-scarred but triumphant face.

"That's the perimeter fence," he said. "The rest of the base is underground."

# Chapter 9

Laman insisted they were where they were supposed to be, but he had no idea how to get in.

Leaving the children and the twins in the truck with Dave and Norman to watch over them, he led Michelle, Bridget, and Charlie to the place where he'd sighted the remains of the perimeter fence. When they shined a flashlight on the surviving uprights, Michelle saw that the posts were blackened by fire and as fragile as twigs. A few steps beyond, their boots scuffed against concrete, so cracked and unstable they were afraid of falling through. They retreated and walked along what was left of the fence, but they didn't find a single structure or any indication of where to access the supposed underground level.

Laman's finger jabbed furiously at the tablet. "There's got to be *something* here."

"At least there's no sign of Skaldi," Michelle offered.

"We don't know that. They could be under our feet right now, and we'd never see them."

"Since when are you such a pessimist?"

"Since this piece of crap won't work!" he said, much more loudly than Michelle thought was advisable. She laid a hand on his arm, and he stared at her, the bruises making his face look ghoulish in the light of the unresponsive tablet. Then he took a deep breath, letting it out slowly.

"We're going to have to wait until daylight," he admitted. "I'll take first watch. You get some sleep."

The way he said that reminded her of Arachne, and she shook her head. "I'll stay up with you. We can wake Bridget when it's time for her shift."

He grumbled a little more, but didn't say no.

Everyone walked back to the truck, stepping carefully in case there might be hidden fissures that opened onto the underground area. When the others were settled in the back to sleep, the two of them sat in front, Laman in the driver's seat and Michelle beside him. The heat lightning had died, and when he powered down the tablet, he became nothing but a black hole in a blacker hole. They had a brief debate about putting on the headlights so they wouldn't have to stare into complete darkness, but they decided it was better not to draw attention to themselves or risk draining the truck's battery.

For a long time, they sat without talking, Michelle shifting uncomfortably in an attempt to make her bladder stop feeling like a water balloon about to pop. Then she heard, not saw, Laman turn to her.

"I'll get us in there," he said. "I promise."

She looked at where he would have been if she could see anything. "I never said you wouldn't."

"I know you didn't. I just wanted you to know … I mean, what we were talking about earlier, I want you to know that I would never … "

His next words were swallowed by an enormous yawn.

"Why don't you get some sleep?" she asked. "So you're ready for the morning."

"There's no way I'm going to be able to sleep tonight," he said sulkily.

"Okay."

"I mean it."

"I know you do," she said quietly, and then listened as his frustrated breaths leveled and turned to snores.

Morning found them asleep in the front seat, her head cushioned against his shoulder.

She sprang awake when the light revealed their position. She couldn't decide what felt worse, that the two of them had been derelict at guard duty or that she'd fallen asleep beside—touching—another boy while she was carrying Kareem's baby. Nervously, she scanned the dusty plain for any sign of movement, but the dawn revealed nothing except the spindly verticals of the fence posts and the squat globe of a lone cactus. Her ears strained for the slightest sound, but that was missing too, not even a chirp of bird or insect to interrupt the mummified silence.

"Laman," she said softly, and was relieved to hear her own voice. "Wake up. It's daytime."

He shook himself awake then sat there, looking bleary and sheepish. She wondered if he'd woken at any point during the night and found her leaning against him. She decided that was one question she'd never ask.

"Let's get something to eat," he said. "Then start searching."

Michelle felt bloated in her too-tight pants and top, but she accepted a breakfast bar and a canned Monster energy drink. That gave her enough of a jolt to climb out of the truck and meet up with the rest of the colony, all of whom were stirring except the little girls. It also gave her—but what else was new?—a desperate need to use the bathroom, so she slipped off to find someplace private, or as private as the flat, open land would afford her. She wondered how long it would take before she gave up her old-world squeamishness and took to squatting in front of everybody like a dog.

When she returned, Tyris and Petra had joined the group, though they looked cross at having been awakened. Laman was putting the finishing touches on the two-person teams he'd commissioned to spread out and search the grounds. He was obviously reveling in his promotion: the high school loser elevated to a position of authority by virtue of being just a tiny bit less lost than everyone else.

"Diana," he said, "why don't you come with me?"

"What about the girls?"

"They can come, too," he said, though he didn't look entirely happy about Tyris and Petra ruining what he seemed to think of as a date.

They unloaded flamethrowers from the back of the truck and helped each other strap the bulky equipment on, with everyone except Michelle and the four girls carrying one of the weapons. Laman looked as if his skinny frame would collapse beneath the weight, but he panted out final instructions before the teams went their separate ways.

"Keep an eye out for anything that might be an access point," he told them. "That could mean a door, a tunnel, a manhole cover, anything. It'll probably be well disguised even without all the dust, so don't let anything pass you by just because it doesn't look promising on first sight."

"And be extra alert for Skaldi," Michelle added. "If you encounter anything that doesn't feel right to you—even if it's only a prairie dog—hit it with the flamethrower before it gets too close."

Laman stared at her. "But what if it's—"

"We don't have the luxury of *what ifs*," she said, and the grownups' nods showed that they agreed.

Laman gripped the nozzle of his flamethrower and avoided her eyes. If he only knew whose life she'd already taken with a flamethrower, he probably wouldn't be so quick to turn his back on her.

The teams fanned out, each heading to a different point of the compass. Michelle and Laman's team crept westward at a snail's pace, not only because of the weight he was carrying but because he insisted they stop to check every anomaly in the barren terrain. While Tyris chattered excitedly about useless discoveries, such as the time she "found" her own footprints, Petra grew even quieter than usual, her eyes flicking over the landscape. She was the one who noticed things no one else bothered to see: a pile of sand slightly higher than the norm, a faint outline in the ground that looked as if it might be an iron plate buried beneath the surface. It turned out to be nothing but a large, flat rock, but Michelle was impressed that Petra had picked its shape out of the random ripples of windblown dust. Every so often, when the girl lagged behind, Michelle would get the eerie feeling that Petra had vanished, disguising herself against the nothingness of the desert with Skaldi skill. Then she'd turn and spot Petra pacing silently in her rear, leaving footprints so light Michelle couldn't believe the solid little shape had passed over the ground at all.

She wasn't surprised when Petra made the first real discovery of any of the teams. Near a row of scrubby bushes no one had thought to check because they were well beyond range of the perimeter fence, she came across a divot in the ground that was too perfectly circular to be a mere desert depression. Laman called the other teams over, then told everyone to stand back while he poured a stream of fire over the ground. Nothing emerged from the flames; the only casualty was Laman himself, who staggered and fell when he turned the nozzle off. Shedding their flamethrowers, he and the grownups dug away dust to a depth of several feet until they struck something solid. Michelle stood to the side, anxiously watching but forbidden to participate, and so she was the first to see Laman lift a dust-covered but gleeful face from where he stood waist-deep in the hole.

"This is it," he said. "It's the roof of an access tunnel, built with reinforced concrete. That's good news for us, because it means the base won't have been too badly damaged by what happened at ground level."

"Is there a door?"

"Not that I can tell."

"Then how are we supposed to get in?"

"Keep searching. It's only a matter of time before we find the entry point."

Michelle scanned the dusty ground. "It could be anywhere."

"True." He climbed out of the hole, shaking himself to free his clothes of dust. "But we've got a scout with eyes like a hawk."

Petra glanced up at him, displaying one of her devilish smiles.

With the little girl in the lead, they paced along the track that was their best estimate of the tunnel's direction. Every so often, Petra angled left or right as if following contours only she could see. Had it been any other child, the procession would have looked like a group of adults being led on a wild goose chase by a mischievous kindergartner. With Petra, there was no hint of playfulness: her eyes were fixed on the ground, her pug nose wrinkling as if she were picking up a scent on the dusty air. Now that the sun was fully up and the heat had climbed, Michelle's heart hammered and her breath grew short as they covered what seemed like miles of winding ground, but not even Laman urged her to stop and take a break. She was about to do so herself when Petra issued the first sound she'd made all morning, a short victory cry.

"She's got it!" Laman exulted. He seemed ready to scoop the girl into his arms, but she danced away, giggling as she gripped Tyris's hand.

Everyone clustered around the spot Petra had identified. There, flush with the ground, was a metal plate roughly four feet square when they swept the dust off to expose its corners. The plate was set in a concrete housing which Laman, stooping to inspect it, announced confidently was the roof of the tunnel. It wasn't bolted down, he said, so they should be able to pry it loose in a jiffy.

Michelle didn't want to burst his bubble, but she also didn't want him to grab a crowbar only to look like a fool. "It won't come free."

Laman squinted up at her. "Why not?"

"Because of that," she said, pointing to a dust-covered keypad beside the plate.

He bent down to take a look. "Damn."

"It's a top-secret military base," Michelle pointed out. "They're not going to let just anyone in."

"We could try blasting it loose."

"You brought explosives?"

His face and neck flushed. "You never know."

They debated the situation for a few minutes before deciding that was their best bet. While Bridget hiked back to the truck to get the plastic explosives, Laman tried a number of codes on the keypad, but none of them produced the desired effect. Michelle shook her head as she watched him. Did he honestly think the creators of this base would be so careless as to use a code that a sixteen-year-old hacker wannabe could crack? Wasn't it more likely that the plate was wired to self-destruct after a number of false codes?

Bridget returned, bearing the bricks of plastic explosive, along with a length of wire and a detonator. While everyone except Laman stood back, she molded the putty around a corner of the metal plate. Michelle doubted that their de facto leader had any idea if his plan would work, but his face, furious with concentration, didn't allow for questions. After Bridget spooled out the wire that led to the charge, he grabbed the detonator and hunkered down behind a lowly dune no more than a hundred feet away.

*He's going to get himself killed*, Michelle thought as she watched from afar. *And then where will we be?*

The ground shook and dust plumed upward with the force of the explosion. It was stronger than anyone, Laman included, had guessed, and when Michelle ran—not walked—to his inadequate hiding place, she found him lying on his back, blinking up at the sky.

"That better have worked," he said weakly.

She helped him stand. He said nothing about her over-exerting herself; in fact, he leaned against her when his legs gave out. She held him loosely as he limped toward the acrid smoke that rose from the ground.

When they reached the metal plate, they found it blackened by the explosion but perfectly intact.

Laman stared, then let out a laugh that sounded an awful lot like a cry. "I should have known. Let's hear it for another of Lame Man Genn's A-plus ideas!"

Michelle wished she could say something to soothe him, but the thought made her feel awkward. "What do we do now?"

He kicked dust over the scorched plate. "What do I always do? Give up. Walk away. Let someone else figure it out."

"So quickly?"

"We've been screwing around half the damn day. With my luck, that little stunt sent out a wake-up call to every Skaldi in the tri-state area. What else am I supposed to do?"

"You could try again."

"I'm sick of trying. I'm going back to the truck."

She moved close to him, speaking in a voice for his ears alone. "Don't you remember what you said yesterday? About not giving up?"

"That was yesterday," he said. "Don't you remember what *you* said?"

"I said that I can see how some people might give up. I didn't think you were that kind of person."

"Well, I guess you don't know me as well as you thought you did."

"Laman," she said in exasperation, "you're the one who brought us here. You made a promise to me, and now you're backing out. Is that what a leader would do?"

"I'm no leader, Diana," he said. "Thanks for calling attention to the obvious."

He lurched away from her and stumbled toward the truck. Michelle stood there, breathing sharply through her nose to control her temper. She was trying to figure out whether to follow him or let him go when Petra appeared at her side, clutching Tyris's hand.

"It moved," she said.

"It looks the same," Michelle answered, caught off guard not only by hearing the little girl speak but by her surprisingly husky voice.

"No," Petra said. "There."

Michelle followed her finger to a spot far beyond where they stood. "Laman!" she called, then took Petra's hand and, forming a chain with Tyris, set off for the surprise only the little scout had seen.

When Laman and the others caught up to them, Michelle pointed at the eighteen-inch wide hole in the dusty ground, too dark to see bottom.

Laman stared in wonder. "It must have opened up when the explosives went off," he said. "The tunnel was probably damaged in the earlier bombing, and the shockwave widened the seam at the stress point." This time, he caught Petra and swung her into the air, while the girl squirmed to liberate herself. "I'm putting *you* in charge!"

She burst into a riotous laugh and shook free of his arms, running hand-in-hand with Tyris to a spot they judged safe from further abuse. Michelle smiled at them, but when she turned back to the hole, she was due for another disappointment. "Damn it," she said.

"What?" Laman asked.

"It's not wide enough."

He cocked his head. "I think it's okay."

"Not for a cruise ship like me. Or probably even for Bridget and the other grownups."

He dropped to the ground and pointed his flashlight into the hole. "I'm pretty sure I can see bottom. We could ask Petra to—"

"There's no way you're sending her down there," Michelle said. "I'll park my oversized load on you if you even try."

He grinned, not seeming totally opposed to the idea. Then he slipped both of his feet into the hole and wriggled downward. Skinny as he was, his hips barely fit through, but before she could stop him, he'd lowered himself halfway and was using his arms to brace himself. The next second, he let go and fell, landing with a thud and a grunt. She rushed to the hole, but couldn't see any sign of him.

"Are you okay?" she called into the dark.

"I'm fine," his voice floated up to her. "There's a floor down here and everything. It was just hard to make out from up top." His flashlight clicked on, and she saw his pale face, grinning maniacally as he waved at her from ten feet below.

"You're lucky you didn't break your neck," she said.

"A leader has to take risks," he answered. "Now stay with the girls, and I'll see you soon."

The words *be careful* were on her tongue, but he was gone, his footsteps echoing briefly before the earth swallowed all sound of him.

138

# Chapter 10

Michelle had never expected to feel so worried when one of Udain Genn's sons disappeared from her life.

She called to the girls, who skipped over to take her hands. While everyone waited for word from Laman, she led them to a spot close to the metal entrance plate and tried to get them interested in a game. She even drew a hopscotch grid in the dust with a loose stone and, when they stared blankly at it, started to explain the rules. The two of them, however, preferred to sit by themselves, heads close together, conferring on some very important five-year-old matter. Or was Tyris six by now? Michelle was surprised by how quickly the girls had formed such a tight bond, though maybe she shouldn't have been. Seeing them together made her long for all of the female friendships she'd had and lost: her mom, Rosie, Janine, even Tyris's mother, though Michelle had only known Helene for a little while before she died. It made her feel as if she'd been surrounded by nothing but men since the day the bombs fell.

She was so absorbed in watching the girls' private play, it was a while before she realized how long Laman had been gone. Certainly long enough to walk down the tunnel from the place he'd entered to the spot where she was sitting, unless he'd lost his way or encountered an obstruction. Under the pretense of stretching her legs, she left the girls and walked the short distance to the hole where he'd disappeared. Feeling stupid, she cupped her hands around her mouth and leaned down to call his name, but she received no answer except the echo of her own voice. She stood indecisively for a minute, debating whether to try cramming herself through the gap in the tunnel, but she decided that would definitely violate Dr. Melan's no-overexertion policy. Instead, she walked the well-traveled path back to where the girls sat. Their game, if it was a game at all, hadn't changed much; it seemed to involve little more than trading Tyris's dusty doll back and forth between them, touching hands as often as possible while they did so.

They continued playing placidly for what had to be a half hour at least, Michelle growing more anxious by the minute. Dire possibilities crowded her mind: he'd gotten lost, gotten hurt, gotten killed by whatever was lurking in the depths of the base ... And she'd been the one who'd goaded him into it, without even knowing why. When it had seemed the lower level was inaccessible and Laman had been eager to wave the white flag, shouldn't she have helped him to the truck and gladly kissed this place goodbye? She was still trying to answer that question when the metal plate beside her released a hiss of trapped air, and she jumped at the sound.

"Laman?"

"You were expecting someone else?" His voice sounded thin and faint, and Michelle saw why: the plate was raised less than an inch above its sealed position.

"What took you so long?"

"Exploring. Lots of cool tunnels down here."

"How are we … " She slipped her fingers into the crack, but she knew at once that the metal plate was far too heavy for her to lift. "How did you open this thing?"

"There's an emergency release. But the cement must have shifted or something, because it's stuck pretty bad."

Michelle thought about it a minute, then the solution came to her. "Wait right there."

While Tyris and Petra continued playing as if there were nothing more vital in the entire world than the feel of the doll's rubbery skin against their fingers, she explained the situation to Bridget and the men. It took a while to find what they needed amidst all the equipment they'd piled into the rear compartment of the truck, but eventually they rigged up a system with cables tied to the back bumper and hooked to the metal plate. Michelle told Laman to move away, and when he gave the all-clear, Bridget inched the truck forward. Laman was right: the hatchway resisted even the power of the truck, and Michelle feared the straining cables might snap. But finally, with a grinding sound that made her shiver in the quiet desert air, the plate came free, exposing the square opening that led to the tunnels.

A second later, Laman's head popped out. "There's a ladder, so it shouldn't be too hard for you."

*Thank you for your concern*, Michelle thought. For all her worries, she found herself less than thrilled to have him back. Maybe that had something to do with lowering herself into another possibly monster-infested tunnel.

"How do I know you're you?" she asked.

"What?"

"You were down there a long time. So how do I know you're you?"

141

"Come on, Diana. Do you seriously think the Skaldi would want to take *me* over?"

She frowned, grating at his quip. His hand was only inches from hers, his face shining. Yet for some reason, she couldn't bring herself to validate his conquest.

"Cut yourself," she said.

He looked shocked. "What?"

"Skaldi don't bleed," she said in case his dad and brother hadn't explained it to him. "Here, give me your knife."

"You're serious?"

She held out her hand for the knife. If he had any doubts about how serious she was, her face dispelled them.

"I'll do it," he said, his own face falling.

Taking a Swiss Army knife from his pocket, he gave himself the tiniest nick at the end of his index finger, little more than a paper cut. Wincing nonetheless, he squeezed the finger and presented it to Michelle for inspection.

She leaned close to see. A droplet of blood welled, grew, then followed gravity's course down his finger. She felt instantly ashamed, and handed him a tissue without looking at him.

"Thank you," she said.

"It's okay," he said. "So you trust me now?"

She met his eye. His hand was out, the one that wasn't bleeding. She took it and let him guide her to the ladder.

"Better get out of the way," she said, striving for a carefree tone. "Diving bell descending."

Laman backed down the ladder while she lowered her unwieldy body into the hole. He shined his flashlight upward to help her see the rungs, and all she could think of was what kind of view she was presenting him from below. If he said anything, anything at all, she was determined to kill him right then and there.

Luckily for both of them, he kept quiet. The ladder was short, and in moments, her feet touched the solid cement of the tunnel floor. The twins came next, bringing the reluctant Tyris and Petra with them. When everyone had assembled inside, the adults taking longer than the others as they transported their heavy flamethrowers down the ladder, Laman shined his flashlight around the space to show them what he'd found.

At first glance, Michelle's memory kindled with the layout of the Skaldi facility back east. There were the same blank gray walls, the same stale, plastic-smelling air. But instead of the linear layout of that dungeon, this place was a labyrinth, Laman's beam reflecting off a circle of metal doors heavily reinforced with steel plates and bars. Some of the doors were closed, while some stood in the open position, their keypads blinking a pinpoint of red light. Michelle could easily imagine what had happened: Skaldi pouring into the facility from the surface, or escaping from within, to consume the inhabitants as they tried to flee. When Laman headed toward one of the open doors, she held out a hand to stop him. "We need to leave a guard."

He froze in mid-stride, looking puzzled or annoyed. "What for?"

"To watch the entrance. Just in case."

"Look, I know you're antsy about being here—"

"*Antsy* doesn't begin to describe it," she said. "That hole over our heads is one of only two ways out, and some of us can't fit through the other. Wouldn't a *leader* leave someone behind to make sure we can evacuate if we need to?"

"A leader never leaves anyone behind." The way he said it sounded like he was repeating someone else's words, maybe his father's. "Which is why we're all going together."

He turned from her, but she grabbed his arm.

"Please, Laman," she said. "This might seem like an awesome adventure to you, but it's not to me."

He looked at her with poorly disguised frustration, and she knew she'd read him right: in his excitement about calling the shots for the first time in his life, he'd forgotten that this wasn't a game. Minding her own rule about not touching, she let go of him and beseeched him with her eyes, and after a moment, he threw his hands up and let out a hard breath.

"All right," he said. "Who's staying?"

Bridget and Charlie volunteered, and since it seemed reasonable to have a team guard the exit, Laman decreed that they could both remain. Calling everyone else together, he arranged the colony in a sensible order: himself and the other two adults with their flamethrowers up front, then Michelle and the little girls directly behind the lead team and the twins in the rear. As an extra precaution, Michelle insisted that Laman hand over his tablet for her to draw a rough map in case they got disoriented or needed to retreat quickly.

"No one separates from the group," she said. "No one goes into a hallway or a room until it's cleared. And when it comes to survivors, shoot first and ask questions later."

She glanced at Laman, but this time, he had nothing to say.

They started down the tunnel Laman had chosen, moving slowly with only his flashlight and the beams mounted on the flamethrowers to show the way. They passed numerous doorways, most of them closed, a few yawning open, but none of the rooms they peeked into contained anything tempting enough for them to linger. Most, in fact, were completely empty. The corridor intersected others from time to time, and at each branch, Laman paused so Michelle could record their position in Dr. Melan's tablet. She tried to keep them on a straight course, but that soon proved to be impossible, since there were times when the main tunnel split into two or three branches and they were forced to make a choice. It was wearying to the eye when everything looked so much the same, bedeviling to the mind when they had no idea where they were going or how far the tunnels extended. Michelle realized that during the half-hour or so that their fearless leader had been "exploring," he was lucky he didn't get himself hopelessly lost, and she was determined not to let that happen to them.

They'd been walking for a good hour, the unvarying emptiness and silence of the place starting to fray her nerves to the breaking point, when they came across a door much different than the ones they'd seen earlier.

For one thing, it was huge. It filled the corridor in front of them, a metal monstrosity that looked more like the portcullis of some medieval castle than a doorway inside a modern military facility. For another, it seemed to be the end of the line; there were no other tunnels at this point, the last intersection having been several minutes before. If the maze was designed to mislead intruders who were trying to breach this final bastion, it seemed that Laman's fledgling colony had successfully defeated the designers' system.

Except for one problem: the portal was closed.

Laman stepped up to the door, next to which his scrawny body looked like a grade schooler's. Everyone except

Michelle and the little girls joined him. Together, they pressed their shoulders against the door as if they might be able to force it open, but Michelle wasn't surprised when it didn't budge. Laman resorted to holding his ear close to the metal and tapping various parts of the door, something he must have seen in an old spy movie. The result was that, when he touched a spot in the approximate center, there was a whirring of machinery and recessed turrets slid out with the clicking sound of rounds being engaged. Laman jumped back, but thank goodness, the turrets didn't fire.

"I think we better go back," he said shakily.

"That's probably a good idea," she said, and they retreated down the corridor, keeping an eye on the turrets that swiveled in their housings as if tracking the colony's movements. When they reached a safe spot beyond the most recent intersection, Laman drew a deep breath.

"I'm guessing that was the situation room," he said. "It's where the top commanders assemble in case of a nuclear strike or any catastrophe of national scope."

"Do you think they're in there right now?"

"I doubt it. If the base was on lockdown, all the other doors wouldn't be open. I wonder if there was a malfunction here, so they had to escape another way."

"Or they didn't escape," Michelle said. "Not in their own bodies."

Laman's mouth fell open as if that was the first time he'd ever heard of such a thing.

"We should head back the way we came," he said. "Maybe we'll find another safe room, or a place with food and water. Or," he added, nodding significantly at Michelle, "somewhere for you to get some rest."

146

"I'm not the only one," she said, but he didn't seem to hear her as he turned to lead the way back down the tunnel.

Michelle followed, holding Tyris and Petra by the hand. She didn't fully understand why she was acting out her rapidly changing moods on Laman, why she felt like comforting him at one moment and strangling him the next. *Hormones*, she thought, but she knew that didn't explain it. Maybe it was just that she was tired, less from actual exertion than from wandering through this maze with only the dancing circles of the flashlights to show their way. Or maybe it was because her baby hadn't checked in since they entered the base—none of the lazy, aqueous ballet moves she'd grown accustomed to feeling. That might only mean the spud was sleeping, but if she didn't receive a visit soon, she wasn't sure what she'd do. Still, Laman wasn't responsible for what was going on inside her body, so why did she feel as if the baby was keeping quiet in fear not only of this place but of him?

She'd succeeded in talking herself into a near panic when Laman startled her by letting out another of his ill-advised cries of triumph.

"I told you!" he gloated. "I told you this was the place!"

They'd retraced their steps almost all the way back to the entrance, using Michelle's map—which, she couldn't help but notice, Laman had never thanked her for drawing. Now he ducked down a side passage and waved for the others to join him. When Michelle caught up, she found him aiming his flashlight into a room that had the unmistakable look of a cafeteria: shiny floor, tables folded against the walls, glass-and-metal food line bouncing back the beam of light. It was similar enough to the dining hall from the Skaldi lab back east that Michelle's gut churned. But like the cafeteria in that place, this one was empty of inhabitants, and the others flooded inside after Laman, searching for food.

"Keep the flamethrowers ready!" she called out, then instantly regretted how loud her voice sounded. "We don't know if it's safe," she added in a sharp whisper.

Laman made a sour face that looked unpleasantly like his younger brother's, but he didn't contradict her. While Dave stationed himself at the door and Norman covered the room, Laman led the little girls in an attack on the cabinets behind the counter. Somehow, he restrained himself from whooping with joy when he discovered packaged food, canned goods, and powdered milk stacked neatly inside as if waiting for them. The twins' search was less successful: no sooner did they open one of the tall metal lockers that stood in the shadows than the stench of spoiled food wafted over the room, making Michelle's stomach clench before they slammed the door shut. There was one positive outcome to that: her baby, as if feeling her discomfort, awoke and snuggled against her insides. Tears sprang to her eyes, which Laman mistook for a show of gratitude toward him.

"See," he said, his arms full of boxed crackers and cereal. "I knew this was the place to be."

"There's no water."

"The sink must be in the back," he said, with a smile that announced there was no way she could bring him down from his current high. "Or we can find a bathroom."

"And if the water's shut off? Like the lights?"

His grin widened. "We turn it back on."

Michelle looked away from him, balancing her stomach with both hands and speaking silently to her reawakened traveler. She wished she could find it in her to cheer for

Laman while he ran his victory lap; if he was right, then they *had* found the perfect spot, a place where they might live indefinitely. She hated to admit the possibility that this was the reason she felt so resentful—because he was right.

The twins unfolded one of the tables while Laman opened a box of crackers and handed them around. They were nothing special, some sort of snack cracker in an unmarked box, but Michelle's mouth watered at once when the smell of buttery sweetness reached her. She let the cracker sit on her tongue for a second before chewing, savoring the way the flavor dissolved in her mouth. Dave and Norman set down their flamethrowers and joined the party, which got even more festive when the twins found juice pouches in another of the cabinets. Sitting there, sipping fruit punch through a tiny plastic straw and passing crackers to Tyris and Petra, Michelle was taken back to the days when she'd visited Rosie's preschool classroom. She remembered feeling like such a big kid, occupying the undersized plastic chair beside her sister while all the other four-year-olds goggled at her. She tried to smile at her present companions, but all she could think of was that Rosie would never meet her niece or nephew, and the baby would never know the world Rosie had known. Forces no one was aware of had swept away the fantasy they were all living in, and there was no going back to the days of snack time and Show and Tell.

They finished the first package of drinks, and Nausikaa and Aristodeme rose to find more. Laman was opening a second box of crackers, butterfly shaped this time, when one of the twins emitted a short shriek.

Michelle turned to see Nausikaa pointing at a spot on the shiny floor, her sister gripping her arm as if to keep her from

149

falling. It was so rare for either of them to make any noise at all, Michelle knew at once that something was terribly wrong. She crossed the cafeteria with jerky strides and looked down at the thing the twins had discovered.

Her first thought was that she couldn't understand what had upset Nausikaa so much about a large pile of brown plastic tape, the kind you'd use to seal a shipping box. The girl wasn't just frightened but beyond panic; she fell to the floor despite Aristodeme's support and backed away in an uncoordinated crab walk, her arm rigidly pointing, her mouth emitting an almost inaudible whimper. When Michelle squatted awkwardly to look more closely at the pile, she saw why.

It wasn't tape. It was skin.

Her half-digested meal rose to her throat. The pile was about the size of a beach ball, but she could imagine its shape when unfolded: a complete human skin, arms and legs and head, with a few strands of hair clinging to that part. There was no odor, nothing damp that might have been vessels or viscera. There was just the empty sac of a human body, lying in a disheveled heap as if the person it had belonged to had been emptied instantly. Norman prodded it with the toe of his boot, and Michelle saw that something held it to the floor, a black paste with the consistency of Gorilla Glue. It wasn't blood, but beyond that, she couldn't tell what it was.

"We're getting out of here," she said.

The men retrieved their flamethrowers while Michelle gripped the little girls' hands and Aristodeme helped her sister up. Laman was on his feet too, but for some reason he lingered in the room while everyone else ran for the exit. Michelle paused at the door, expecting him to join them. When he didn't, she hurried back. "We have to go. Now."

He stared at the pile, shaking his head in dismay. "I don't understand it. This seemed like such a safe place."

"I wanted to believe that, too," she said. "I was so desperate to believe it, I let you lead us here. But there *is* no safe place. Not here, not anywhere. Not anymore."

"But the Skaldi could be gone," he protested. "They could have been here before and be gone now." He turned to her, spreading his hands helplessly. "If we leave, where else are we supposed to go?"

"If we stay, we're all going to die." When even that didn't shake him out of his stupor, she added, "Not just you, but Tyris and Petra and the twins. And"—she felt ashamed to say this, but it was her last card—"my baby. Do you want to be responsible for that?"

His defeated expression didn't change, but he backed toward the door with her. He took one last look at his shattered kingdom before joining the others as they raced for the exit.

It was a short run, just down the cafeteria hallway and then fifty yards to the anteroom where they'd entered the facility. The moment they took the turn onto the main corridor, Michelle knew that something was wrong.

They'd left a team to watch the exit. Now, there was only the imposing figure of Bridget. Flamethrower in hand, she stood in the dusty sunlight that fell from above, while a mound of material—possibly Charlie's flamethrower, possibly something else—lay at her feet. She opened her mouth as the rest of the colony drew near. The light was too weak to make out her expression, whether she was about to shout a warning, bare her teeth, or peel open from forehead to chest to swallow her prey. Michelle never found out which, because at that moment, one of the adults leading the charge depressed the trigger of his flamethrower, and the tank roared to life.

"Don't!" she shouted, but it was too late.

The stream of fire shot down the tunnel like a dragon's breath, engulfing the figure who stood there. Reacting instinctively, Michelle threw herself on top of Tyris and Petra. Laman shouted something incomprehensible as he did the same with the twins. They all hit the floor in a tangle of arms and legs just as the fuel tank of Bridget's flamethrower exploded, rocking the tunnel and sending a fireball searing above Michelle's head. The grownups' screams were cut short as the tunnel caved in, mercifully crushing them before they could burn to death. Darkness fell, but the avalanche that Michelle expected to smother her and the girls never came. The fallen cement that had killed the adult members of their colony must have saved her and the others, creating a barricade the fire couldn't penetrate.

Michelle coughed on the smoky air. Faintly, she heard someone screaming—possibly Bridget, or whatever Bridget had become—but that sound faded too, leaving nothing but the stink of burning fuel and burning flesh. The tunnel shook once more, followed by another crash, and whatever had been left to burn on the other side of the debris was snuffed out as surely as the light.

She reached for Petra and Tyris, pinching them to make sure they were alive. Two cries answered her wordless question. She could see nothing, so she felt for Laman's body and found it closer than she expected, trapped by two pairs of bony limbs that had to belong to Nausikaa and Aristodeme. She shouted against the ringing in her ears.

"Laman! Are you all right?"

"No need to yell," he groaned, though his voice sounded muffled. "I'm fine. Only—damn it!"

"What's wrong?" she asked in what she hoped was a quieter voice. She could barely hear herself.

"My leg. There's something on it. I think it's—" He cried out. "I think it might be broken."

She sat, scrambling blindly for the tablet to provide light, but it must have fallen in her haste to protect the girls. "The flashlight?" she asked Laman.

"Lost it. When that idiot—"

"He thought Bridget was Skaldi. He might have been right."

"Or Charlie might have just stepped outside to use the bathroom," Laman grunted. "Now I guess we'll never know."

With the assistance of the twins and one other pair of hands—probably Petra's—Michelle managed to clear enough rubble from Laman's legs that he could pull himself into a sitting position. She ran her hands inexpertly over his shins and up to mid-thigh, but she couldn't detect anything that felt like a break. "Where is …?"

"It hurts all over." Her hearing was starting to come back, and it sounded as if he was gritting his teeth. "Let me see if I can—"

He grabbed her shoulder and tried to stand, but he collapsed at once, moaning in pain. She felt for his hand, and he gripped convulsively. His skin was clammy with sweat.

"It's my hip," he said. "I can't put any weight on it."

"Laman." She tried to keep her voice soft so the girls wouldn't hear. "What are we going to do?"

He didn't answer, but in his silence, she heard his words from earlier in the day.

*Give up. Walk away. Let someone else figure it out.*

Tyris began to wail in the dark, and that was when Michelle knew they were truly alone.

# Chapter 11

The little girl's wretched cries echoed in Michelle's ears. She reached for Tyris and pulled her close, trying to stifle the girl's sobs against her chest, but it did no good. Even when Petra cocooned against her friend and mimicked Michelle's shushing noises, Tyris only cried harder, a sound of such utter desolation it made the pitch-dark vault seem as if it were already a tomb. Michelle understood Tyris's distress. The girl had lost both her mother and father on the same terrible day, and she'd counted on Michelle to take their place. Now, Michelle had failed her, too.

Anger coursed through her veins as she held the desperate child against her. Anger not at Laman, not at the creators of the Skaldi, but at herself. After all she'd suffered at the hands of Udain Genn's oldest and youngest sons, how could she have trusted his middle child to chaperone her to safety? And of all the places he might have chosen, how could she have let him lead her to yet another of the military installations that seemed to exist everywhere in the country, buried like poisonous mushrooms beneath the unsuspecting public's feet? Laman himself was probably less a villain than an imbecile, his head too full of adventure novels and superhero movies to admit that not all stories have happy endings. But *she* knew, and still she'd set judgment aside and allowed him to shepherd her and the others to their deaths.

When Tyris finally cried herself to sleep, another voice emerged from the fathomless darkness—Laman's, babbling empty words that Michelle could only assume meant he was crazy with pain, if he hadn't lost his mind altogether.

"They shouldn't have been here," he said. "This was supposed to be a safe place. Maybe we were wrong. Maybe there wasn't anything back there in the lunchroom. We could go and check it out, if I could just get up … "

She heard him trying to raise himself, then his gasp of pain. His body sank to the floor, and his voice resumed.

"They never should have used the flamethrower. That was stupid. We could go back and check, and I bet we'd see it was nothing, just a little pile of string … "

On and on, he tried to convince himself, or to convince her. All he succeeded in doing was make her feel as if he was blaming her—for contradicting him, for getting everyone so worked up they'd shot at the first thing that moved. Eventually, she couldn't stand to listen to him anymore.

"Laman," she said. "If you don't have anything constructive to say, just shut up."

He did, for about a second. Then he went on exactly as he had before.

"I was so sure of it. Everything was going exactly the way it was supposed to. There was the entrance, and there was food, and everything was working out. I'm going to go back right now. I bet it wasn't anything at all in the lunchroom, and that stupid guard … "

Michelle shifted the sleeping Tyris from her lap to one of the twins', then reached out in the dark toward the sound of

Laman's voice. When she found his skinny arms, her fingers curled around them and held tight.

"You know something," she said.

"It was supposed to be a safe place … " he repeated weakly, before his voice trailed into silence at last.

"You and Dr. Melan planned to bring me here," she said. "You chose this location before we left your dad's base, and then you lied to me about the mountains to convince me. Didn't you?"

He said nothing. Though she couldn't see him, she could feel him shrink from her.

"Didn't you?" she nearly screamed.

"No!" he protested. "I admit I lied about the mountains. But the doc never told me to come here. He mentioned it is all. He said he worked here before, and … "

Michelle dug her nails into his arms to stop herself from trembling. He didn't even wince. "He tricked you, Laman. He *wanted* us to come here."

"But *why*?" His voice sounded as bewildered as the little boy she couldn't help thinking he'd always be. "Why would he help us escape only to lead us here?"

"I have no idea. Maybe he and Athan wanted to work on me without your father's interference. Maybe this place has a better lab. There's no limit to what those two will do. What I can't figure out is how *you* could have done this to me."

Her final word echoed and fell silent. He made no answer, and she couldn't tell if he was too ashamed to say anything or if he truly had lost his mind. Then, very quietly, he began to talk again.

"I wanted to be the one to save you," he said. "I didn't want you to think coming here was anyone else's idea. I wanted you to trust me. To believe in me. Because then maybe I could believe in myself."

She loosened her grip on his arms and fell back against the rubble that blocked their escape. "Oh, Laman. If you only knew what you've done."

"I'll … I'll make it up to you. I'll get us out of here, I promise. And then I'll … "

She felt his hand hovering near her. Roughly, she pushed it away.

"You've broken enough promises to last a lifetime," she said. "I'll never trust you again."

He said nothing. The only sound was the quiet breathing of the twins, along with the occasional whimper from Tyris. Michelle pulled her knees as close to her chest as the baby would allow and let her head sink into her hands. There was nothing more to say, nothing more to do. After six months of running and fighting, she was trapped at last, and the thought that Laman might find a way out was beyond laughable.

*So why not end it now?* she thought. *Why struggle any more?*

She felt around on the floor until she found a jagged sliver of stone, then squeezed it so tightly in her palm it must have drawn blood. A seductive voice seemed to call out to her from half-forgotten dreams: *never to know pain again, never to know loss …*

She hurled the stone away, and heard it clatter to the floor as she sank back against the pile. Shards of stone clutched her like the Skaldi's claws, but with nothing to fill the emptiness inside her, she fell asleep before she knew it.

SHE WOKE SOMETIME during the night, or maybe it was the next day—who could tell?—to a faint scratching sound. Like fingernails against a chalkboard, the noise tickled her spine, which must have been what awakened her more than the sound itself. It surprised her that she was still capable of feeling anything at all. But then the baby moved, and its presence made her thankful she hadn't given in to the impulse to slit her wrists. Even with nothing to live for, even with her baby as trapped as she was, she still clung to life.

She sat up in the darkness and held her breath, listening for the sound to repeat itself. Minutes passed without her hearing anything except the soft exhalations of the others. She wondered if Laman was still there or if he'd dragged himself toward the room where they'd found the emptied skin. How far would he get? Would more damage from the ceiling block his way? If he arrived, would he find what he was looking for, or only the waiting arms of the Skaldi?

*Scratch, scratch.*

Her ears tuned in instantly to the sound, fainter than when she'd first heard it. Was it coming from farther away? From behind the wall of rubble? Or was her hearing failing her again? The darkness seemed to have stripped away her sense of direction along with her power of sight. Maybe the sound was Laman pulling himself down the debris-strewn corridor, or trying to break through the barricade with his fingernails. Knowing him, he'd be more likely to succeed in dislodging the one piece of rubble that would bring the whole structure crashing down on their heads.

Rising to her knees and guessing at the location of the scratching sound, she inched away from the wall with her hands held in front of her. She touched a body—one of the twins', from the size and whittled-down musculature of the frame—and then someone softer lying in their arms, probably the sleeping Tyris. Laman she didn't feel, and didn't try to. Carefully, making an effort not to wake anyone, she clambered over the bodies and continued to move forward in pursuit of the sound. It had stopped again, so she held still, hoping that the next time she heard it she'd be able to lock onto its position.

*Scratch, scratch.*

It was there, close by, though she still couldn't tell exactly where it was coming from or what it was. Frustrated, she felt around on the floor, seeking either a clue or a weapon, she couldn't say which.

Michelle jumped as something grazed her hand. The sensation was light and feathery against her skin, reminding her of those awful furry centipedes that used to scurry around her basement back home. She recoiled at the thought, but then the thing hardened into a solid shape and gripped her wrist, and she knew what it was.

Fingers. Reaching up from beneath her, trying to pull her down.

She wrenched her hand loose, so hard she fell back against bruising rock. The thing followed, issuing from the abyss with the stealth of a cat. It flowed over her, grappled with her, pinned her hands down. She rolled violently to the side, sent the thing flying—

"Ouch!"

The husky voice didn't belong to any Skaldi. And now that she thought of it, the hands that had clung to her were warm, not icy cold. They weren't trying to pull her down. They were trying to pull their owner *up*, and they couldn't have done that so easily if the body they belonged to wasn't as light and nimble as a child's.

"Petra? Where did you …?"

"Out." The word was as short and definite as a stone dropped in a pond. "See?"

Michelle was about to tell her she couldn't see anything when she heard a rapping noise, followed by a weak repetition of the sound as if from an echo. She didn't know what Petra was doing until the child took her hand and knocked her knuckles against the floor where they were sitting.

"Hollow," Petra said.

"There's a sublevel? How'd you find it?"

She could picture the imp's goblin grin. "Ty-Ty's sad."

Michelle reached for her and pulled the solid little body into a hug, and for once, the girl didn't resist. Tears welled in Michelle's eyes at the child's affectionate nickname for her playmate, and even more, at the realization of what she'd done to help her friend. While everyone else—herself included—had given in to despair, the girl had drawn on her scout's intuition to seek an escape route. She kissed Petra's forehead, then whispered in her ear. "Wake Ty-Ty up and tell her what you found."

Petra giggled and skipped free of Michelle's arms. Even in the pitch dark, she moved with the agility of a gymnast.

The girl roused the others. She spoke mostly in grunts and monosyllables, with Michelle supplying a whispered word or two when needed, but she was efficient, and the exodus was quickly arranged. It felt unbelievably good to hear Tyris and her friend laughing together again. Miraculously, Petra had even salvaged the doll, though when Tyris pressed it against Michelle's hand to show her, she could tell that its head was missing. Laman was there after all, sleeping with the others; Michelle recognized his pathetic groan the moment

161

she heard it. She braced herself for the scene she knew was about to follow.

"You go without me," he said. "I can hardly move."

It took an effort, but she said, "We can help you."

"Forget it. I'd just screw everything up."

"Nobody likes a martyr, Laman."

"Nobody likes me anyway," he said, further proving her point. But she had to admit he was right; with her pregnancy and the twins' weakness, they couldn't carry him into the unknown depths of the base.

"We'll come back for you," she said, and then added, feeling spiteful but unable to stop herself, "if we can."

"No rush," he mumbled, before retreating into a sulky silence she didn't need to see to feel.

With Petra's invisible shape in the lead, they joined hands and threaded through the rubble to the spot where the girl had emerged. Michelle discovered that Petra's instincts had been aided by luck: the collapse of the ceiling had freed a floor panel from its housing, which enabled the persistent child to pry it open a crack. By sense of touch, Michelle and the twins found the edges of the loose panel and peeled it back to accommodate larger bodies. When her fingers told her the opening was wide enough, she edged toward the hole, only to be stopped by Petra's surprisingly firm grip on her wrist.

"Careful," the girl said.

She guided Michelle's hands to the top rung of a ladder that descended into the hole. Once again, Michelle had a moment to be amazed at the child's uncanny faculties; how a girl her age had found the loose panel in the total dark, possessed the presence of mind to make sure there was a ladder, and then gathered the courage to climb down into yet another depthless darkness was a mystery she couldn't resolve. A vague misgiving struck her, probably no more than leftover distrust from her argument with Laman—but it *did* seem strange that this superhuman companion had connected herself to Tyris so quickly, followed them to the new base, found a way in, and now discovered a new route that might lead out. Should she be thankful for their good fortune, or distrust this apparent angel too?

*You're being paranoid*, she told herself. *That's what the Skaldi do to you: they make you suspicious of everyone you love. If you let them do that, then they've already won.*

"I'll go down first," she told the others. "Petra, you come right after. Nausikaa and Aristodeme, help Tyris. When you reach bottom, stay right where you are. I don't want to lose anyone."

*Anyone else*, she added silently, remembering the boy they were leaving behind.

She got onto her stomach and searched for the first rung of the ladder with her feet. When she found it, she started down. In the dark, it was impossible to tell how deep the pit was, and when her feet touched the floor only seconds later, she was so surprised she would have fallen if Petra hadn't scampered down the ladder and helped her regain her balance. The girl took her hand and snuggled up to her belly while the others descended, and Michelle told herself again that her doubts about the warm, solid little scout were ridiculous. When everyone reached the bottom—Tyris making more noise than Michelle would have preferred, but that was Tyris—they formed a chain and peered into the void.

"Which way?" Michelle asked Petra.

The girl tugged her hand. "Here."

"Not so fast," Michelle warned, and Petra slowed to a pace that normal human beings could maintain in utter darkness.

They inched forward, Michelle holding tight to Petra's hand in front and Tyris's behind. She couldn't see the dimensions of the place where they were, but a sixth sense she must have inherited from the darkness told her it was narrower than the tunnel above. There was nothing to hear except their own cautious footsteps, not even the hum of machinery she might have expected in the guts of the base. Even Tyris, for once, was quiet. Michelle's nose picked up the scent of what might have been diesel fuel, and her skin detected the tiniest trace of humidity, so faint she probably wouldn't have noticed it if she hadn't spent the past days in a desert and a climate-controlled facility. Absent those sensations and the assurance of the small hands in hers, she might have been walking in outer space, or in the kind of dream where there's nothing to see except your own fears.

"There," Petra announced.

Michelle stared but saw nothing. "I can't … "

"More," Petra clarified.

She pulled harder on Michelle's hand. For the first time since they'd begun their underground journey, Michelle had the sensation that their guide was following a serpentine path, maybe to avoid some obstruction only she could see. The girl led them in this fashion for as much as a half hour, and in all that time, she hesitated only once, for a moment or two, before plunging ahead again. When Michelle listened very closely, she heard Petra muttering to herself as if she were counting off steps.

All was darkness for another few minutes after that until a wall passed before Michelle's eyes and she realized that she could separate its black outline from a lighter patch behind it, as if they'd rounded a corner and entered another part of the subterranean system. The smell of exhaust or motor oil was thicker here, as was the stuffiness in the air, but the most miraculous thing remained that she could *see*—only enough to make out a formless gray space ahead of them, but she'd take that after complete blindness. Glancing down, she identified Petra's squat shape; behind, she found Tyris's slimmer silhouette, then the gawky figures of the twins. She breathed a sigh of relief so loud it was as if she'd been holding her breath for the past hour.

Petra squeezed her hand. "No more."

"This is as far as you went?"

The girl squeezed again, and Michelle felt pleased that she was learning to decipher Petra's telegraphic language.

Firmly gripping the little scout's hand, Michelle took a step forward until she was fully inside the gray space that had supplanted the dark. The gray was concrete, her feet told her that, but the walls and ceiling were hidden in pitchy blackness. Whether to march the girls into the unknown—and, the reminder came back to her, to abandon Laman in the process—seemed a much harder decision than the natural impulse to follow Petra in hopes of escaping the prison up above. Laman's words came back to her, breeding fresh guilt: *A leader never leaves anyone behind.* Even if that was only a military slogan he'd adopted from his father, it didn't sit well with her to ignore a call that she knew in her heart was right.

But heroic as those words had sounded when he'd said them, they rang as hollow down here as the sound of her own footsteps. She couldn't gamble six lives—counting her baby's—to try to save one person she probably couldn't save anyway, what with his injured hip. Horrible as she felt about leaving him to his fate after all he'd risked for her, she couldn't see a way to return for him that didn't involve losing everyone else.

*I'm sorry*, she voiced a farewell. *I hope you understand.*

She switched Petra's hand to Tyris's. The two hugged immediately, as if they'd missed the separation of only a few hours. Michelle was beginning to be able to make out faces, and she saw Tyris's cheek pressed lovingly against Petra's.

"Follow me," she said. "We're going to find out where this goes."

# Chapter 12

S he strode forward more confidently than she felt, and the girls followed.

A hundred or so yards ahead, they discovered the source of the illumination: running lights embedded in the floor. The lights were too dim to show her the dimensions of the room they'd entered, but from the way the oppressive darkness crowded above and all around them, she had the impression that it was simply enormous, the size of a convention hall or even an airplane hangar. The only problem with that theory was that she saw no planes, no loaders or ramps or those long strings of cars that carry suitcases at regular airports. She supposed a military hangar would look different from a civilian one, but still, shouldn't there be planes of some sort? Fighter jets or whatever? Unless—and this was the craziest thought she'd had all day—the Skaldi that had overrun the base had taken the planes and departed, flying all over the country to bomb the ruined cities she'd seen in Athan Genn's protograph.

*Can Skaldi fly planes?* she thought.

The answer came back immediately: *If they took over the bodies of pilots, they could. They can do anything the people they used to be could do.*

Even—maybe—fall in love.

"*K'chortu*," one of the twins swore.

For a second, Michelle thought the words—which meant something like "to the devil"—were a response to her own thought. She turned to find Aristodeme on the ground beside the running lights, her sister helping her to stand. Michelle rushed over to the two of them, dreading to discover that the girl had tripped over another pile of hollowed-out skin.

Instead, she found a single metal track in the cement floor, rising to a height of a foot or so above the concrete. A monorail, it came to her, like the kind they had at Disneyland, though that one was aboveground and elevated on a much higher track. There was no train, and even stranger, there were only a few yards of track, as if someone had started building the rail but stopped—or been stopped—before they got very far. Squatting so she could inspect the track more closely, she discovered that the part that jutted above the ground was only a small segment of a much more extensive track recessed in the floor. Apparently, the track could rise and sink, and this part must have gotten stuck in the extended position. Now that she'd figured out the design, she realized that the track had probably been beside them the whole time, hidden beneath floor level.

*A subway tunnel*, she realized. *Not an airplane hangar.* The cars were nowhere to be seen, nor could she hear their rumble or feel their vibrations. There was also no platform for passengers to stand on, and no escalators or stairs to the outside. But if this base had a subway system, there must be a way back to the surface.

She took the little girls' hands again and started walking rapidly alongside the track. Despite the dim light, she would have run if she'd thought Tyris and the twins could keep up. Dr. Melan's warning about overexertion was nothing but a distant memory; for all she knew, he'd only said that to prevent her from trying to escape this place. She knew that that magic word—*escape*—was nothing but a word, not a real thing she could cling to for any length of time. But if *escape* meant no more than breathing the outside air for a few precious moments then immediately looking for the next place to run and hide, she preferred that option to being a prisoner of Athan Genn and his father. If that's what her life was going to be like from now on—always fighting to survive for one more day, never escaping for any longer than that—then she would just have to face it. And, she allowed herself to hope, if her baby was okay after all, she wouldn't have to face such a future alone.

It helped her mood that the tunnel grew lighter, enough so that she could see the girls' faces clearly, with Nausikaa and Aristodeme their typical expressionless selves while Tyris and Petra smiled serenely in each other's presence. The extra illumination came from lights at the base of the walls, which showed her that the tunnel was circular in shape, something like London's subway tubes though constructed of featureless gray concrete. The ceiling remained shrouded in darkness, but it was safe to walk along the track, all five of them abreast, without fear of tripping over segments of the rail that were randomly locked in the extended position. It made Michelle a bit uneasy that the lights still worked, but then she remembered what Laman had said about autonomous technology. With the advanced science that had gone into building this place, it would be surprising if it didn't have the ability to keep the power on without anyone staying behind to flip the switch. But being reminded of Laman depressed the spirits she was trying to keep up for the girls' sake as well as her own, so she focused instead on the lights dwindling into darkness far ahead and imagined the exit that might appear at any moment.

She'd been listening for the sound of trains since they started walking, but the tunnel remained silent except for the echo of their feet and the almost noiseless hum of a tune Tyris improvised on the spot. Michelle decided the absence of trains was a good thing; without a platform to stand on, she wasn't sure how they'd get out of the way if one should rumble through. Every so often, they came across a recessed metal door in the tunnel wall, but when she pulled on the handles, hoping they might lead up and out, she found the doors locked. Probably they were nothing more than service entrances like the ones in the tunnels along the Pennsylvania Turnpike. In a pinch, she and the girls might be able to squeeze into one of the recesses. But she didn't want to test that theory, and her heart jumped to her mouth every time she thought she felt the slightest vibration in the floor.

They walked for several hours, long enough for Michelle's legs to grow weary and her bladder to demand attention. Feeling embarrassed that she couldn't hold it longer than a pair of five-year-olds, she made the others stop for a minute so she could lose herself in the darkness and pee on the floor, an expedient that was immediately copied by Tyris and the twins. When they reassembled by the track, Michelle paused to assess their progress, but nothing seemed to have changed: the lights continued straight ahead, while the darkness crowded the space above. Looking at her companions' expectant faces, though, she realized that an imperceptible change *had* occurred: the humidity she'd barely sensed before had thickened, laying a sheen of sweat on the twins' brows and drawing perspiration from her own cheeks and forehead. She was sure they must have passed under the surface-level perimeter fence and were deep beneath the desert by now, so it puzzled her that there should be this kind of climate inside the tunnel. It had to be artificial, but what was producing it— and for what reason—remained a mystery. She felt a new urgency to push forward, and so she rallied the girls, taking Petra and Tyris in hand and willing them to keep up. She even tried to skip with them, since that seemed to be their favorite form of locomotion, and clumsy though she was with her bulging belly, her tactic got them to pick up the pace and even giggle a little.

But not for long. The humidity grew denser by the minute, and soon Nausikaa and Aristodeme were streaming with sweat. Tyris was half-dead on her feet—the skipping probably hadn't helped—and though Michelle had convinced herself that Petra was immune to fatigue, it became evident that even the little scout was staggering under the added burden of supporting her friend. Michelle herself felt drained, both from the humidity and from the letdown of not finding an exit. She wondered if she'd mistaken the nature of this subterranean railway; maybe it was like the transit that took you from the security line to the terminal at the Pittsburgh airport, a self-contained system for traveling around the base instead of a commuter line with access to the surface. She wished she'd been able to bring food or water on this journey, though in her case, a single sip might have been enough to push her over the edge. For the others, and especially for Tyris, there was simply no choice but to take a break.

She called a halt at the next recessed door—locked, of course—and crowded into the small space with the rest of them. Tyris and the twins fell asleep at once, but Michelle stayed awake, watching as Petra's eyes flicked restlessly up and down the tunnel. The little girl's lips moved without making a sound, and Michelle wondered if she was practicing one of the melodies Tyris had made up to amuse her bosom friend.

Then Petra was clutching her hand, and Michelle sat up with a start, realizing she must have nodded off. When she shook her head to clear it of cobwebs, she saw that Petra's face was uncharacteristically troubled, her eyes wide. The next thing Michelle knew, the five-year-old had pulled her, baby and all, to her feet. She was about to ask Petra what was wrong when the girl put a finger to her lips.

"There," she whispered.

Petra didn't indicate where "there" was, but Michelle's eyes moved automatically across the tunnel to find the one and only thing the girl could have meant.

A door. Identical to the ones they'd passed before, identical to the one they were sitting in now, with one huge difference.

This one was open.

Michelle looked at her miniature partner in alarm. When they'd sat down to rest, she was positive the door on the other side hadn't been open; surely she would have headed for it if it had been. Now that she thought about it, she couldn't distinctly remember seeing a second door at all, which must mean she was woozier from fatigue and dehydration than she'd realized. She had no idea how many minutes or hours she'd been asleep, and it seemed possible that in however long her eyes had been closed, Petra might have gone exploring and discovered a door no one had noticed. Discovered it—and opened it? Yet if that was the case, why did the intrepid little girl seem so fearful of what lay inside?

"Petra," she whispered. "Do you know what's there?"

The girl shook her head, her eyes refusing to meet Michelle's.

"Scary," was all she said.

"Stay here," Michelle cautioned, without much conviction and with even less effect, as Petra gripped her hand and followed her across the track.

Michelle approached the door and laid her fingers lightly on it. The room was as dark as the tunnel where they'd left Laman. Heart pounding, she took a tentative step inside. The lights came on so suddenly it was like the bang of a starter's pistol, and she gasped aloud before her eyes took in her surroundings.

The room was tiny, even smaller than the one she'd been placed in at Udain Genn's facility. It had the same hospital look of that room: white walls and floor, glaringly bright fluorescent panels above. The only furniture in the room—the only thing in the room at all—was a metal bed with a white sheet stretched over it. The unmistakable shape under the sheet made Michelle's knees weaken despite her companion's steady grip.

A body.

There was no odor of decay or embalming fluid. Yet Michelle had to believe the body had been there for some time; the thought that it had appeared recently, as if someone had planted it for her to find, was too much to believe. Could it have been there so long it had lost its smell? Or was it possible that it wasn't a body at all? The room definitely looked like it belonged in a hospital; could it be that the occupant of the bed was nothing but an anatomical dummy, the kind medical students used for practice?

But practice for *what*?

She knew she couldn't leave this room without finding out. Even if the only scary thing about what Petra had discovered was its resemblance to a dead body, she would torment herself with wondering if she didn't pull that sheet back. Inching forward with her breath in her throat and the pulse throbbing so hard in her wrist she couldn't tell if it was hers or Petra's, she closed the distance to the bed and sank her fingers into the starched sheet. With a motion like a magician revealing the vanishing lady, she tore back the corner where the head would be.

When she saw what lay there, horror clutched her, and she would have fallen if not for the girl at her side.

It was Kareem.

His eyes were closed and his face gray, but she'd been dreaming of that face for so long, she couldn't be mistaken. His thick black hair and lashes, the strong curve of his nose, the sunken look of his cheeks—even with his features frozen and waxy as if he truly were an anatomical model, this was the father of her child, the boy she'd loved and killed. But it *couldn't* be him, not like this, not here. She'd incinerated him thousands of miles from this place, leaving no trace of him but the ashes in her lost collection jar. It could only be a horrible joke, a nightmare. This couldn't be Kareem.

And yet, it was.

He was dead, that much was certain. His motionlessness and pallor would have told her that by themselves, but even more disturbingly, his lips were pulled back like a mummy's, revealing his teeth to the roots. The expression was totally unlike what Michelle remembered from her grandmother's viewing several years ago, that too-perfect peacefulness crafted by the morticians from dead flesh. Kareem's face was fixed in the rictus of someone who had died in terrible pain, and recalling the torture chamber where Athan Genn had prepared his instruments to operate on her, she trembled to think what had been done to him.

But she had to know. She couldn't spare herself. She owed his memory that.

She folded the sheet down to uncover his neck, his throat, his shoulders. Gray skin, freezing cold to the touch, met her with every inch of him she revealed. She paused, her heart pounding, before yanking the sheet free to expose the rest of him.

When she did, she screamed and fell despite Petra's support, the sheet clutched in her hand like a burial shroud.

She'd seen it, the empty cavity where his chest should have been, the bloodless gray opening with no muscles or bones or organs inside. Not the result of an operation. Nothing had been surgically removed. He had simply opened like a monstrous orchid, the Skaldi's scar splitting him in two. Below that awful scar, there was no stomach or legs, only a snaky appendage that trailed from the edge of the bed.

Her cries brought Nausikaa and Aristodeme and even Tyris running. Without a glance at the corruption on the bed, they clustered around her, rocking her in their arms while she moaned more piteously than Tyris had ever done. She felt their warmth pressed against her, heard the little girls' awkward attempts to soothe their surrogate mother along with the twins' almost mute sounds of sympathy, but she was beyond comfort, beyond hope. To have taken his life once, only to watch him rise from the grave as this grotesque, inhuman thing ... She'd told herself she could survive any pain, any grief, but she couldn't survive this.

In a daze, she felt the others half-leading, half-carrying her from the room. In a swoon, she saw Kareem's face, heard him whisper the name *Chelle*. Then she watched his face peel back until the awful maw consumed his whole body, and she was too weak to pull the trigger that would burn his life and hers away.

SHE SPOKE TO him out of a fever dream, pleading for his forgiveness, desperate to make him understand why she couldn't go on. He sat just out of reach, but the sadness in his eyes was that of someone a million miles away from everything he loved.

*I tried, Kareem*, she said. *I told myself I could do this, and I did try. But I'd lost too much already, and when I lost you, there was nothing left for me to live for.*

*There are plenty of things to live for*, he said. *The girls. The twins. Our baby.*

*Our baby?* she repeated. *Our baby is a monster. The devil's spawn. It's everything we hate, everything we've been fighting to destroy.*

He was silent for the time it takes fires to burn and dreams to die.

*Then live for yourself*, he answered at last. *Live because your life is beautiful, and not to be thrown away for anyone or anything.*

*I can't. I thought I could, but I can't. Don't you see that I don't want this life anymore? That I wish you'd taken me with you, so we could be together forever, free of this place?*

176

*But I don't want that. What joy would it bring me to know that, in giving my life, I deprived you of yours? You speak of monsters. What kind of monster would I be if I could desire such a thing?*

*Oh, my love*, she said. *You don't understand.*

*What? What don't I understand?*

*That you betrayed me too. Not willingly, but all the same. You were supposed to be the one thing I never doubted, the one thing I never lost faith in. But you failed. When I took the flamethrower in hand and stole your life away, I knew that I would always hate the thing I loved, and hate myself for loving it, and for losing it. I'm sorry.*

He was quiet. His face was fading into night and flame, graying to dust. He bent down and left a kiss on her lips.

*You do what you have to do. I'll never come here to try you again.*

Then he was gone, and she sobbed in a darkness as deep as the space between life and death.


GRADUALLY, THE WETNESS on her cheeks gave way to warm, soft pressure. The soft thing touched her forehead, her closed eyes, her cracked lips. Her mouth was forced open, and she heard a gruff voice.

"Drink."

She did, unwillingly; a few drops of fluid went down, but she choked on the rest and coughed, spitting up. She tried to turn her head, but she was too weak. A hand turned it for her, another hand cupping beneath her lips to catch the water and bile.

"Try again. Slowly."

Water dribbled onto her tongue. She wanted to close her mouth, wanted to push the canteen away, but all her hand could do was flex feebly by her side. *Please let me die*, she said to herself, her tongue too clumsy to form the words out loud.

177

*Please don't make me have to open my eyes and see what I've seen ever again.*

"That's better," the voice said, while the cloth patted her chin dry. "Now let's see if we can get some food into you."

Michelle's lips parted. A sound emerged from them, though even she wasn't sure it amounted to an actual word.

"What did you say?" the voice asked.

Michelle tried again. "No."

"No what?"

"No … food."

"You're sick. Dehydrated and malnourished, mostly. If we don't get something in you, and fast, you'll die."

"Let me."

"I can't do that. Not now."

Michelle's eyes fluttered. The world was so blurry it was as if she was looking at it through warped sunglasses, but she saw a dark shape leaning over her, felt its hands lift her chin and press something between her lips. The food was salty but tasteless, and she would have spat it out if she could. Instead, the hands moved her jaw to make her chew the morsel, and eventually, saliva-slickened and compressed into a tiny lump, it slid down her throat.

"Much better," the voice said before forcing another grain of the salty substance between her teeth.

It went on like that for minutes, maybe hours. Bite by bite, the person who was feeding her got most or all of the food—a cracker? an energy bar?—into her stomach. By the time it was finished, Michelle felt utterly drained, the mere act of chewing and swallowing having taken all the energy she possessed. She tried to focus on the person hovering over her, but even raising her eyelids was beyond her ability. Instead, she felt herself spinning back into sleep, entering the shadow realm where Kareem might come to her again.

"Don't," she tried to say.

"Don't what?"

"Don't let … " *Don't let him find me.*

"I won't," the voice answered, as if the person understood. "Sleep, Michelle. We've still got a long way to go."

By the time she heard the person pronounce her name, Michelle could no longer marshal the strength to ask how they knew it.

KAREEM DIDN'T RETURN.

She was thankful for that; in her weakened state, she could never have fought him off. Somehow, she sensed that the person who had fed her was guarding her as well, making sure he didn't return. If he did, she wondered what her protector would do, if they'd have to burn him to nothing all over again.

She drifted in and out of sleep several times, and each time her eyes flickered open, she saw the dark figure leaning over her, felt a hand patting her face with a damp cloth. Her vision remained blurry, but she was pretty sure she was still in the tunnel, judging from the gray light and the echoes. She couldn't tell where the others had gone, Tyris and Petra and the twins. Had Kareem taken them away? Had they become Skaldi, too? But no, she felt certain that the person who'd saved her would save them.

Even if, like her, they didn't want to be saved.

The next time she came out of sleep, she heard Tyris and Petra's hushed voices. No giggling for once. More than anything else, that told her how close to death she'd been.

179

This time, though, when her eyes opened, a hand went behind her head and lifted her torso enough from the floor that she could feel the tightness in her belly. That, at least, hadn't changed. The baby was still there—had she really called it a monster?—and so, in a way, Kareem was still there too. She couldn't decide if that made her want to live or die.

"Careful," the voice said. "This is hot. But it'll fill you up a lot better than a lousy ration bar."

Michelle's lips twitched at the spoonful of steaming liquid the person offered her. Soup, she guessed. It didn't have much more flavor than the ration bar, but it did do what the person said: with each spoonful, her stomach felt fuller. Warmer, too. Energy crept back into her limbs from the glowing spot in her center, and at last, she felt strong enough to move on her own. The first thing she tried to do was pull away, but the person wouldn't let her.

"You're something else," they said. "I track you halfway across the desert, and this is the thanks I get?"

Michelle's lips tingled with the effort to talk. "I didn't ask you to."

"I didn't want to, believe me. But as the Stones so memorably remind us, you can't always get what you want."

"Then why ...?" she started to ask, before words failed her again. *Why are you helping me?*

"Because there's a debt I had to repay," the person said. "A debt to a boy who gave his life for mine."

Something clattered; maybe it was the bowl and spoon being set on the floor. Michelle was lowered back to the ground, and realized for the first time that she was lying on something soft, a blanket or sleeping bag. She raised her head to see the dark shape stuffing supplies into a huge pack, the kind hikers use to cross the mountains. Though her vision refused to cooperate fully, she made out a camp stove, pots and pans, a lantern, a bedroll—an extra one—and more. Something that looked suspiciously like the stock of a rifle protruded from the top of the pack. When the person was done buckling up their bag, they stood.

"You should get some sleep," they said. "We've got to start moving soon."

They were about to walk away when Michelle held out a hand. "Wait."

The person turned back. Michelle tried to focus on their face, but for some reason, she couldn't.

"Who are you?" she asked.

The person returned to where Michelle lay, squatted before her, and dug inside the pack. Something appeared in their hand, something that glittered dark green in the light of the tunnel. When Michelle saw what it was, her heart jumped as if it had started for the first time.

Kareem's collection jar.

Her eyes found the person's face. The veil seemed to drop from her vision, showing her the dark eyes, olive skin, and shaved head of another companion raised as if by magic from the dead.

"You're not the only one who's been keeping secrets," Arachne said. "Starting with the boy you wanted to believe was yours."

# Chapter 13

Michelle stared at the dark-garbed sentry, who met her look with a sardonic smile that was closer to a sneer.

"They told me you didn't make it," Michelle said.

"Yeah, well, *they* can be pretty cavalier when it comes to the truth." Arachne held the jar aloft, turning it slowly so it caught the light. "Then again, I guess we all can."

"But then you … " It seemed a hundred years since she'd left Udain Genn's base, and her foggy mind had trouble reconstructing how she'd gotten there. "The sandstorm … "

"Classic case of bad timing. I'd alerted Udain to our arrival a few minutes before the storm hit. I figured you wouldn't want me around, so I made myself scarce."

"*You* alerted Udain? Then you knew about … you *brought* us there?"

Arachne lowered the jar and sighed. "It's a long story. And we're not out of this funhouse yet."

"Tell me. I need to know."

Arachne sighed even more deeply. She turned and barked an order at Petra and Tyris, who took flight at the sound of the woman's voice. Michelle saw them huddling with the twins farther down the tunnel.

"You asked for it," Arachne said.

She sat, cross-legged, and set the collection jar on the ground. Michelle longed to take it from her, but Arachne kept it close, her hand hovering nearby and her eyes darting toward it every few seconds as if she knew what was on Michelle's mind.

"All right," she said. "Yes, I was working for Udain. And yes, I delivered you right to his doorstep. You"—she touched the jar—"and this."

"*This?*" Michelle repeated. "*This* is mine—you had no right to take it."

"I had every right," Arachne replied, color rising in her cheeks. "More right than some bimbo who knew him for all of a week, and who just happened to have the dumb luck to—" She stopped, letting out a strangled laugh. "Look, I'm not going to fight you over some dead boy. I gave up that kind of drama when I was your age."

"Then you knew him?" Michelle asked. "Kareem?"

"Kareem Reza, yes," Arachne answered. "But not *your* Kareem. The boy you knew was only a shadow of mine. A duplicate, courtesy of the Skaldi trials."

*Reza.* Michelle ran the name over her tongue, wishing it didn't call to mind the fleshless thing that lay in the room just out of sight. But what did Arachne mean by a *duplicate?* "How did you meet … your Kareem?" she asked cautiously.

"It was in Iran," Arachne said. "On my first and only tour. I was all of eighteen years old at the time. He wasn't much older."

"You were in the army?"

"Private military. Covert operations. You don't need to know the details."

Michelle's mouth twisted. "A mercenary."

"That's right," Arachne said. "But if it wasn't for me, your precious Kareem would have died long before you were born. And that bundle of joy you're carting around would have been less than a twinkle in anyone's eye."

She stared a challenge, but when Michelle said nothing, her features relaxed.

"My job was to infiltrate the local resistance," she said. "I spoke the language, had the right look. I was young and cocky enough to think I could pull it off." She shook her head. "It didn't go well. I was taken. I would have been just another dead Mata Hari if our hero hadn't intervened."

"He helped you get away."

"Fool that he was. He came to my cell, removed my restraints. I wasn't the trusting type in those days. I jumped him, got my hands on his weapon. I was ready to blow what little brains he had out, but he managed to sweet-talk me out of it." She laughed bitterly. "That was the first time I had him in my sights and couldn't pull the trigger."

"The second time?"

"In Jason's camp. When the two of you escaped. I saw him coming at me, knew it wasn't really him, but choked."

She was silent, staring at the collection jar, its green light reflected in her dark eyes. Possibly wishing she'd pulled the trigger the second time she had the opportunity, or the first.

"Why didn't you do anything to protect him at the end?" Michelle asked. "When Jason brought him back to camp? When you *helped* Jason bring him back to camp?"

Arachne lined her up with her eyes. "I was outnumbered. Jason didn't know my history with Kareem. All I could do was stay close and hope for a miracle. You know better than anyone how that turned out."

Michelle tried to meet the woman's fierce stare, but she was forced to look away. Arachne was right. If anyone could have saved Kareem then, it was her—and she'd killed him instead.

"What happened to you and him?" she asked. "Before?"

Arachne's expression softened the slightest bit. "We got out of the war zone. Barely. But he was hurt. His legs … " Grief flashed across her face, only to be replaced by a stony glower. "Back in the states, my CO told me about a project, something off the books. He said he could pull some strings, get Kareem admitted. I thought he was doing me a favor."

"The Skaldi trials?"

"Phase One. Udain was top dog, but his background's in engineering, so the science was beyond him. That's where people like Melan came in."

"And the project?"

"Using Skaldi genes to patch up wounded warriors and send them back onto the battlefield. But send them back *different*. As stealth fighters, undercover agents. Except unlike me, their cover would be so perfect they'd never be detected. Not until they'd eaten their way through the unit where they were planted and moved on to the next."

Michelle shuddered at the thought of Kareem—her Kareem, Arachne's Kareem—being turned into such a ruthless weapon of destruction. But wasn't that exactly what had happened? Wasn't that why she'd had to kill the boy who'd fathered her child?

"Why him?" she asked.

"No idea," Arachne said. "Maybe it was easier to make a non-U.S. national disappear. Or maybe they found something in his blood that made him a better match for the Skaldi genome. I never asked. By the time I realized what was going on, Udain had me in so deep there was no way *to* ask."

"Did they … did they torture him?"

She flinched when Arachne let out a vicious laugh. "What do you think? As if it wasn't torture enough for him to wake up one morning and discover that the scientists weren't satisfied to tinker just with *his* body, but someone had the even more warped idea to use the Skaldi's ability to mimic human cells to breed hundreds of copies of him. So now there's a whole schoolhouse full of genetically identical children running around that are partly him and partly something else, which means he doesn't know who he is anymore or if there's even any *him* left. And then, to learn what they plan to do with all those precocious little monsters, to realize what his life has become … I'd say they tortured him. I'd say that thing in the room back there was lucky—at least it didn't survive the operation. The Kareem I knew *did* survive, long enough to watch everything about himself die … "

To Michelle's amazement, the woman buried her head in her arms. She wasn't crying—at least, she wasn't making any noise—but she looked so lost, so defenseless, Michelle reached out a tentative hand toward her. As if she sensed the movement, Arachne's head snapped up, her eyes wild. She snatched the collection jar and backpedaled frantically.

"Don't touch me!" she screamed.

Michelle held her hands out in surrender or supplication, but it was many minutes before Arachne's breathing returned to normal. When she spoke again, her voice was purposely flat, as if she were reciting data from some boring report.

"The western experiments turned up a number of unexpected results," she said. "Such as the hybrids' ability to store enough energy that they could be used as bombs. Udain got excited by that and decided it was more in his wheelhouse, so he created the eastern facility and moved out there to personally oversee the production line. He must have figured that manufactured beings could be planted in hotspots with less political fallout than veterans—plus, if things went sideways, the little devils could be detonated to destroy the evidence. A new batch of 'children' were minted for that particular phase, all of them designated Subject K-1. The way it worked out wasn't according to plan, but what else is new?"

"So Kareem—*my* Kareem—was half-Skaldi from the start?"

Arachne's eyes bored into her. "Half, two-thirds, one-eighth, who knows? But yes, he was a hybrid, as much as any of them."

"But that doesn't mean his purpose was … I mean, that he was designed to … "

"Udain Genn is a sick man, but his sickness has to do with bombs, not babies," Arachne said. "He had no idea there was something different about his latest creation, something in their blood or brain that made at least one of them human enough to take the next step."

"The next step?"

"Do I have to spell everything out for you?" Arachne rasped. "Human enough to want to learn its own history, to adopt the name it must have overheard Udain or Jason or one of the other scientists using. Human enough to resist their plans for it while it was growing up, and, once it was grown, to want for itself what the boy who first bore its name had wanted." She glared. "Even if it was with a bubble-headed blond like you."

Despite Arachne's anger, despite everything the woman had said about Kareem's past, Michelle felt her heart lighten the tiniest bit. It would have been one thing to learn that her lover's sole reason for existence was to track down a mate, to seduce her, to pass on the monstrous genes deep inside him. Those genes might still lie within her baby, and if they did, she might still have to do what she'd sworn to do. But if it was true that there was more to her baby's father than that, wasn't there hope for his child as well?

"I didn't know any of this," Michelle said. "I didn't know about you and him on the night we … "

Arachne's eyes narrowed, and she gripped the collection jar and drew her arm back as if she was about to hurl it in Michelle's face. Then she let out a rush of air and set the jar on the ground by her side.

"I know you didn't," she said. "And I know that the boy you were … involved with wasn't the same as the boy I knew. But when I found out you were carrying his baby, it became hard for me to split that difference. I almost killed you, Michelle," she admitted in a low voice. "I was itching to do it. Fortunately for both of us, I had just enough sense to realize that if I did, I'd be throwing away the life I wanted to kill you *for*. Udain had made it painfully clear what would happen to *my* Kareem if I didn't deliver the goods I'd promised."

"Me," Michelle said.

"And *this*," Arachne said with mocking emphasis, touching the jar. "When the eastern trials blew up in Udain's face and the Skaldi were released, he was desperate to recover the source material he'd lost. So when I told him I had that material in two forms—in what was left of the boy you killed, and in what that boy had planted inside you—he ordered me to march you straight to him. I doubt he realized what Athan had in mind. All he wanted was to get his hands on Kareem's genes so he could start building his drone warriors all over again."

"But he was halfway across the country by that time," Michelle said. "How did you tell him about me?"

Arachne held up her arm, pulling down the sleeve of her black jacket. There, on her wrist, was a cuff identical to the ones Udain and Athan wore.

"It was Udain who sent me to Jason's camp in the first place," she said. "Seems the old man didn't trust what his number one son was up to, so he assigned me to keep tabs on him. And to help protect his assets, should any of them happen to show up." Her eyes strayed to the jar before snapping back to Michelle's. "You nearly made all his dreams go up in smoke, and Udain Genn is not known for being the forgiving type. I'd say you were lucky to get off his base with your goodies intact, wouldn't you?"

She lapsed into silence, her eyes fixed on the gleaming jar. It seemed to Michelle that there was no bottom to the Skaldi horror—that the more she learned about it, the more she realized she would never be able to grasp it in all its dimensions. Faced with the enormity of that crime, all she could do was look out for the things that belonged to her, the things she could still try to save. Starting with her own and her baby's life.

"Why should I trust you?" she asked Arachne. "If Udain's got you under his thumb, what's to make me think you won't turn us in?"

Arachne's eyes flashed dangerously, but she answered in that deliberately neutral voice. "Udain's got nothing on me anymore. I arrived at his base in Texas to discover that the boy I knew is dead, probably had been all along. The man lied to me, used me, the same way he used Kareem. I'll be damned if I'm going to let him or his twisted little son start messing around with the last bit of Kareem that's left."

She stood, snatching the collection jar from the ground and shoving it deep in her pack. There were still questions Michelle wanted to ask—about how Arachne had tracked them to this base, whether she'd found Laman too and, if so, what she'd done to him—but it was obvious their conversation was over. She tested her own legs and found that they held her—unsteadily, but that would have to do. Arachne shouted an order to the others, who came dashing down the tunnel. Before they arrived, Michelle spoke softly to the sentry who'd saved her life.

"I'm sorry," she said.

"I don't want your pity," Arachne said in a voice dripping with venom. "All I want is for you to keep your mouth shut and your ass moving." She pointed at the bedroll Michelle had left on the ground. "And if you think I'm going to treat you like some kind of fragile flower just because of the cells you're incubating, you can think again."

ARACHNE WASN'T KIDDING.

The pace she set would have been grueling if Michelle was in perfect shape, fresh from pre-season training. As it was, she was exhausted, sick at heart, and six-plus months pregnant—with a baby that Arachne didn't seem to care might pop out at any moment. Michelle understood now why the sentry had been so careful with her before they reached Udain's base: she'd been trying to protect the prize she hoped to trade for Kareem's life. What she couldn't understand was why, if Arachne wanted to keep Kareem's last living memory from harm, she refused to make any allowances for Michelle's condition now. Had she brought Michelle back from the brink of death only so she could torment her personally? Was this her passive-aggressive way of punishing the girl who carried her lover's genes?

*Hardly*, Michelle thought. Arachne was aggressive enough for any two people put together, but she was never passive about anything.

They marched along the monorail track, Arachne in the lead and the others stumbling to keep up. Arachne had her rifle out, a flashlight mounted beneath the barrel, but its beam didn't show Michelle anything new.

"What is this place?" she felt safe to ask.

"Subsurface ICBM rail line." When Michelle looked blank, Arachne added, "For moving warheads to their launch sites throughout the U.S. It's meant to be a deterrent against an enemy strike, since they don't know where the missiles are at any given time."

"Warheads? You mean like nuclear bombs?"

"Would it make you feel better if I said no?"

"I thought it was a subway."

Arachne's face cracked a small smile. "Subway to hell, maybe. It goes on like this for hundreds of miles without any breaks except the launch silos. If we're lucky, we'll find a service ladder to take us topside before then."

"What if we don't?"

Arachne looked at her sharply, but declined to answer.

They continued their march, Michelle keeping her ears open for the sound of missiles—whatever missiles sounded like—instead of trains. They found no ladders, though from time to time, they passed a door, a few of them cracked open like the one leading to the lab Petra had discovered. Even if Michelle had wanted to peek in to learn what other nightmares had been born in this facility, their guide didn't pause for a second or waste a glance to either side. She didn't waste time on food or water or bathroom breaks, either; they ate and drank on the move, and Michelle was convinced her bladder was going to explode if they didn't find someplace for her to pee. From the way the others, especially Tyris and the twins, kept well clear of Arachne, it was obvious they'd picked up on the woman's foul mood. Only Petra, who hadn't had the pleasure of knowing Arachne until now, was brave enough to risk foot-dragging when something in the tunnel caught her keen eye—but every time that happened, a jerk of Arachne's head was enough to send even the bold little scout scurrying back into line.

The tunnel unspooled before them, banded in light below and shadow above, vanishing to a point that never seemed to vary. The only thing that changed was the air, the humidity that had troubled Michelle settling over them like a fog she could almost see in Arachne's flashlight beam. There was no obvious source for the mugginess, no moisture on the smooth cement, no clank of radiators behind the walls. Michelle thought, but couldn't be sure, that with the thickening of the atmosphere came a change in the smell of the place, the whiff of diesel blending subtly into a fouler scent that made her nose twitch with animal warning. It was like a faraway bog that taints the dry land for miles leading up to it. She couldn't understand how something moist and earthy could exist in this sealed cement tube burrowing for hundreds of miles beneath the desert, and it frustrated her more than she could say that she could sense it, smell it, yet come no closer to seeing it than she could to a desert mirage.

"We'll take a break," Arachne announced without warning. "Two minutes."

Michelle saw that the stoic sentry's face dripped with sweat, while her black uniform was stained even blacker at the armpits. Her nose wrinkled, too, as if she smelled what Michelle did and was equally puzzled about its origin.

"I need to use the bathroom," Michelle said.

"Be my guest." Arachne gestured with her rifle to a spot where enough of the floor-level lights had gone out to create a patch of darkness. "If you take more than thirty seconds, I'm coming back there to drag you out."

Michelle frowned as she walked away. Arachne did, however, hand her a package of tissues before she went.

She dropped her pants and—disconcerting as it was to pee on the floor while the others were clearly visible not fifteen feet away—squatted in the darkness. Discomfort yielded to the relief of letting her distended bladder relax, and though the sound of piss hitting concrete was loud enough that she knew everyone could hear her, she closed her eyes and pretended she was alone, if not in her bathroom back home, then at least out in a field somewhere. She was just finishing up when Arachne called out.

"Ten seconds."

Michelle couldn't believe the woman was actually keeping count. She tried to hurry, but the baby got in the way of tugging her pants back on and she stumbled, falling on her butt in something warm and wet. Her own pee, obviously, which made her stomach twist with disgust. When she attempted to stand without putting her hands in the liquid, her insides heaved even more violently than before.

"Arachne—"

"What the hell is it this time?"

The sentry was marching toward her, gun leveled as if she deemed peeing a capital crime. The flashlight beam fell on the place where Michelle sat, and Arachne clamped her lips shut and simply stared.

A puddle of darkness spread on the floor around the seated teen. It was as sticky as tar and glistened like oil in the gleam of Arachne's flashlight, yet it moved with a seeming will of its own, swirling and squiggling as if worms agitated it from within. The sickly smell that Michelle had noticed before was stronger here, as if this clinging pool was the swamp she'd been anticipating all along. She reached behind her to push herself up against the wall, but Arachne held a hand out to stop her.

"Don't touch it," she said.

Michelle turned her head to discover the same fetid sludge dripping down the wall. She craned her neck, but the ceiling was too high and too dark to see where the stuff was coming from. Yet when she held her breath and listened carefully, she heard something up there in the shadows—a sound like children's hands playing in mud puddles, stirring the slop to fashion make-believe pies. Arachne aimed her flashlight at the sound, and Michelle saw a slimy mass overhead that moved in the same slow, squelching way as the pool she was stuck in. With panic, she realized that this substance must have been above them the whole time, oozing down the sides of the tunnel, waiting for the right moment to descend and swallow them all.

Arachne gripped her hand and pulled her free of the puddle, which clutched at her as if with invisible fingers before yielding. Michelle's nose wrinkled with revulsion as she turned to look at the seat of her pants, but to her surprise, the goo that had seemed so sticky and foul hadn't soiled her at all. It wasn't a pool of liquid, she realized. It was a living creature that had tried to hold her but, failing to equal Arachne's strength, had let her go.

"What is it?" she asked.

"I don't know," Arachne answered. "I have a pretty good guess, though."

"Skaldi?"

"Or something like it." Arachne searched in her pack and held out a fresh pair of camouflage pants. "Better put these on. No sense taking chances."

For once, Michelle was only too happy to drop her pants in front of the others and exchange them for Arachne's clean pair. While she dressed, Arachne kept her gun at the ready and shined the flashlight in a slow circle all around them, but nothing moved except the slime that hung above.

"What is this … this stuff doing down here?" Michelle asked, not expecting an answer.

To her surprise, Arachne supplied one. "It's being transported."

"What?"

The sentry pointed upward with her rifle, then traced the trail of slime down the wall and across the floor to where it ended several yards from the embedded rail line. Michelle watched black fingers grope feebly toward the rail, though they always fell short as if they lacked the energy or the willpower to achieve their objective.

"Someone's shipping it from place to place via the missile system," Arachne said. "Or at least, they were." In the glow of the flashlight, her face appeared ghastly as realization dawned on her. "But that means … "

A voice, chillingly familiar, spoke from beyond the beam of Arachne's light.

"Congratulations," it said. "Looks like you two just hit the jackpot."

# Chapter 14

Michelle spun to see Athan Genn step into the light. His petite hand held a large silver pistol. With it, he gestured toward Tyris and Petra, whose arms were wrapped protectively around each other.

"I'd drop your weapon," he said to Arachne. "Unless you want to lose Piglet and Roo."

Michelle saw the calculation in Arachne's eyes, and she feared the sentry was about to gamble with the girls' lives. But Arachne decided better of it, placing her rifle on the ground and sliding it with a toe toward Athan Genn.

The boy smiled. "Nice. Now we can all get along."

A metallic clatter followed his words. A hulking shadow joined Athan in the tunnel, while a smaller shape moved behind it in a lurching way. Michelle couldn't tell where they'd come from, but when they reached the spot where Athan stood, she saw that the one who trailed Udain Genn was supporting himself on crutches, his bad leg held off the ground and his arms quivering with exertion.

"See, Dad?" Laman Genn crowed. "I told you we'd find them here!"

"Yeah, now all you've got to do is explain why you brought them here in the first place," Athan responded. "If, that is, you don't want to end up in solitary when we get home."

Laman cringed at his brother's words, but Udain stood mute, his eyes as black as bullet holes, his face as blank as an automaton's.

"Laman had nothing to do with Diana being here," Arachne spoke up. "*I'm* the one who brought her."

Michelle looked at her in surprise. Why would Arachne take the fall for Laman?

"Nice try, Ash," Athan said. "Thing is, Melan told us all about the great escape plan. He said it was Laman's idea to squire her away, like a knight out of some pathetic teen romance novel."

"Melan was lying," Arachne said evenly. "To save his own neck. He and I planned the escape, while Laman came along at gunpoint. Otherwise, why would he have helped you find us?"

Athan looked back and forth between his brother and the sentry. Laman ducked his eyes under his younger brother's scrutiny, but Arachne—or was her real name Ash?—didn't even blink. At last, Athan shrugged and let out a hard breath.

"Well, there's enough trucks outside for a regular rodeo," he said. "And Lame Man's never come up with an original idea in his entire life, so I wouldn't be surprised if it was your doing after all. Not that it matters, now that we've got you both."

He waved his oversized gun, and Udain moved forward mechanically to relieve Arachne of her pack and search her for weapons. A knife came free of a sheath strapped to her thigh; a semi-automatic pistol was pulled from a holster below her armpit, with spare magazines on the other side. Her communication cuff came off last of all. Michelle found it obscene to watch the giant hands roam over Arachne's body, all the more so since Udain seemed to be completely unaware of what he was doing. When the mountain of a man finished with his search and reached for her and the girls, Michelle held perfectly still and tried to imagine she was somewhere else. Finally, after he'd patted them down and shown his son that they had no weapons, Udain retreated with Arachne's pack and took his place by Athan's side.

"What have you done to him?" Michelle asked.

"That's for me to know and you to find out," the boy said with a smirk. "Don't worry, he'll snap out of it once I cut the power. And the beauty of it is, he won't remember a single thing."

He gestured again with his gun, directing them to a door a few steps up the tunnel that had been hidden in darkness. Udain opened it, and fluorescent lights sprang on to reveal a flight of stairs leading up. In the glow of the lights, Michelle saw that a tiny wire snaked up the giant man's neck to connect to a spot behind his ear.

Laman entered the stairwell first, clumsily steering himself through the doorway on his crutches. Michelle tried not to hate him, tried to remember that she'd given him plenty of reasons to get back at her. When she thought about what he had to look forward to on their return to Udain's base, she almost felt sorry for him. But when she imagined what awaited *her*, sympathy was drowned in a tide of anger and dread.

Athan stood beside the door, waving the others through with his gun. Udain could barely squeeze into the small space. The girls came next, followed by Michelle and Arachne, who gave Athan one of her select scowls as she passed. He grinned back, then paused at the doorway, taking a final look at the tunnel.

"So this is the factory floor," he said. "And that black stuff must be some kind of birthing gel, I guess." He shined a pinpoint light from his wrist cuff at the ceiling, where the gel hung like a grotesque mold. "I can't believe Melan kept all this secret. The things I could *do* with this place!"

"Which is exactly why Dr. Melan didn't want you to know about it," Michelle said.

Athan turned to her, anger distorting his features. "Now do you understand why we can't fight them the way my dad wants to? Someone's launching that stuff"—he waved a hand at the black mass—"with freaking *missiles*, spreading it in seed form all over the country, maybe all over the world. There's no way we can keep up with that."

"You sound as if you actually admire them," Michelle said.

He eyed her coldly. "I admire anything that adapts to survive. You should know that by now."

"I know only one thing," she said. "And it's that I'm going to live to see them destroy you and all your little boy dreams."

He bared his teeth, and Michelle saw that she'd pushed him too far. All self-control gone, he lifted his gun as if to strike her.

The blow never fell.

A clattering noise made them both turn their heads, just in time to see Laman stumble down the stairs and collide with his father. Taking advantage of the distraction, Arachne wrapped an arm around Michelle and pulled her out of

Athan's reach, simultaneously chopping at his hand. There was a crunch, and the boy cried out, his gun falling to the floor. Before he could issue another command to his father, Arachne spat something from her mouth and hurled it at the black growth that hung overhead, then threw herself on top of Michelle.

"Get down!" she shouted, just as the world exploded.

The tunnel rocked. The ceiling came down where they'd been standing a moment before, drops of the black gel pelting them like hailstones. High-pitched screams, maybe from Tyris and the twins, maybe from Athan and his older brother, replaced the sound of stone striking stone. Michelle was pulled to her feet, pushed down the tunnel the way they'd come. She looked back, expecting to see Udain lumbering after them, but what she saw made her cry out in dismay.

The ceiling had collapsed right in front of the stairwell, completely blocking the tunnel at that point. On this side of the mountain of shattered concrete, the floor was covered with the birthing gel, pools of oily gunk smeared everywhere like black blood. Streams of it were in motion, slithering across the cement, joining with other clumps to form solid shapes. Some of these had grown to man-size, and were pushing themselves from the floor on long, skeletal forearms. Like the lifeless figure of Kareem she'd found in the tunnel, their night-black bodies ended in snaky tails that whipped against the floor. When one of them turned toward Michelle, she saw that it had no face, nothing but a ragged scar that split its skin where its features should have been. The scar extended the length of the creature's body, and the odor of decaying flesh was so strong Michelle had to struggle to keep from puking.

"What did you do?" she screamed at Arachne as the woman pulled her arm.

"The only thing I could think of!" Arachne yelled back. "Now move!"

Michelle stood rooted to the spot as the creatures grew in number from five to ten to twenty. She searched desperately to see if Tyris, Petra, and the twins remained in the custody of Athan and Udain Genn, but the rubble from the ceiling and the swarming bodies of the Skaldi made it impossible for her to see anything.

"Now, Michelle!" Arachne screamed in her ear, and she turned and fled at last, the sentry's hand on her back and the moans of the newborn Skaldi echoing behind her.

They raced down the tunnel as fast as Michelle could go, Arachne gripping her uniform top to urge her on. A swishing sound warned Michelle that the Skaldi were in pursuit, but she didn't look back. The weight of her baby had never felt greater, and the memory of Dr. Melan's words—*avoid overexerting yourself*—flashed through her mind. She was breathing heavily and staying upright mostly thanks to the hand on her jacket when a door appeared in the tunnel and Arachne steered the two of them toward it. Miraculously, it opened, lights flashing on inside before it clanged shut behind them. Bodies flung themselves against the door with metallic shudders, reminding Michelle of the night she and Kareem had spent in the barracks back east. Arachne was pulling her toward the stairs when the creatures figured out how to remove the impediment and the door creaked open.

"Up the steps!" Arachne yelled, and Michelle's feet complied. The sentry alternately pushed and pulled her up the flight toward a landing where there was another door. The stink of decay told Michelle that the Skaldi had made it through the door below, while the scratch of their claws meant that they were dragging themselves up the cement stairs. Arachne shouted at her, but Michelle couldn't make out the words. Her vision narrowed as she stared at the exit, which seemed to be receding as fast as they climbed. At last, Arachne gripped the door and threw it open, then shoved Michelle to the other side, where she collapsed onto her stomach. There was another clang and the snapping of a bolt, then the sound of the Skaldi hammering against the metal.

Michelle sat up and stared at the door, which seemed not only to be shaking from the impact of the Skaldi's bodies but slanting and warping in its frame. Darkness crowded the sides of her vision, and she would have fallen if hands hadn't held her upright.

"Breathe," Arachne said in a low voice. "Like this."

She modeled slow, deep breaths, and Michelle tried to copy her. A sharp pain in her side made it hard to fill her lungs, but breathing cleared her head enough to realize there was no trauma to her body, just a stitch from exertion.

"I haven't … run … like that … in months," she gasped. "Not since … "

"Save your breath," Arachne said. "We can have the 'joys of pregnancy' conversation at the baby shower."

Michelle looked into the sentry's dark eyes. Out of no-where, she wondered if Arachne had ever been pregnant, and if so, with whose baby.

"Feel better now?" the woman asked.

"I … " The question about Arachne's obstetrical history slipped away as fast as it had come. "He called you *Ash*. Athan did."

"He would," the sentry answered with a grimace. "That's short for Asheh, the name my parents gave me. They told me it meant 'blessed,' but I googled it a few years back, and it actually means 'born at a time of grief.'" She shrugged. "I like the name I got from my unit better."

"So Jason didn't give you … "

"Jason didn't give me anything but hell. Especially on the nights when he needed to get his rocks off."

"You *slept* with him?"

"I was undercover. I was supposed to be a good little soldier. I did what I had to." When Michelle continued to stare, she said, "Spiders have sex too, Cupcake. It's about survival, not senior prom."

She gripped Michelle's hands and pulled her to her feet. The Skaldi continued pounding against the door, but Arachne didn't seem worried. She brushed something from Michelle's sleeve—a spot of the black birthing gel, which slithered away when it hit the floor—then braced her until she could stand on her own. Something like a look of concern crossed her face as she jockeyed Michelle into position, and the thought entered Michelle's mind that maybe all the tough talk in front of the girls was just an act.

That was when she remembered.

*The girls.*

"We have to go back," she said. "Athan has Tyris and Petra and the twins."

Arachne cocked an eyebrow. "So?"

"*So?*" On second thought, maybe the vestige of motherly concern was the act. "So there's no telling what he'll do to them. He'll start experimenting on them, or torture them just for spite … "

"You do realize he's completely inside your head, don't you?" Arachne asked. "That he *wants* you to try to get the girls back? He's sitting there right now waiting for you to come galumphing after them, which gives us the time we need to get the hell out of here."

"But when he knows we're gone … "

"I can't be responsible for every virgin or near-virgin who falls into Athan Genn's hands," Arachne said. "My job is to get *you* to safety. You, and this."

She reached inside her dust-covered jacket and withdrew the collection jar. Michelle stared as if it were another body resurrected from the grave. "How did you …?"

"Udain dropped my pack when I set off the charge. I grabbed the jar before we cleared out. I'm sure as hell not going to let you waste my heroics by racing back there on a fool's errand."

"You don't have a choice. Because I'm going."

Arachne glared at her. Michelle held her ground, glaring right back.

"I could knock you out and carry you the rest of the way," Arachne said.

"I weigh a ton. You'd never make it."

The small woman looked her up and down. "Then I'll leave you here."

"You won't do that either. The ashes in that jar"— Michelle swallowed, admitting this to herself—"they're just dead cells. The baby inside me, *that's* Kareem's body and soul. You'll do anything you can to save it, even if that means taking orders from someone you'd just as soon let die."

Arachne chewed her lip in silence. Her eyes could have drilled holes in steel, but Michelle was almost confident enough to crack a smile. Almost. There was no reason to push her luck with a woman like Arachne.

"You realize I have no weapons," the sentry said. "I used up my last dime."

"Your last what?"

"D-I-M-E. Dense Inert Metal Explosive. It sealed off the tunnel, though it seems to have fed that black crap the energy it needed to spawn full-grown monsters. And they're out there waiting for us, just like Athan and Udain."

The door banged again, hard enough that the floor shook. Michelle thought she could hear the creatures' enraged moans through the heavy metal barrier.

"I'll take that chance," she said.

Arachne gave her one more look before throwing her hands up in defeat. She tucked the collection jar inside her jacket, then started marching resolutely down the dimly lit corridor that lay in front of them. Michelle hurried to catch up, but when she reached Arachne's side, the woman picked up her pace and left Michelle in the rear again.

"I like the name Asheh," Michelle called out.

"Which is exactly why I don't use it," the sentry said without looking back. "It helps me remember that I'm nothing like you."

ACCORDING TO ARACHNE, who answered one last question from Michelle before clamming up completely, they'd exited the stairwell on the top floor of the base, just below the surface. Lights were on in this part of the complex, but the bulbs were barely bright enough to see by. They must have been emergency back-ups. Michelle wondered whether the lights had remained on during the whole time the base was abandoned, or if the fact that they were on now meant that Udain and Athan Genn were waiting to pounce around the next corner, or the next.

They'd turned a number of such corners without incident before she concluded that Arachne's intuition must be right: Athan and Udain—and Laman too, if he was alive—weren't in pursuit, but were waiting for Michelle to deliver herself to them. At about the same time, she sensed an easing of the tension in Arachne's shoulders, as if the woman had accepted the inevitable. Though her guide remained one step ahead of her, Michelle felt safe to pick up the conversation that Arachne's rebuke had put such a sudden stop to.

"Why'd you cover for Laman?" she asked. "Telling Athan that you were the one who helped me get away?"

"It wasn't totally untrue. I had the intention, but Laman got to you first."

Michelle made a face, even though Arachne wasn't looking. "Come on. You don't put your ass on the line for anyone without good reason."

Arachne glanced over her shoulder just long enough to look annoyed. "It's basic protocol. When you're taken by the enemy, you do what you can to sow the seeds of doubt. Find their fault lines and exploit them to your advantage."

"What if the enemy's doing the same thing?"

Arachne snorted. "All the more reason."

She faced straight ahead and continued to stalk down the corridor. Maybe it was because all the highs and lows Michelle had gone through today had scrambled her brain, but she decided to go for broke.

"I think you're lying," she said. "I think you did it because you like Laman."

Arachne stopped dead, which caused Michelle's protruding stomach to ram into her. "You think I *what?*"

"Well, maybe *like* is too strong a word. But you care for him. The same way you do for me."

Arachne put her hands on her hips. "Why are you doing this, Michelle?"

"Doing what?"

"Trying to make me into someone I'm not."

"Because *I* like you," Michelle said. "And I refuse to believe I could like anyone who's as hard as you pretend to be."

"Then you'd better stop liking me," Arachne said. "Because there's no *pretend* about it."

She turned to stomp off, but Michelle lunged and caught her hand. Arachne ripped it free with such force Michelle nearly lost a nail.

"What in hell is the matter with you?" Arachne barked. "Are you hopped up on some kind of crazy pregnancy hormones?"

Michelle couldn't be sure. She did feel a little loopy, plus the goober was doing nonstop backflips in her belly. The touch of Arachne's hand in hers, however brief, had brought a tightness to her throat, and when the pressure worked its way upward, tears tickled the corners of her eyes. Arachne's expression changed from disgust to horror.

"We are *not* going to do this," she said. "Not now, not ever. Understood?"

Michelle nodded, sniffling. The baby did something she couldn't remember it doing before, something like a head-stand or a very deep dive.

"We're going to track down Athan, using mostly our sense of smell," Arachne said. "We're going to liberate the girls—again, with nothing but our bare hands and a few deft card tricks—and then we're going to make a run for it, even though you can't run for two minutes without popping a seam. In the unlikely event that we find someplace safe from Skaldi and other noxious life forms, you're going to have your bouncing baby whatever, I'm going to capture those first precious moments on my nonexistent phone, and then I'm never going to see you or your brat ever again. Got it?"

"Sure," Michelle said.

"Then stop your blubbering and let me get to work on the first part of the plan. You know, the part where I track down our quarry like a lioness out on the savannah."

She turned her back and stormed away. Michelle waited a moment for the tears to dry then caught up to her, walking one pace behind as before.

"We all done?" Arachne asked, looking at Michelle out of the corner of her eye. Michelle nodded, and they continued down the corridor without saying another word.

The area where they were walking was as much a maze as the part Laman had found, with multiple branches and intersections that would have made it easy to get lost. Arachne seemed to know where she was going, or at least she did a good job of faking it. She paused periodically to glance down passages where the corridors split, but once she made her choice, she threaded the labyrinth as confidently as if the hallways were strands of her own web. Michelle couldn't keep up with all the twists and turns, but she got the impression that they were backtracking, possibly moving toward the barricaded door that led to what Laman called the situation room. That made sense, she supposed; if Udain or Athan knew how to unlock the door, the installation's heavily fortified nerve center would be the perfect place to wait for Michelle and Arachne to arrive. The perfect place, once they did arrive, to make sure she and her baby never left.

Her edginess rose as the minutes passed. It didn't help that the baby was going crazy inside her, twisting and fidgeting in a way that made her back and belly ache. The thought popped into her head that the baby knew Arachne was right and was trying to talk some sense into its mother. Michelle tried to silence its voice, but that didn't stop the *what ifs* from sounding louder and louder: what if Athan had chosen another place to lie in wait for them, what if he had already taken the girls' lives in a fit of childish pique, what if they encountered the Skaldi army before they found their way to the situation room? What if, for that matter, Arachne's assessment *was* right, and Michelle was risking all on an impossible hope? The woman was a combat veteran; she knew how to gauge the enemy's strength against her own. Maybe, given what Athan would do to her and her baby if they were caught, it was better to sacrifice the children's lives to be free of the Genn family for good.

But the moment she had that thought, Michelle felt sure that Arachne *wasn't* right. There were some things you couldn't measure in strategic terms, some things that mattered more than safety or good sense. Some things, she whispered to the squirming noodle inside her, that were worth giving your life for.

As if approving her decision, the baby ceased its restless acrobatics and settled down to sleep.

Michelle's back was absolutely killing her by this point, so they rested briefly along with the baby then continued on their way. Arachne had walked briskly till now, in fact a little too briskly for someone in Michelle's condition, but after their break she slowed down and proceeded much more cautiously, with frequent pauses to check around corners, fist raised in a signal to Michelle to stay put. Finally, at the most complex intersection they'd come across so far, with at least eight different branches radiating outward like the blades of a fan, Arachne put up the *stop* sign and didn't release her partner by flicking her fingers the way she usually did. Instead, she flattened herself against the wall, gesturing for Michelle to join her. The sentry's eyes were narrowed and, of all things, her nose was actually twitching.

"What is it?" Michelle whispered. Her voice sounded hollow and unreal after hours of silence.

"Not sure. Something … "

She leaned out to look down one of the hallways, but pulled back instantly, her hand flying to cover Michelle's mouth.

"They're there," Arachne said. "What's-her-name and the other one."

"Nausikaa and Aristodeme?"

"Whatever. No sign of Tyris or her little friend, and I'm pretty sure I would have picked up the stench of Athan's poopy nappies if he was anywhere near."

Michelle had thought the whole smell thing was a joke, but she wasn't about to argue. "Do you think the twins got away?"

"Possibly. But it's more likely they're being used as bait."

Very slowly, she leaned out to peek down the corridor, then gave Michelle the go-ahead to do the same. When Michelle complied, she saw Nausikaa and Aristodeme standing in the weakly lit hallway, their hands linked and their eyes roaming vacantly over the area around them. Additional passages branched off from the spot where they stood, and they seemed as lost in this maze as Michelle felt.

She pulled back. "I didn't see anyone else."

"That's what worries me."

"The twins are quick. They might have gotten away."

Arachne mulled that over, her mouth working silently. "I still don't like it."

"We have to try. That's what we're here for, right?"

"That's what *you're* here for. If it was up to me, we'd be mailing postcards by now."

"Then I guess it's a good thing it's not up to you," Michelle said, and ducked around the corner before Arachne could stop her.

Her foot slipped in the new corridor with the first step she took, then she righted herself and headed for the girls. Nausikaa and Aristodeme looked up with broad smiles she didn't usually find on their faces. The two dropped hands and reached out as Michelle came near.

"Michelle, wait!" Arachne cried out.

Her footsteps sounded in the corridor. The twins smiled even more widely as they spread their arms to embrace their friend.

Then their faces peeled back, and the suffocating stink of the Skaldi enfolded her.

# Chapter 15

The cavity of the twins' bodies was more horrifying than anything Michelle had ever seen.

It was moist and black and dripping, not with blood but with the same sticky stuff that had seeped from the ceiling in the subterranean rail line. It bubbled and flowed as if agitated by the Skaldi's breath, except Skaldi had no breath, no lungs to breathe with. The sisters' shapes oozed together, forming a single conjoined being, now connected at the wrists, now at the shoulder, now at the throat. Black fingers reached out from inside the shapeshifting mass, and when those fingers touched Michelle's face, the terrible sensation of losing herself paralyzed her, making her limp and pliant in the monster's hands. She was dimly conscious of the Skaldi tugging at her waistband, could vaguely see a flood of viscous black pouring down the walls around her, but even that didn't wake her from her stupor as the oily strands knitted themselves with her hair and drew her into the darkness.

Then the creature's arms released her, and her sense of self returned as she fell to the floor. The counterfeit twins were screaming, flailing black limbs that seemed to have multiplied into hundreds of tentacles. A white mist covered them, but the more they struggled to free themselves, the more the mist wrapped them in milky filaments like a chrysalis. At the edges of her vision, Michelle watched the black flood climb the walls like a waterfall in reverse. It disappeared into cracks too small to see, and all that was left was the swirling mist that filled the corridor.

Arms held her, strong and warm. Sounds without sense gradually resolved into a woman's voice. "… ana! Can you hear me? Are you still there?"

"I'm … " She looked into the woman's black eyes, which were wide with unaccustomed panic. "I'm … okay. I'm … "

"What's your name?"

"Diana."

"Your *real* name."

*Chelle*, she thought. "Michelle."

"And who am I?"

"You're … Asheh. Arachne."

Arachne's face softened. Michelle reached up to touch her cheek, and this time, she didn't pull away. Instead, she drew Michelle closer and held her in arms that trembled despite their strength.

"Can you stand?" she asked.

"I think so."

Arachne lifted her to her feet, then helped her back into the pants that the Skaldi had unaccountably pulled halfway down her legs. Michelle's eyes fell on the blackened remains of Nausikaa and Aristodeme, their bodies merged into a single shape without limbs or faces, the whole mass encased in a smoking shell like a block of dry ice. "The twins … "

"They're dead." She said it harshly, but Michelle could have sworn her voice broke. "There's nothing we can do for them now."

"We can ... " *Bury them*, she wanted to say, but couldn't. Grief spilled from her at the death of the two silent, wraith-like companions who'd been with her for so long, and she fell to her knees beside their corpses. Arachne let her cry for a short time, then lifted her to her feet as easily as if she were a child.

"We need to go," the sentry said. "I don't know what that smoky stuff is or where it came from, but I doubt it'll keep the Skaldi away forever. I'm sorry, Michelle."

"But Tyris and Petra ... "

"We can't save them," Arachne said. "We never could. And we're almost out of here, so there's no way I'm going back to look for them now."

Michelle caught her breath in mid-sob to stare at Arachne's face. The sentry looked back at her without tears, though the lines around her eyes had never seemed deeper. "You led us ... out?" Michelle asked.

Arachne nodded.

"Then you never ... you never meant to find ... "

"I meant to do what I meant to do all along," Arachne said. "And that was to get you to safety if I could."

Realization of how the sentry had tricked her stole the last strength from Michelle's legs, and she fell against the smaller woman, who clutched her and held her close. Michelle would have screamed at her, fought to free herself, but she knew it was useless. She couldn't find her way through the labyrinth without Arachne. She should have known that the battle-hardened sentry would be willing to make the devil's bargain she couldn't bring herself to make— to abandon four children Michelle had come to love in order to save the one child who'd not yet come to be.

Arachne held her while she cried, the rough hands awkwardly stroking Michelle's hair. Michelle wished she could find it in herself to hate her protector, but she couldn't muster the energy for that or anything else. She felt as empty as the Skaldi must feel, if Skaldi felt anything other than hunger. Maybe this *was* what they felt. An aching, eternal emptiness, one that could never be satisfied no matter how many bodies they consumed, how many lives they took. She could take a life too; she could even create one. But she knew it would never be enough to make up for all the ones she'd lost.

When Michelle's last tear had fallen, Arachne held her at arm's length and looked gravely into her eyes. "Are you all right?"

*Yes. No.* "I'll be fine."

"You're a tough kid. Much tougher than I had you pegged for at the start."

"Can we please not talk?"

"Whatever you want." She reached inside her jacket—checking for the jar, Michelle knew—then nodded toward one of the radiating passages. "This way."

Michelle followed, not looking back.

Now that she knew they were close to the base's exit, she gave up on her effort to determine where they were and simply let her steps copy Arachne's. The hallways looked the same as everywhere—dim lights, random intersections—but she trusted Arachne's instincts as the woman took a rapid succession of turns. Michelle tried to summon excitement at the prospect of freedom, but failed. At least Arachne wouldn't expect her to *act* excited when they reached the outside. Unlike Laman, she had no illusions about what freedom really meant.

216

They'd been walking for no more than fifteen minutes when Arachne laid a cautioning hand on Michelle's arm. "Someone's following us."

"Who—?"

"If I knew that, I wouldn't have said *someone*," Arachne answered with an edge to her voice. "All I know is they've been on our heels since we left the … the place where we were before."

Michelle resisted the temptation to look over her shoulder. She listened for footsteps, but they were too soft to be heard over the beating of her own heart. "What should we do?"

"Pick up the pace. I doubt we can lose them, but it's worth a shot."

Arachne quickened her stride, and Michelle tried to follow suit. She felt clumsier than ever, as if her belly kept getting in the way of where her legs were supposed to be. She remembered the day she'd set the state record for the 400 meters in interscholastic competition, but that race seemed as long gone as everything else about the world she'd once known.

They walked at this pace for another minute before Arachne whispered again. "Nothing doing. You're a blimp."

"Thanks a lot."

"Might as well put your disability to good use. Trip."

"What?"

"Hit the deck. After we take the next turn. Act like you tripped over your own stomach or something. Our footpad isn't making much of an effort to conceal himself, so I think he'll fall for it."

"You can hear him?"

"I don't need to hear him. Try to make a noise like you're hurt when you go down. I seem to recall you have a flair for the dramatic."

Michelle glowered. It felt like a lifetime since her theatrics in the desert, but evidently, Arachne was never going to let her live that down.

The next fork in their path approached. Arachne turned left, and Michelle performed on cue: she stumbled and fell, letting out a yelp as she did. It wasn't hard to fake pain; she'd been a little too convincing an actor, and in her attempt to protect the baby, her chin had hit the ground when she landed.

A second later, someone tripped over her. A second after that, Arachne launched herself at the person and laid them flat on their back.

Michelle climbed painfully to her feet and looked down at the prostrate figure. It was impossible to tell who the culprit was, because they were wearing a yellow hazmat suit, with gloves and boots and oversized bubble headpiece. She could hear the soft rasp of the suit's ventilator, but couldn't see a face through the black visor. Whoever it was didn't put up a fight; they raised their gloved hands over their head and went limp in Arachne's grasp.

"Who are you?" the sentry snapped. "Speak up!"

"Please—" the voice came, distorted by the ventilator.

"Try *pretty please with sugar on top*," Arachne said. "Maybe then I'll decide not to cut the answer out of you."

Even through the ventilator, Michelle heard the quaver in the person's voice. "I can explain—"

"Explain fast. And lose the headgear. I like to see who it is before I kill them."

218

She undid the clasp that held the visor in place and swung it open. In the deep shadows of the hood, the frightened eyes of Dr. Praneet Melan blinked back at them.

Arachne stared at him for a moment, then started to laugh. She took her weight off of him and slid to the floor by his side, as if she considered the doctor too much of a joke to pose any kind of threat. "Melan! You getting paid to chase after *me* now?"

Seeing the face of the man who'd betrayed them, Michelle found that she *was* still capable of feeling. "Go ahead and kill him, Arachne. We don't have time to waste on his *explanations*."

"Wait!" the little man squeaked, throwing his arms in front of his face. "Please, you must listen to me. I followed you to this facility to help you. Your own lives are at stake, as are those of your colony."

"My colony is dead," Michelle told him. "Because of you. Those children"—her finger shook as she pointed back the way they'd come—"were my family. Now they're worm food, and nothing you say can change that."

His face fell. "I have children, too."

"Then you should have known better than to let other children die." She nudged Arachne more roughly than she'd meant to. "I've heard enough of this shit. Kill him."

To her surprise, the sentry made no move to carry out her order. "I think," she said in a careful voice, "we should hear what he has to say. He used to work here, and he might know something valuable to us."

Dr. Melan nodded enthusiastically inside the hood.

"I think differently," Michelle said. "Now get out of my way."

She lunged at Dr. Melan, who recoiled and curled into a ball. Arachne caught her before she got far, and though Michelle felt angry enough to break Melan's neck if she could get her hands on him, the truth was, Arachne was much stronger than her. The sentry gripped her wrists, gently forcing her arms down and holding them at her sides. Michelle fought her briefly, but soon gave up and slumped beside Melan. Arachne watched her anxiously for another moment, but when Michelle didn't move, she turned back to the doctor.

"Tell us everything," she said.

Dr. Melan struggled into a sitting position against the corner of the wall, as far from Michelle as he could get. He reached up and removed his hood, showing all of his sweat-covered face. In the bulky suit, his head and neck looked even punier than usual.

"I tried to do as Miss Diana wished," he began. "To keep her departure secret for as long as I could. But the general, and his son … " His eyes entreated Arachne. "You know there is no appeasing them."

"Wild guess," she said. "They threatened your children."

He nodded. "Athan told me that my son and daughter were being held in an undisclosed location within the base, and that if I did not reveal everything I knew, he would have them killed. I had not realized that he would go to such extreme measures to retrieve Miss Diana. I had thought … "

"That there were limits to the depravity of Udain Genn and Son?" Arachne asked. "What planet have you been living on?"

The man looked stricken. "I am a doctor, sworn to preserve and protect life. My own wellbeing I was willing to risk for Miss Diana's sake, but the lives of my little ones … "

"The twins were twelve years old," Michelle said in a hollow voice. "Tyris and Petra would have been six."

Tears sparkled in Melan's eyes. "I am sorry … "

"Why did you rat out Laman?" Arachne cut in. "How was that supposed to help?"

"The general can be harsh to his second-born son," Melan answered. "But the boy is a member of the Genn bloodline, and his father would never purposely allow him to come to harm. I thought that, if he believed Laman was solely responsible, I could—"

"Save your own neck," Michelle said. "Not your children's. Your own."

Melan's face crumpled. Arachne laid a hand on Michelle's shoulder.

"I understand how you feel," she said. "But you're not helping right now."

Michelle shook Arachne's hand away, then wrapped her arms around her knees. She could barely hold that position; it seemed as if her stomach had grown larger or dropped lower in the last few minutes. She forced herself to stay like that anyway, as if her own discomfort could make up for the pain she'd caused everyone else.

Arachne hovered over her for a moment, her hands held out as if she feared Michelle might topple. Then she resumed her interrogation of Dr. Melan. "You said you could help us. How?"

"By delivering you from this place," he answered. "As you deduced, we are very near the surface. But you will never win your way to freedom without my assistance. The creatures will swarm the only exit as soon as you make for it, and you will not be able to fight them off without this."

He opened his gloved hand, revealing a small metal object that looked something like a miniature propane cylinder. Arachne stared at it, and then at him, as if Melan had completely lost his mind.

"This pressurized gas neutralizes the Skaldi, as it did those that attacked you before," he explained. "It was developed specifically in this laboratory to keep the creatures under control. But," he added needlessly, "it failed."

"What about fire?" Arachne asked.

The doctor shook his head. "The Skaldi germ plasma was designed to absorb energy from combustible materials. Far from destroying the creatures, fire catalyzes their maturation from seed to larval form. This specially formulated cryogenic gas slows their growth potential and is unavailable to them as an energy source."

"Christ," Arachne muttered. "What the hell has been going on in this madhouse?"

"Experiments of a most fatal nature," Dr. Melan said. "It was here that the Skaldi were first mass-produced, grown from the germ plasma for purposes of research and development. But the scientists who developed the line—"

"Got sloppy," Arachne finished for him. "And ended up as lunch, right?"

Melan hung his head. "It was even more dire than that, I am afraid. The germ plasma infected and replicated members of the team. The outbreak spread rapidly, and under its influence, those who were charged with containing the Skaldi—"

"Bred an army of the little buggers instead," Arachne interrupted once more. "And then began launching the plasma around the globe via ICBM. Does that pretty much sum things up?"

Dr. Melan said nothing, but he covered his face with his hands. Arachne let out one of her typical humorless laughs.

"So how'd you miraculously fight your way to freedom? With your impeccable manners?" Her voice sank to a whisper. "*You're* not Skaldi, are you?"

The man's head snapped up. "Of course not. I would know if I were—"

"No, you wouldn't," Michelle said. "They don't know what they are. Not at first."

That stopped him. His eyes darted nervously between Michelle and Arachne before he removed a glove from one hand and held it out to the sentry. Lacking any better weapon, she dug her nails into the back of the doctor's hand, eliciting a small cry. When blood leaked from the marks she'd left, he met their eyes and resumed.

"I was reassigned to the Texas facility years ago. Though it became obvious within past months that a security breach had occurred at this site, I took courage in the belief that, under the general's leadership, we would find a way to arrest what we had started." He shook his head. "I was wrong."

"You were dead wrong," Arachne said.

The doctor made no reply.

"I don't trust him," Michelle spoke up. "He's the one who told me you were dead back at the base in Texas. With him, it's always one horror story after another, and each time, he's only covering up for something worse."

"Point well taken," Arachne agreed. "What do you say to that, Melan?"

The doctor's face struggled for a long time before he came up with an answer. "I wish to atone for past mistakes. To prove to you that I am not who you think I am."

"You don't have the first idea what I think you are," Michelle said. "If you did, you couldn't sit there with your smug little slogans and your—"

Arachne placed a hand on her arm, and Michelle quieted, though the words she hadn't said burned on the tip of her tongue.

"Jury's still out, Doc," Arachne said. "You're going to have to do a lot better than that."

Melan looked pleadingly at them. "I am not a bad man."

"You're not a man at all," Michelle let the words come. "You might bleed like one, but you're as much of a monster as they are."

His head fell again. With his small body clothed in the oversized suit, he looked like a Trick-or-Treater who'd been scolded by his mother for hogging candy.

It was Arachne who broke the silence. Standing, she said with another short laugh, "Well, that was refreshing, but now that we're all caught up on recent history, I suggest we move out. I can't believe I'm saying this, but I don't see how we have any choice but to trust him." She pointed at the cylinder in Melan's hand. "Is that little gizmo enough to stop an army of Skaldi?"

Melan's face shone at the unexpected stay of execution. "I exhausted this canister to neutralize the Skaldi that attacked Miss Diana. Luckily, there is a much more plentiful supply in a locked storage vault. Assuming the codes have not been changed, I can provide access."

"Then let's go," Arachne said. "And just so we're clear: if a single word you've said turns out to be untrue, I'll peel the skin from your bones one strip at a time. On second thought, maybe I'll let *Miss Diana* do the honors."

The doctor looked back and forth between them, and what he saw made him shake in his clown-size boots.

Arachne offered Michelle her hand. Despite the sentry's aid, it was even more of a production than usual to hoist herself from the floor. She had the distinct and unpleasant sensation that the baby was dragging her downward, as if it was sick of the whole business and was determined to stay put. When she finally fought off its desperate gravity and climbed to her feet, she felt moisture trickle down the inside of her legs, as if she'd peed her pants. The first few steps she took were more of a waddle, her legs spread wide like some ridiculous gunslinger from a cowboy movie.

When Dr. Melan saw her, he flew to her side. "Miss Diana—"

Michelle jerked away from his outstretched hands. As she did, a lightning bolt of pain shot through her midsection, forcing a gasp from between clenched teeth. The doctor's beady eyes nearly popped from his head.

"We must hurry," he said. "Asheh, can you assist Miss Diana?"

Arachne's eyes widened. "Is she …?"

"Contractions have begun," he affirmed. "We must consider the birth of Miss Diana's baby to be imminent."

# Chapter 16

Michelle clutched Arachne's arm as a second white-hot dagger sliced through her abdomen.

"*Imminent?*" Arachne shouted at Melan. "What the hell do you mean by *imminent?*"

"I cannot predict the course of this delivery!" Melan yelled back. "So much of Miss Diana's pregnancy is unprecedented—the baby is three months short of term, and the onset of labor was more sudden than I—"

Another contraction crashed through Michelle, drowning out his words. She knew the pain came from inside, but it felt like a fiery current hitting her as she stood in a lava river. She fell from Arachne's grasp, and was barely able to get a hand out to prevent herself from face-planting on the concrete.

"What's going on?" Arachne snapped at Melan as she knelt by Michelle's side. "Should it be hurting her this much?"

"Miss Diana's case is unprecedented," the doctor repeated unhelpfully. "We will need to carry—"

Arachne didn't wait for him to finish before scooping Michelle into her arms. "Which way?"

Dr. Melan's mouth opened and expelled a series of phrases—"operating theater" and "heart monitor" and "possible C-section"—but Michelle couldn't string them together into a sentence. She might have marveled at Arachne's strength as the small woman sprinted down the corridor after Melan, but everything was consumed by an agonizing barrage of contractions that hit so close together they were like a single continuous wave battering her against the rocks.

She snatched wildly at Arachne's arm. Her fingers caught something solid, dug in. She knew she must be hurting Arachne, but she couldn't control herself.

"It's … Skaldi," she gasped. "It's trying to—"

Another contraction came so suddenly her teeth clamped down on her tongue, biting hard enough to draw blood.

"It's opening me up," she said when she could free her tongue again. "It's tearing me apart … "

"We'll be at the lab soon," Arachne said calmly. If she felt Michelle's nails puncturing her flesh, she didn't react.

"Kill it," Michelle said through her teeth. "Or kill me. Don't let it … "

Arachne didn't slow her pace, but she looked down, meeting Michelle's eyes. After the brief moment of panic when Michelle's contractions started, the sentry's face had returned to its customary implacable mask. Gently, she pried Michelle's fingers from her arm and transferred them to her hand.

"Squeeze," she said. "Break every bone in my hand if you have to. We'll be there in a minute."

Michelle squeezed as if she were dangling from a cliff and Arachne's hand was the only thing preventing her from falling. "You'll … help me … You won't let it … "

"If the time comes," Arachne said, "I'll do what needs to be done."

Michelle breathed a soft sigh that turned into a gasp when another contraction ripped through her. She squeezed Arachne's hand so hard she was sure she would squash it to a pulp, but Arachne never even flinched.

They raced through the hallways, light and shadow flickering in Michelle's periphery as she tried to keep her eyes focused on Arachne's stoic visage. There was no time, no space; there was only an endless stream of pain, and the sole thing that anchored her to sanity was the feel of Arachne's hand in hers. She was conscious of the doctor and the sentry exchanging words, but she had no idea what they could be talking about. She had stopped hoping for the contractions to cease when she felt herself being lowered onto a bed, which might have been soft if her back wasn't twisted in pain. She grabbed for Arachne's arm, only to find that their hands were still locked together.

Arachne's face hove into view, dark eyes and calm mien. "Relax, Diana. We're here. The doc's going to give you something for the pain."

"I should not be doing this," Michelle heard Dr. Melan muttering to himself. "So close to delivery, there is some risk of—"

"Just do it!" Arachne snapped, and the man shut up. Michelle felt herself being rolled onto her side and a needle sliding into her lower back. It pinched, but after the pain of the contractions, she welcomed the novelty. She bucked involuntarily when the next contraction came, and she heard Dr. Melan yelp.

"How long does that take to work?" Arachne asked him.

He appeared beside her, tugging a rubber glove from his hand. Michelle saw blood where the needle must have nicked him. "No more than fifteen minutes," he responded. "In normal cases."

Arachne looked down at Michelle with a tight smile that crinkled the skin around her eyes. With the hand that wasn't currently being pulverized, she smoothed hair from Michelle's brow. "See? It'll be better soon."

Michelle tried to smile back, but her teeth felt locked in place. "I'm anything but normal," she said weakly.

"You got that right." She gave Michelle's cheek a surprisingly gentle caress, then carefully disentangled her other hand. "I have to help the doc get some things ready. I'm not going anywhere, so if you need me"—she raised her eyebrows—"just scream."

Arachne's face disappeared, and there was a brief noise as of something squeaking across the floor. Michelle let out an involuntary cry, but the empty space above her was instantly filled by the sweat-sheened countenance of Dr. Melan, a blue surgical mask looped around his throat.

"Screaming will not be necessary," he said with a grisly approximation of a smile. "I have placed you on a monitor, and given you an epidural. I will be here to attend the birth, while Asheh assists me."

As if conjured by her name, Arachne reappeared and gripped Michelle's hand. Dr. Melan popped out of view, and when Michelle searched for him, she discovered two things: her legs were spread wide, and her pants had vanished. The doctor's head poked up from where he'd been inspecting her, but instead of mortification, she felt only relief that the two of them were staying with her.

"You are almost fully dilated," he reported. "The contractions—"

"So fast?" She tried to raise herself to see what was going on down there, but Arachne gently held her back.

"No two deliveries are alike," he said, the unconvincing smile still on his face. "And time has been known to telescope for women in labor. Nearly two hours have passed since contractions began."

"But—"

A contraction stronger than any other stole the question from her lips and made her do exactly what Arachne had given her permission to do: scream. Good to her word, Arachne held her hand tightly and mopped sweat from her forehead with a towel. Michelle panted, then took a deep breath to regain control of her voice.

"There's something you're not telling me," she said to Dr. Melan.

The doctor raised a rubber-gloved hand to his brow. He'd shed his hazmat suit and donned blue scrubs, though Michelle couldn't remember when.

"Asheh told me about the explosive device she planted in the Skaldi germ plasma," he said. "I am making an educated guess that your baby was affected by the energy discharge, which might explain the rapid course of labor."

"Because it's … Skaldi."

"Because of its genetic history, yes. But take comfort, Miss Diana. We will not know anything with certainty until the baby is born."

"When … when will that be?"

His strained smile softened, looking almost natural. "Soon. Do you feel strong enough to push?"

Michelle felt another contraction coming and gathered herself to force the baby from her body. She was somewhat numb below the waist—the shot beginning to work, she guessed—but her muscles clenched and bore down as if she'd been training for weeks to perform this action alone. Another contraction rippled through her a few seconds later, then another and another and another, and each time, Dr. Melan encouraged her to push, Arachne echoing his instructions as soon as she caught on. For whatever reason, the epidural or something else, Michelle barely noticed the pain anymore. Her head felt light and unsteady, her vision flickered in the operating theater's strong overhead bulbs, but her body felt amazingly solid, strong, even powerful. The baby no longer threatened to tear her apart from within. She would survive this birth, and whatever followed, she would face it.

Even if that meant she had to kill it herself.

"The baby is crowning!" Dr. Melan announced in an excited voice, his mask ballooning outward with each word. "Push, Miss Diana! Push now!"

Michelle pushed, and experienced an immediate lessening of the pressure on her pelvis and back. She could feel the baby's head exiting her and then, a moment later, its slick and slippery body flowing from her as if it were swimming in its own water. Arachne made a sound somewhere between a laugh and a cry, and planted a quick kiss on Michelle's forehead. Her exclamation was followed by another cry, loud and piercing, that stirred Michelle's heart like nothing she'd ever known. Dr. Melan reemerged from between her legs with a small, bloody form wrapped in a blanket. It howled and howled, and with each sound it made, the ache in Michelle's chest grew stronger.

"A girl," Dr. Melan said, and placed the baby in her arms.

With trembling fingers, Michelle pushed the blanket from its face. It—*she*—continued to cry, mouth open and eyes squeezed shut. She was warm and slippery from the birthing process, with flecks of blood covering her fine hair, which was blond like her mother's. Michelle searched the face for signs of Kareem, but when that search proved fruitless, she touched the baby's lip and traced a line down the tiny chin to the chest. Anxiously, she looked up at Dr. Melan. "She's so small."

"This is to be expected with a premature birth. And yet, to my eye, she appears almost perfectly developed."

"But you said she wouldn't be … "

"That was my fear. I can only speculate that the energy boost she received not only hastened labor and delivery, but accelerated her development."

Michelle's heart sank. "Then she *is* Skaldi."

"She bleeds," he said in a quiet voice.

"She—?"

"I collected a specimen of her blood for analysis," he clarified. "I will need to perform additional tests on the placenta to be certain, but as you know, the Skaldi do not bleed."

"Then—" Michelle looked at the screaming infant, so alien and yet so familiar. "What is she?"

"She is the product of two human beings, one of whom bore Skaldi genetic material. She is exceptional in every way, a miracle whose future we can scarcely predict. And," he added, "she is hungry."

His words startled her. Then she realized what he meant, and while Dr. Melan and Arachne withdrew, she unbuttoned her uniform top and placed the baby at her breast. It took an effort of will not to recoil at first contact, but as soon as the little lips latched on, she felt another something new inside her, a warmth that came from the exchange of life-giving fluid she had no idea she'd started producing. Everything was happening so fast, too fast, before she had time to ask, much less answer, the thousands of questions that whirled through her mind. She watched the baby suckle, but even with the eyes closed, she had to admit the newborn looked nothing like the immature Skaldi she'd fought in the lab back east, much less the fully grown monsters that had haunted her days and nights for as long as she could remember. Her daughter looked human, completely human, and when she'd drunk her fill, she fell asleep on Michelle's chest, breathing sweetly in her face.

*They all look human*, Michelle thought. And that thought was followed by another: *She is mine.*

She cried, and Arachne came to shush her, and held her until she fell fast asleep with the baby in her arms.

# Chapter 17

The baby's cries woke her.

Michelle didn't know how long she'd slept; she only knew she was still exhausted from the birth. But the baby was hungry again, so she mechanically unbuttoned her uniform top and moved the lips into position. She remembered lectures about childcare in Health class, all of them dedicated to warning girls like her not to have unprotected sex. What stuck out now was the part where students were told that newborns have tiny stomachs and need to nurse more or less constantly. The teacher explained that this was an evolved trait to strengthen the bond between mother and child so crucial to neonatal development, but she also cautioned her students that it meant nursing mothers could count on getting pretty much zero sleep for the first three to six months of their baby's existence.

As Michelle glanced down at the puckered face, watching the little lips expertly tug and slurp, she forgot about the sleeplessness part and felt only the overwhelming love of caring for this helpless life.

Dr. Melan's words returned to her: *She is the product of two human beings, one of whom bore Skaldi genetic material. She is exceptional in every way, a miracle whose future we can scarcely predict.* The boy who was her baby's father hadn't been born in the usual way either; if what Arachne said was true, he'd been less born than bred. But did that matter? Did the fact that he was a copy of someone else, someone who'd lived a life completely separate from his, make him any less human? She turned the thought over and over in her mind, but all she could conclude was that he'd been human enough to bring her joy in a time of despair, to fight to keep her safe, to whisper that he loved her. If that wasn't human, then what was? Even at the end, when the pressure of what the scientists had planted inside him became too much for him to contain, he'd told her that he *wanted* to be so much more than his makers intended him to be.

And the reason he'd wanted that was because of her.

*I will protect you,* she said as she stroked the baby's cheek with her index finger. *I will never let you go. I will not let dark's dominion claim you, and I will teach you to be what your father was: human not so much by birth as by choice.*

Gradually, she came out of her trance to the sound of Arachne and Dr. Melan puttering around the room. They'd draped a towel over a couple of IV racks to give her privacy, but when the baby was done nursing, a shadow fell on the makeshift screen.

"Knock, knock," Arachne's voice came. "You decent?"

"As much as I'll ever be."

The sentry came around the curtain, smiling more broadly than Michelle had seen yet. That lasted less than a second before her nose wrinkled.

"Honey," she said, "that kiddo stinks."

"Does she?" Michelle checked the washcloth Dr. Melan had wrapped around her daughter's butt, and sure enough, it was filled with a thin yellow gruel. Strangely, the sight and smell of her daughter's first poop didn't bother her.

"I'll clean her up," she said. "Just help me get out of—"

"That's a negative, Private. Until the doc gives the all-clear, you're staying put. Here," she said, holding out her hands as if to disarm a wired explosive, "I'll do it."

Michelle felt an unexpected reluctance to give her baby to another person, even for a moment, but she overcame the primal instinct and handed her to Arachne. "Hold her head," she said while the sentry fumbled with her daughter's flimsy body parts. She smiled to herself as Arachne retreated behind the screen. How she'd ever thought the woman might have been a mother was beyond her.

It took longer than she expected—or maybe that was just maternal anxiety—but at last Arachne reappeared, a fresh washcloth tied lopsidedly around the baby's legs and a look of triumph on the sentry's face. The baby hadn't cried once, and now she curled up on Michelle's chest and blew a few milk-breath burps. Michelle inhaled the scent of fresh baby and beamed at her unwilling nurse.

"Adorable," Arachne said. "Remind me to call the guys from Hallmark." But she was smiling when she said it.

They were quiet for a few companionable moments, Michelle stroking her baby's downy hair and Arachne watching with an indescribable expression on her face. It was the sentry who broke the silence. "Melan and I are going to have to leave for a couple of minutes. To get the gas cylinders and some other things."

"Right now?"

"No time like the present. We had to take a detour to the birthing suite thanks to a certain someone, and—"

"This is a birthing suite?"

Arachne shrugged. "It's nowhere near hospital-quality, but it's the closest thing to one on this haunted hayride."

"What's a birthing suite doing in a military base?"

"You know, that's what I asked Melan," Arachne said with a scowl even worse than the one she'd worn when she was handling the messy baby. "But as you might have noticed, he can be really good at changing the subject."

Michelle was about to ask a follow-up question when Dr. Melan's head poked around the screen. She had the feeling that his interruption was no accident, but Arachne's look warned her not to give voice to her suspicions.

"And how are we this morning?" he asked brightly.

"Is it morning?" she asked, wondering why doctors always referred to their patients as *we*. Then she remembered that this time, she *was* a we.

"It is morning indeed," he said. "And a perfect hour for a quick check-up before we depart."

He came out from behind the screen, wearing plastic gloves and a stethoscope around his neck. While Arachne held the baby, he examined Michelle, timing her pulse and having her sit to take a few deep breaths before unceremoniously throwing the bedsheet aside to peer between her legs. Apparently satisfied that everything below her waist was where it was supposed to be, he turned to the baby, checking her heartbeat and breathing, opening her mouth to look inside, tickling various parts of her and watching her scrawny legs and doll-like fingers flinch reflexively. The baby nodded off sometime during the inspection, and when he handed her back to Michelle, she raised a concern she'd had since the birth. "Why haven't her eyes opened yet?"

"Sometimes newborns take days to open their eyes," he said. "Premature babies in particular."

She nodded, though the answer didn't entirely mollify her. The next question, though, was even harder to ask. "What about the tests you said you were going to run? The ones to see if she's ... "

"I performed a preliminary genetic mapping while you slept," he said, pointing to a squat black machine with a screen and a keyboard that sat in the corner of the room. "As was to be anticipated, there is some small degree of Skaldi genetic material, but it is of minor significance compared to the predominance of the human genome. We will have to be watchful, of course, but I feel cautiously optimistic in pronouncing your daughter a successful fusion of Skaldi and *Homo sapiens*."

Michelle clutched the baby even closer to her side. The warning voice that whispered *You can't trust him* was drowned out by a much louder voice that said, *She is human.* Superhuman, maybe—the dominant species Athan Genn was trying to create. But he didn't have her, and she told herself she would die before she allowed him to get his hands on her or her baby ever again.

Her throat felt raw and her voice came out husky when she asked the next question that was on her mind. "What about me? Arachne says I'm not allowed to get out of bed until you say so."

Arachne frowned, but the doctor answered in a chipper tone.

"Asheh is correct that I ordered bed rest through the night. But I think, if you feel up to it, now would be a good time to test your strength."

Both he and Arachne reached out toward her, but Michelle gave them a look until they turned their heads. It took some doing to pull her pants on while she held the sleeping baby to her side, but when she was done, she rose without assistance. Standing barefoot on the tiled floor, she found that her legs felt as strong as ever—stronger, possibly, than they'd felt in the past six months. The only issue was the dull ache between them, which she had no intention of asking about. The doctor, however, must have noticed her discomfort and spoke up.

"I had to suture you," he said. "There was some tearing of the perineum during delivery." When her eyes widened at the word *tearing*, he hastened to add, "This is very common during childbirth, particularly with first-time mothers."

"And the perineum," Michelle said, trying to remember the drawings in the gynecologist's office. "That's my ... "

"Yes," he said, then launched into a painfully detailed lecture in front of Arachne.

"Can I walk?" Michelle cut him off before he got too far. She noticed a wheelchair folded in the corner, but the last thing she wanted to do was be wheeled out of this place.

"Judging by what I have witnessed with my own eyes and from Asheh's quite thorough report," Dr. Melan said, "I would venture to say that you can do most anything you set out to do."

"Except help us with the gas cylinders," Arachne jumped in. "You've already got your hands full."

Michelle resisted the urge to argue. "How long will it take?"

"No more than an hour," Dr. Melan replied. "You can page me at any moment and for any reason."

He pressed a palm-size device into her free hand. Its operation was immediately obvious: the only moving part was a red button. When she pressed the button to test it, the pager at his belt emitted a steady beep until he switched it off.

"I would advise you to use the time we are gone to prepare for our departure," he said. "Moderate exercise will do you good, and we will need to leave as soon as we return."

Arachne squeezed her hand, then the two of them ducked behind the screen and were gone, the door closing softly behind them.

Michelle looked around the room. There wasn't much to prepare, though she did find her boots lined up neatly beside the bed. She also found a metal cabinet with extra washcloths, packages of wet wipes, and individually wrapped gauze pads. She grabbed an armload of all three items, figuring she might need the latter in case of bleeding. A distant memory of her mom caring for the newborn Rosie came to her, and she laid the baby down on the bed to swaddle her in a bath towel. Though she didn't really know what she was doing, she managed to get the baby burrito snug and not too sloppy, with more than enough left-over towel to tuck in at the end. She rested the bundled newborn in a plastic tray atop a wheeled cart, then sat on the edge of the bed to tie her boots. For some reason, she'd expected her stomach to return to normal the moment the baby was born, but she must have missed that lecture in sex ed, because the gut was still there, if less inhibiting than before. Offsetting that small increase in mobility were the sutures, which hurt when she bent over. When she was done, she experimented with using another towel to create a sling for the baby, just in case she needed her hands free. But she couldn't tie it properly without someone's help, so she eased herself onto the bed again and waited for Arachne and Dr. Melan to return.

It couldn't have been more than twenty minutes when a shadow fell on the screen. She hadn't heard the door open, but maybe they were being extra careful not to wake the baby. She rose to meet them, only to find herself face to face with Dr. Melan, who flung the screen aside and gaped at her with frightened eyes.

"There has been an accident," he said. "One of the canisters burst unexpectedly, and Asheh—"

A chill shot through her. "Is it dangerous to humans?"

"In its concentrated form, extremely so. I have attempted to remove her from the room, but I will require your assistance—"

"I'll be right there," she said, glancing at the baby asleep in her cart. The impulse to stay with her was incredibly strong, but Michelle knew she'd be useless to Arachne if she were carrying the baby as well. Surely the newborn would be all right for a few minutes? Or she could take the cart with her, roll it down the hallway to wherever Arachne was ...

"We must hurry!" Dr. Melan said, and Michelle made her decision. Scooping the baby into her arms and cramming a washcloth and pack of wipes into her jacket pocket, she stepped past the doctor toward the door. His face seemed to register momentary anger, but she was moving too fast to be sure.

Her foot slipped in something wet, then stuck and wouldn't budge. She turned in alarm to look for Dr. Melan.

What she saw brought a choked scream to her throat.

The doctor was gone, replaced by a pool of the Skaldi germ plasma. Black tentacles extended from it like snakes' tongues sniffing the air for prey. From the ceiling over the door—the only exit—more of the black stuff was dripping, streaming down the wall to join the pool as it spread across the white-tiled floor. It held both of her feet now; she could feel its fingers climbing up her boots and twining around her legs. She pressed the pager button before she realized that was useless if the Skaldi had taken Dr. Melan. One of the tentacles, as if sensing her intention, knocked the remote from her grasp. A second tentacle circled her chest and constricted, squeezing the air from her lungs. A third groped for her arms, where the still-sleeping baby lay. Her mind fogged as she held the bundled form above her head, but the tentacle followed.

With her last breath, Michelle screamed.

The door burst open, and Arachne appeared, followed—impossibly—by Dr. Melan. The two of them wielded gas canisters as large as flamethrower tanks, which shot powerful streams of vapor directly at the black ooze at Michelle's feet. The plasma recoiled when the spray hit it, the tentacles unwrapping themselves from her body as it tried to slither away. It had no mouth, but Michelle was sure she heard it scream, unless her addled brain was playing tricks on her. The room grew dark as if consciousness were fading, but then she realized the darkness wasn't in her mind—it was all around her, black rot creeping like ink stains across the walls, the floor, the bulging ceiling. Arachne aimed the canister at the nearest mass, but then she threw her weapon aside and lifted Michelle and the baby over her shoulder. Michelle, facing back, saw the ceiling burst and the pent-up flood of black sludge pour into the room. She shouted Dr. Melan's name, then found that he was at Arachne's elbow as the sentry raced down the corridor with her burden.

The baby was shrieking now, hungry or terrified or both, but Michelle could do nothing to comfort her. The black tide swept down the hallway after them, so much of the tar-like fluid it seemed as if every ounce from the missile rail had percolated up to this level. Dr. Melan turned repeatedly to spray it with the gas, which halted the organism for a moment—but every time he let go of the nozzle to catch up with Arachne and her two passengers, parts of the creature that hadn't been neutralized by the gas surged forward to continue the pursuit. Michelle had no idea how much gas the canister held, but she couldn't believe it would be enough to stop a monster that filled the corridor behind them.

She was right. The canister sputtered, spraying a last gossamer cloud of mist that did nothing to slow the black wave. Dr. Melan flung the tank away and joined Arachne, the Skaldi organism biting at their heels.

At the last second, just when Michelle thought the flood would overwhelm them, Arachne threw herself through an open doorway and the doctor slammed it closed. The germ plasma struck the portal with a resounding boom, but the door was like the ones on a bank vault, reinforced with bands of riveted steel. Dr. Melan spun a circle in the center, and locks engaged. From Arachne's shoulder, Michelle saw that the room they'd entered was filled with shelves of both sizes of gas canisters, the large and the small. Several of the larger size models had been placed on a wheeled cart. A second door, reinforced like the first, stood at the far end of the room. Unless the Skaldi could break through the ceiling or surround the room, there was a way out.

Michelle's feet hit the floor, Arachne leaning against the wall and drawing deep breaths. The sound of the Skaldi battering the door was drowned out by the baby, who was red-faced with screaming. Michelle knew immediately that these weren't hunger cries, but much as she shushed her daughter, rocked her, crooned to her, she wouldn't stop squalling. Dr. Melan held out a small object.

"I had meant to … give you this … before," he panted.

Michelle stared at the plastic pacifier on his palm, then backed away, hugging her frantic daughter to her chest.

"It was you," she said. "The Skaldi looked like you."

He shook his head in confusion, opening his mouth like a fish gasping for air.

"It looked like you!" she repeated. "It told me Arachne had gotten hurt, and it … it must have been trying to lure me away. From her," she said, remembering the strange behavior of the infected twins, how they'd seemed to be trying to get at the baby even before it was born. "It wants her, and it pretended to be you to get her."

The doctor looked dazed. "You must be mistaken," he said. "Once the Skaldi have taken a human body, they are not able to revert to their original state."

He took a halting step toward Michelle. Before he got there, Arachne blocked his path, a fresh gas canister pointed at him. "What's going on, Melan?"

He held his hands up, the pacifier dangling ridiculously from his curled thumb and index finger. "I do not know. It seems as if the plasma possesses properties of mimicry that the mature creatures do not. I was with you at every moment, Asheh," he pleaded in response to her skeptical expression. "I could not possibly be infected with—agh!"

He grabbed his palm, which Arachne had poked with a hypodermic needle she must have swiped from the birthing suite. Everyone, the doctor included, watched tensely as he squeezed his hand, until finally a drop of red welled from the puncture wound. At the sight, he looked up at Arachne with relief, as if he'd doubted it himself.

He offered Michelle the pacifier again, but she mutely shook her head. The baby's screams raked her nerves, but even after the blood trial, there was no way she was going to put anything he'd touched in her daughter's mouth.

Dr. Melan's face fell, and he stowed the pacifier in his pants pocket. "Try your finger instead," he said softly. "She needs to suck for comfort."

Michelle turned from him and placed her pinky finger in the baby's mouth. The screaming infant latched on, sucking voraciously, and in a few minutes, her breathing calmed. The sound of the Skaldi hammering the door had ceased as well, and Michelle took a deep breath in the sudden silence before facing the others.

"We can't go on like this," she said. "Or she can't, anyway. It's not enough to escape from this place—the Skaldi will just come right after us. After *her*. We have to stop them for good."

Dr. Melan looked at her helplessly. He was about to say something when Arachne interrupted.

"Is the gas flammable?" she asked.

"Not in itself," Dr. Melan said. "But the canisters are under high pressure, and will explode if incinerated or improperly vented."

"Even better," Arachne said. "So what we do is—"

"But fire, as I explained, will not serve our purposes," Dr. Melan added. "It will simply feed the germ plasma the energy it needs to form mature creatures."

"Seems to me it already has energy to spare," Arachne said with a scowl at the doctor for the interruption. "But that's not what I was thinking of anyway."

Quickly, she outlined her plan.

"There's only one way in or out at the moment, right? The rail line was blocked when I blew up the germ plasma belowground, and the tunnel Diana and Laman busted through collapsed. So other than the way Melan and I got in, the base is sealed."

"So far as we know," the doctor answered.

Michelle said nothing, holding her baby and rocking her gently from side to side. She couldn't help thinking that, if she and Laman had known there was another way in, all of this could have been avoided.

"So," Arachne continued, "we set up a bunch of canisters by the exit. Then we blow the place all to hell, sealing the only way out. The Skaldi are trapped inside. Permanently. Does the plasma ever die?"

"It has survived in a dormant state far longer than I would have believed," Dr. Melan said. "But in theory, if it were deprived of a source of energy for an indefinite period of time, its molecular structure might break down and the organism to which it gives birth might, in effect, 'die.'"

"That's good enough for me," Arachne said.

"Except for one thing," Michelle put in.

Arachne frowned at her. "Which is?"

"You told me you don't have any explosives left. So how are we supposed to blow up the canisters?"

To her surprise, Arachne's frown turned to a smile.

"Honey child," she said, "just watch me."

# Chapter 18

They waited for the baby to fall asleep before they left. Michelle nursed her one more time, then cleaned and diapered her with the one remaining washcloth she'd taken from the birthing room. Dr. Melan wanted to perform another neonatal checkup, but Michelle warned him away with a glare and Arachne backed her up with the gas canister. The doctor looked pale and aggrieved at Michelle's continued distrust, but he shrank back without a murmur, leaving Arachne to help Michelle rearrange the baby burrito so the sleeping infant hung from her chest and gave her free use of her hands.

"Will the gas affect us?" Arachne asked the doctor before they left. Michelle listened intently, waiting to see if he would answer the way his mimic had.

"The gas was formulated to react specifically with the organic polymers that bind the germ plasma," he said. "As such, it should have no effect on us whatsoever."

Arachne nodded, but Michelle wondered whether *he* was lying or the other Melan was. He'd left them in the dark about so many things—the presence of the birthing suite, the unique properties of the germ plasma—she had no idea what to believe. Just in case, she pocketed one of the miniature gas canisters before they left, ready to use it against Melan if it came to that.

They exited the room through the rear door, Arachne stepping outside first and aiming her canister at the ceiling and walls before she let the others join her. When Dr. Melan pushed the cart with the remaining canisters into the corridor, Arachne opened the valve on one of them and rolled it back into the room, where it lay spouting white mist. Within seconds, the room was too full of vapor for Michelle to see the other side.

"That should make them think twice about following us this way," Arachne said with a satisfied nod.

With Dr. Melan in the lead so Arachne could keep an eye on him, they made their way through the hallway. Michelle listened for sounds of pursuit, but there were none. According to Arachne's explanation of the base, they were very close to the only exit, a garage with a sliding metal door that opened onto the desert. When she'd arrived at the base, she'd cracked the code and entered the garage to find a single vehicle parked there, presumably the one Athan and Udain had arrived in. Her own truck was a quarter-mile away, hidden behind a rock formation, while Melan's had been left— foolishly, she told Michelle under her breath—out in the open next to Michelle and Laman's. Once they were free of the base and her plan to seal it had been completed, they could march to Arachne's truck and be on the road in a matter of minutes.

"And Athan and Udain will be trapped inside, too?" Michelle asked.

"That's the general idea," Arachne answered. "Is there a problem?"

Michelle shook her head, wishing she could stop thinking of Laman. She reminded herself that he could have chosen a different path, and if he ended up inside the sealed base
with the monsters his father and brother had unleashed on
the world, that was something he'd just have to square with
his own conscience before the end.

"Almost there," Arachne said in a whisper. "Take it
slow, now."

Michelle peered ahead to see a rectangle of light at the
end of the corridor—the doorway to the garage, she guessed.
The baby fussed without fully waking; Arachne shot Michelle
a look, so Michelle gripped her daughter to her chest and
rocked, hoping she'd settle. She didn't, not entirely, but the
towel she was wrapped in muffled the sound of her short,
coughing cries. That wasn't good enough for Arachne.

"Shut that racket up if you want to get out of here alive,"
she said. "Melan, double-check to make sure the canisters are
ready."

While Michelle did her best to quiet the baby, Dr. Melan
removed a canister from the cart, opening its valve fractional-
ly to release a thread of vapor. He nodded to Arachne to indicate that the canister was working, then shut the valve. By
this time, they'd reached the end of the hallway, and Arachne
leaned through the half-open door to inspect the parking garage. A second later, she pulled back and signaled to Michelle
to join her.

"All clear," she said. "No little beasties, no big ugly monsters. It's your call who I'm talking about."

They entered the garage, Dr. Melan pushing the cart before him. Michelle was surprised at how small the space was;
she'd imagined a huge parking complex that could accommo-

date the cars of all the scientists who used to work here, but it wasn't much bigger than the ground-floor parking garage at her pediatrician's office back home. Evidently it had been built for visiting VIPs, while everyone else lived on the base full-time. The single vehicle that was parked there wasn't like the truck she and Laman had arrived in; it looked more like a Hummer, black and shiny in the fluorescent light that bathed it from above, with tinted windows and the red letters SKLDI printed on its side. The cab was taller than usual—custom designed, Michelle supposed, to accommodate its abnormally large owner. The corrugated metal door at the far end of the parking area was closed, but Michelle could see the keypad on the wall beside it, and her heart gave a brief leap at the thought that they'd soon be free.

Arachne was moving toward the truck, with Dr. Melan and his wobbly cart just behind. Michelle held the fussing baby close and hurried to catch up. In the few seconds it took her to get there, Arachne had already jimmied the driver's side door and popped the hood.

"Lots of combustible materials inside a car," she said as she braced the hood. "But let's go for the battery."

As she worked, she explained that car batteries release trace amounts of hydrogen when they're being charged or discharged, which, in combination with the canisters, should be enough to set off a chain reaction explosion. A simple fuse—she produced a spool of it from a deep pocket Udain had ignored when he frisked her—would start the detonation process; once she was finished setting everything up, they'd position the cylinders near the battery, turn the car on, and exit into the desert. They'd light the fuse—she pulled a Bic lighter from the same pocket—then slam the door and run.

"Essentially," she concluded, "I'm turning the big man's luxury limo into an IED." She was too focused on her work to show any emotion, but Michelle wondered if a roadside bomb was what had injured Kareem years ago and sent Arachne on her quest to heal him, a quest that had led her to Udain Genn's door.

"You're sure this will seal the base?" she asked.

"As sure as I can be when I'm jerry-rigging it on the fly."

"And we'll have time to get away before the explosion?"

"It's a slow-burning fuse," Arachne answered, as if that meant anything to Michelle. "Still, once I've set this up, even a static electricity charge could make the whole thing blow. So if you're feeling the need for a smoke break, I'd suggest you wait until we're outside."

Michelle, who'd never smoked a cigarette in her life, backed away from the Hummer and held the baby close.

It took Arachne a few more minutes to arrange everything the way she wanted, with the fuse trailing from one of the battery's terminals and the cylinders clustered on the floor by the front bumper. She fiddled with the ignition until it started, and with Michelle following her while Melan wheeled the cart out of the way, she carefully unwound the fuse and walked it toward the garage door. When she discovered that it wasn't as long as she'd thought and she would have to light it while standing inside, she let out a stream of curses that Michelle was glad her baby was too little to understand. The sentry's finger was hovering over the keypad that opened the door when she froze, and Michelle felt a silence settle over the room as if all the air had been sucked from it at once.

She turned to see Dr. Melan standing by the hood of the car, his hands in the air. Two figures confronted him, both of them instantly recognizable by their size: the giant command-er of the Skaldi trials and his youngest son. A third person moved out from behind Udain, holding Athan's silver pistol in one hand while he balanced himself on a single crutch with the other. His pale, scrawny arm trembled as he took an un-steady step toward the doctor, and Michelle's heart fell when she saw who it was.

Laman Genn.

"So close, Ash," Laman's younger brother called out. "And yet so pathetically far."

Arachne shot a guilty glance at her companion, and Michelle had the horrible thought that the whole thing had been a trick—the story about Kareem, the escape plan, every-thing. But then she told herself that made no sense; Arachne wouldn't have risked her life in the missile rail line, wouldn't have exposed herself to the threat of the Skaldi, if all she'd meant to do was betray Michelle now. The guilt in the sen-try's eyes had a simpler explanation: she was furious at having been outsmarted by Athan Genn, and she was debating whether to light the fuse to deprive him of his prize, even if that meant destroying Kareem's child herself.

Michelle watched the woman wrestle with the impulse, and she saw the moment when Arachne realized she couldn't do it. Raising her hands above her head, she dropped the fuse and left it coiled on the floor while she and Michelle ap-proached the car.

Athan wore his typical smug grin. Michelle saw that his wrist was splinted and bandaged, probably broken by Arach-ne's karate chop. That explained why Laman was holding the pistol, and also why the younger boy sounded even more gleeful than usual at this culminating victory over his rival.

"Ash, Ash, Ash," he said, shaking his head like a father disappointed with his teenage daughter's report card. "This could have worked out so well for you. Just think where you'd have been if you'd followed orders. The reward, the glory, the everlasting thanks of a grateful world." He clucked his tongue. "You used to be smarter than that."

Arachne said nothing. For the first time since Michelle had known her, she looked utterly defeated, and each word that came from Athan Genn's mouth made her shrink into herself even more.

"We've been watching you all along from the situation room," he said. "Very educational place, that. Reams of data to keep an avid reader like myself occupied. For example, did you know that the good doctor wasn't the lowly functionary around here he tries to make himself out to be? Quite the contrary, he was the head honcho at this place, the one who designed the Skaldi germ plasma." He turned to Melan. "Tell her, Doc. Tell Ash how you bred her boyfriend's clones to test the germ plasma on back in the day, until your little experiment went slightly, shall we say, off the rails."

Melan turned a beseeching look toward Arachne, but even if he'd wanted to say anything in his defense, her face seemed to have lost its capacity for anger.

"But okay, maybe you can't be expected to know everything about the shady Doctor Praneet Melan," Athan went on. "Still, to stroll with him to the only exit in this whole place without stopping to think who might be tuning in?" He displayed the miniature protograph on his unbroken wrist. "I synced this with the surveillance cameras in the situation room. I've got to tell you, I've seen some simply *fascinating* video of our leading lady this past day. In high-def, too."

He leered at Michelle, who sickened at the thought of him watching her give birth, nurse her baby, and everything else.

"But we've got days to chat about Mistress Diana's cinematic talents," he said. "We'll drive to Texas to collect my research, and then we'll be heading back here to stay."

"You're coming *back*?" Michelle found the voice to ask.

"Of course. Why slave away out in the boonies when I have a primo facility like this at my disposal? I'll admit it's a bit of a fixer-upper, but I've got time." With a smirk, he held out his unbandaged hand. "Laman, if you'll kindly escort our Cinderella to her waiting carriage, we'll be on our way."

Laman limped forward on his crutch, pointing the pistol at Michelle. She had a moment when she considered ending it all—jumping at Laman, forcing him to shoot her. But it was one thing to kill everyone as Arachne had contemplated, another to get herself killed. That would only leave her baby even more defenseless than she was now.

"I've got big plans for the both of you," Athan said gaily as he opened the Hummer's back door. "From what I can tell from the doc's data, many of the original test subjects weren't suitable for assimilating with the germ plasma. It could mimic anyone it came in contact with, but the genetic hybridization didn't always produce sustainable lines. A baby that's already part-Skaldi, though—I'm guessing I could clone *that* to great effect. And your eggs must be some kind of special if they were able to accept the Skaldi genome."

Hugging the baby to her chest, Michelle entered the back seat of the Hummer, where Melan already sat with his head in his hands. The opposite door opened, and Michelle gasped when she saw Udain herding the thin frames of Nausikaa and

Aristodeme into the seat beside Dr. Melan. She spun to look at Athan, who stood leaning casually against the door frame.

"Additional test subjects," he said. "Shipped here direct from a Russian orphanage, as I understand it. The ones that attacked you yesterday were pure mimics, born out of the germ plasma."

Michelle didn't know whether it was relief or dismay she felt at the knowledge that Nausikaa and Aristodeme had survived, only to become renewed subjects of the Skaldi experiments. With his affinity for sensing others' pain, Athan kept talking in a conversational way while the twins withdrew ever deeper into their forced blankness.

"I haven't determined which one of these two was the original, or if there was a master that came before them both," he said. "I do know that Dad found them promising enough to take them with him on his jaunt back east, which gives me high hopes for their line down the road. But"—he gestured at the opposite door, where his father was squeezing Tyris and Petra into the back seat beside the twins—"it was the little spy that got the most attention around here after the fabulous Subject K-1."

"Petra?"

"Sure, if that's what you want to call it. There must have been a hundred of the tykes running around this place at one point. This seems to be the only one that got free, though." He reached across Michelle to give Petra's cheek a pinch, but the child pulled away. "Sneaky little sucker, isn't it?"

Petra's eyes flicked around the cabin of the Hummer as if she were hunting for a way out. The girl's familiarity with this place now made sense to Michelle, as did her peculiar gifts and secretive personality. Kareem, the twins, Petra, her own baby, herself—was everyone nothing but raw materials in the hands of the men who'd built this place?

Udain Genn slammed the rear doors of the Hummer and circled to the front to close the hood. Michelle saw the giant form advancing on Arachne, heard his youngest son speaking in an amused voice.

"Now, Ash," Athan said. "Whatever are we going to do with *you*?"

Michelle wasn't sure what happened next. There was the sound of Laman's crutch clattering to the cement, the thud of his body as it fell against the driver's side window. His pistol discharged, loud and close enough that her ears hurt, but when she looked frantically at her baby and the others in the backseat, no one seemed to have been hit. The baby was awake and screaming, probably startled by the noise, and Michelle was trying to comfort her when Arachne's hand reached into the car and yanked the two of them out. Michelle saw the huge black shadow of Udain Genn looming over her and tried to shield the baby with her body, but another shot rang out, and the Tall Man fell beside the car with a ground-shaking crash.

"Laman, you worthless piece of—" Athan swore, then he grew very quiet.

Arachne held Laman's gun pointed at his younger brother. Laman himself sat against the car beside the discarded crutch, grimacing in pain as he pressed bloody hands to his bad hip. The boys' father was sprawled on his back, unimaginably huge even then. His breath came in spasmodic gasps, his blood pooling on the cement from a wound to his stomach. But that wasn't why Athan Genn had run out of words to say.

All around them, the garage had grown dark, the over-head light occluded by a black mass that spread across the ceiling and crept down the walls like a monstrous fungus. Where it touched the ground, figures were growing, child-size bodies with long arms and whipping tails. Across their blank faces, human features flashed and rippled like reflections in water: the twins, Petra, Dr. Melan, Arachne. Herself. Even— Michelle caught her breath—Kareem, looking sad and scared and lonely, his eyes reaching across the empty space to find hers or Arachne's. The only one who wasn't mirrored in the Skaldi's faces was the one they had never touched, the wailing baby she held in her arms.

"Back away," Arachne said to Michelle. "Take the girls."

"What about Laman?"

Arachne cast a careless glance at the boy who sat with his back against the car, his face paler than it had ever been.

"Leave him," she said.

Michelle scooted around to the passenger side of the car and let the girls out. Tyris and Petra grew wide-eyed now that they were this close to the screaming baby, but they obedient-ly joined hands with the twins and followed Michelle to where Arachne waited. The sentry had armed herself with one of the canisters, and had opened the valve enough that a fine mist was rising around her, holding the Skaldi momen-tarily at bay.

Laman lifted his eyes to Michelle's. His face was tight with fear; his mouth formed a single word that might have been *please*. Looking around the garage, she saw that the Skaldi had grown to adult size, standing on two legs and wearing the faces of strangers, men and women who must have worked here before the creatures gained control. All of them carried the same haunted, pleading look she'd seen so often on the doctor's face.

"We're taking Melan," she said. "And Laman. We can't leave them here."

"We don't have time for this, Diana," Arachne warned as the Skaldi took a step closer.

"We always have time for mercy," she said, and leaned into the car where the doctor sat.

He glanced at her, his eyes the same as those of the mimics outside, and then at her baby. An expression of wonder softened his features, but when Michelle offered her hand, he shook his head.

"My children are safe," he said. "It will be better this way."

Michelle could practically feel the icy breath of the Skaldi around her, could smell their noxious flesh. She removed the miniature spray can from her pocket and stepped away from the car, waving the canister at the creatures in warning. When they retreated, she leaned down and held a hand out to Laman.

He took it, wincing as he grabbed his crutch and climbed to his feet. The hip wound didn't look as bad as she'd first thought; the bleeding had mostly stopped, and she couldn't find any damage where the bullet had entered. Hopefully, it had only grazed him. With his arm draped across Michelle's shoulders and the baby howling at the top of her lungs, they backed with the girls toward the garage door. Arachne had opened the valve of her canister wider, and the Skaldi shied from her, closing in instead on the boy beside the Hummer.

Athan Genn hadn't moved, not even to check on his father. He stood by the car, dwarfed by its blackness, surrounded by the even darker forms of the approaching Skaldi. His face was eerily calm, and his voice was as cold and dead as if he were already one of them. "Don't waste your time trying to use Laman as a hostage. You don't think I care what happens to him, do you?"

"I don't think about you at all," Michelle said. "Your brother is the only one of your family worth saving."

Athan's eyes burned into her. "This isn't over, you know. Not by a long shot. No matter where you go, no matter how far you run, the Skaldi will be hunting for you, and for your baby. They'll find it, and bring it back, and I'll be right here waiting." He showed his teeth. "Then you'll *really* find out what this little boy can dream up."

Arachne fired again. Athan gripped his knee and fell, blood spurting from the wound. The Skaldi backed off momentarily, as if they were hesitant to acquire a damaged body. Then they reversed course, and Athan and Udain disappeared beneath the swarm. A thin, childish scream emerged from the blackness before falling silent.

"Be ready to run," Arachne breathed.

They'd reached the door. Arachne closed the valve of her canister and rolled it toward the melee of Skaldi. Quickly, she punched a code into the keypad beside the door, and it rumbled open. When Michelle and the baby, Laman, and the girls had slipped outside, she raised the silver pistol one more time and fired at the canister that lay on the floor.

It exploded, the fireball rushing over the Skaldi on the outer edge of the swarm. Another blast followed as one of the tanks by the car detonated. Michelle could see the Skaldi's bodies through the flames; some had melted into a black slurry, but others seemed to welcome the fire, spreading their arms wide as if to drink it in. Athan and Udain were nowhere to be seen, but a loud hissing noise could be heard building inside the garage.

"Run!" Arachne shouted, slamming her fist against the keypad to close the door.

Michelle held the baby close as she turned to run, but Laman's hip gave out from under him and he fell to the dusty ground. She was leaning down to help him to his feet when the entire garage exploded in an inferno of fire and smoke. She watched the fireball sweep toward them, heard Laman scream. In the instant she had to react, she squeezed the baby to her chest and huddled around her to shield her from the blast. Then something hard struck her head, and with her daughter's wails echoing in her ears, she slid into darkness.

# Chapter 19

Kareem came to her as he had the time before. He looked weak and weary, as if he'd traveled a long way across the desert to reach her. His skin was ashy, his black hair hanging lifelessly beside wasted cheeks. But his eyes were the same as always, and they gazed at her with a tenderness she could never get enough of.

"I thought I told you to stay away," she said.

"This is the last time, I promise. I had to see our daughter just once before I go."

Michelle looked down and was surprised to find the baby in her arms; she'd feared that she'd lost her, too. She handed the bundled form to Kareem, who knelt beside her and held the infant as naturally as if he'd done it a hundred times. Knowing what she knew now, Michelle wondered if the original Kareem had ever fathered a child, if *her* Kareem remembered who he'd been years before, when Arachne, not Michelle, had been the light of his eyes.

He touched the baby's cheek, smoothed her flaxen hair. When he bent to kiss her head, Michelle blurted out, "I wanted her to have hair like yours."

"I like it this way. She's so beautiful. Like her mother."

"Have you looked at me lately?"

"You'll always be beautiful. And now you'll never be alone."

Fear gripped her at the memory of Athan Genn's final words. "She's not safe, Kareem. They'll be searching for her, and I don't know if I can keep her hidden forever."

"You don't think Udain and his son are dead?"

"I don't think evil like that ever dies. If not them, it'll be someone else. You have to help me. You have to tell me what to do."

He shook his head sadly, then handed the baby back to her. She clutched her daughter to her chest as Kareem stood.

"You'll do the right thing," he said. "I trust you."

He bent down to kiss her. The touch of his lips brought something immeasurably sad to her heart, a longing and a loss she knew she'd never outlive. When he pulled away, she saw in his eyes that he felt it, too.

"I love you," she said. "Thank you for giving her to me."

He smiled and turned away. He seemed to be fading into a blur of desert heat, but he looked back just before she lost sight of him.

"I'll be waiting for you," he said, and then he was gone.

SHE WOKE TO the most surprising thing she could think of, though it was something she'd woken to almost every day for the first seventeen years of her life.

The aroma of coffee wafted over her. It was the smell of early mornings in the Simmons household, the smell on her mother's and father's breath when they kissed her goodbye at elementary school, the smell of the first cup they'd let her drink at the kitchen table when she turned fifteen (though they didn't know she'd already shared Starbucks with the older girls on the track team starting freshman year). She'd never become a habitual coffee drinker; she didn't want to turn into Janine, who was a nervous wreck without her daily dose of lattes. But to smell it now, something so normal in the midst of a life that had turned so precarious, made her ache with memory. Without opening her eyes, she drew the smell deep into her lungs, holding it there, never wanting to let it go.

"You're up," Arachne's voice came from the darkness behind her closed eyelids. "Don't try to pretend you're not."

Michelle opened her eyes. Arachne sat a few paces off, tending a coffeepot over a small camp stove. It wasn't morning after all; she knew the difference between a rising and a setting sun, and the red globe that hovered over the desert dunes was definitely on its way down. Tyris and Petra played one of their silent games in the evening shadows by the front bumper of Arachne's truck, pattycake or something else they'd invented that required them to hold hands as often as possible. Michelle wondered what had happened to their doll. That thought made her touch her chest where the baby should be, but there was nothing there. She looked around wildly, then breathed a sigh of relief when Aristodeme came around the side of the truck holding the swaddled infant in her arms. Nausikaa kneeled over a blanketed shape that lay at the rear of the vehicle, but it was only when Michelle propped herself on an elbow that she could tell who it was.

Laman reclined beneath the blanket, his eyes closed. Michelle was momentarily worried, but then she saw his chest rise and fall, while the first aid kit on the ground reassured her that the twins had dressed his hip wound. His face looked pained, his hook nose and gaunt cheeks even more deeply cut than she remembered. His younger brother's taunt came back to her, and it carried a deeper significance than before. Laman wasn't a hostage, that much was sure. But now that he'd survived, could they risk keeping him with them?

"He'll be all right," Arachne said. "I put out the fire before either of you got burned too bad."

She poured coffee into a tin cup then rose, bringing the steaming drink to Michelle. She clucked when she saw Michelle's hesitation to take it.

"Having a little coffee won't hurt the baby," she said. "Plus we've got enough formula to keep her going if you ever want to take a break."

Michelle accepted the cup and inhaled the scent. She took a tentative sip and felt warmth and energy spread through her at once. "Where'd you get formula?"

"Brought it from the compound in Texas. They had cases and cases of the stuff in the dispensary. Now, stop looking at me like that," she said. "It's just the regular, garden-variety kind. Athan Genn might have been an evil genius, but he hadn't cracked the code for baby formula."

Michelle set the coffee cup aside and looked over to where Aristodeme held her baby. The tween had a bottle to the baby's mouth and was watching with intense concentration as the infant hungrily guzzled.

"I should be the one to do that," Michelle said, and was about to rise when Arachne held out a hand.

"Let someone else take a turn. You got a pretty bad knock on the head earlier today, and we're all happy to chip in."

With some reluctance, Michelle settled back. Her head did ache—as did her stitches from the birth—and a few moments of rest seemed like the greatest gift anyone could offer.

"You're *all* happy to chip in?" she asked. "Including you?"

Arachne sipped from her own cup. "I know less about babies than just about anyone on the planet. But considering I might *be* one of the only people left on the planet, that raises my profile significantly, don't you agree?"

Michelle tried to smile, but she couldn't help feeling that the joke miscarried. How Arachne could laugh through a lifetime of pain was beyond her, unless that was the only thing that kept her going. Maybe, someday, she'd learn to do the same.

"When are we leaving?" she asked.

"As soon as you feel up to it. No rush, though. I checked the base, and it's sealed tight as a drum." She sniffed a laugh. "Truth be told, I wasn't sure that stunt with the gas would work. But I wasn't about to tell anyone that."

"And what are we going to do with Laman?"

"We should start by thanking him."

"For what, exactly?"

Arachne cocked her head, looking at Michelle curiously. "You really don't know, do you?"

"Should I?"

"He's the one who got us out of there," Arachne said. "I'm fast, but not *that* fast. If he hadn't tripped, I never would have been able to take the Clone Ranger's gun off him."

"So we should thank him because he's a klutz?"

Arachne shook her head. "He tripped on purpose, Michelle. There's no doubt in my mind. He looked at me, and I saw it in his eyes the second before it happened. If you remember back in the rail line, he was the one who bumped into Udain. He's been trying to help us all along."

Michelle thought back to the moment when Athan had been the one with the gun and Arachne had disarmed him. Laman *had* created a distraction by falling down the stairs, but that was just because he was a hopeless loser, wasn't it?

Wasn't it?

"If you knew he was trying to help us," she asked, "why'd you shoot him?"

"Playing along, naturally. So Athan wouldn't suspect. I barely nicked him. If I'd wanted to kill him, I'd have gutted him like I did his old man."

"But you told me to leave Laman behind."

At that, Arachne's face broke into a wicked grin. "I knew you wouldn't listen to me. And you proved me right as always, thank you very much."

Michelle was silent. The idea that Laman had worked out their escape at the last minute didn't sit right with her; it was as if he was gambling her life, and the life of her baby, on nothing more substantial than covert glances and dumb luck. Then she reflected on the risk he'd taken to save her and her child, the sacrifice he'd made. If he'd failed, it would have meant his death. Now that he'd succeeded, it meant a life of running and hiding, of danger and starvation and fear, and with what as his reward?

"Why did he do it?" she asked Arachne.

The sentry gave her a knowing look. "I think you should ask him that yourself."

Michelle turned toward the truck. Laman was sitting up against the bumper, not facing their way, but Michelle had the distinct impression that he was waiting for their conversation to end. Giving Arachne a *here goes nothing* eye roll, she stood and headed toward the truck. Her baby was done feeding and had fallen right to sleep; Michelle could only hope that would become a regular pattern. She took the bundle from Aristodeme and walked the rest of the way to Laman, feeling a little lightheaded from the coffee or the head injury or something else.

She stopped in front of him. He looked up at her with feigned nonchalance, as if she'd just happened to swing by for a neighborly visit.

"How are you feeling?" she asked.

"I'm okay." He stretched the bad leg out in front of him, grunting as the hip popped into place. "A little sore."

She stood looking down at him, not knowing what to say. She almost wished the baby weren't being so peaceful; at least that would give her something to do. "Are you all right to walk?"

"Should be." He reached for the crutch that lay beside the bedroll, then hopped up on his good leg. The way he struggled across the desert sand, Michelle couldn't decide if the incident in the garage had been real or play-acted. When they reached a spot far enough away that the others couldn't hear, she stopped, and he came to a clumsy halt beside her.

"Laman," she began. "Arachne told me ... she said that you ... "

He waved a hand. "I'm just happy you're okay."

"Laman ... "

"You know," he said, looking out over the distance, "when I was alone there in the dark, I had a lot of time to think things through. I was angry, because I'd tried to help out and then it seemed like, well, like I was being blamed for stuff that wasn't my fault. But then I looked at it the other way, and I thought to myself, how would *I* feel under the circumstances? And I started thinking, what could I do to prove that I wasn't like Athan and my dad, that I was better than the people I'd always been afraid to stand up to? And then, when the two of them found me down there, I knew what I had to do. I was just lucky I had a chance to do it, I guess."

He turned to her, and she leaned forward to kiss his cheek. He reddened, the color deepening when she said, "Thank you, Laman. For saving our lives."

"You're welcome. But I'm afraid we're not out of the woods yet."

Balancing himself on the crutch, he pulled Dr. Melan's battered computer tablet from his belt. The screen was cracked, but the illuminated display showed the map of the tunnels she'd drawn before they found the lunchroom. He touched the screen and brought up a new floor plan, one she didn't recognize. When he zoomed in, three bright red points of light flashed in the middle of the screen.

"This is how Athan and my dad found me," he said. "And how we found you. Everyone on the Texas base must have had some kind of tracker put in them, and the tablets and wrist cuffs show their position. I don't know if the doc knew about the trackers, though you'd think he would, unless it was Athan who implanted them. Maybe he didn't know what their range was. I'm thinking you got yours right after we brought you into the base."

Michelle stared at the screen. "When did you get yours?"

"That's the crazy thing. I have no idea. I don't even know where it is. Mine, or anyone's."

"Did ... do you think Dr. Melan inserted one in ... "

"Your baby?" He reflected for a moment. "Ash was there, right?"

"Every second."

"Then I doubt he had time. But that's not our real problem. Look here."

He zoomed in as much as he could. The red lights flashed the same as before, but at this magnification, Michelle could see what he was pointing at.

"They're moving," she said.

He nodded. "Which either means the three of them are alive, or something is moving their bodies. Moving *in* their bodies, more likely."

Michelle sank to the sand, holding the baby against her. After all this, could it be possible that Udain Genn and his son were still going to come for her, for her baby? Was there anything she could do, anywhere she could go on earth, that they wouldn't pursue her?

Laman sat beside her, sticking his injured leg out straight and tucking the tablet into his belt. His hand lay in his lap for a long moment before he moved it toward hers. "Can I?"

She nodded. He took her hand and squeezed it with the lightest of pressure.

"I'm not afraid of them," he said.

"But I am," she told him. "Laman, you don't know … you *can't* know what it's like to live in fear every moment of your life, not for yourself but for someone you carried inside your own body, someone who's that much a part of you."

"You're right, I can't. But I did think of something that might make it easier for you and your baby."

He released her hand and dug in his jeans pocket. His fingers emerged with a ring, a simple, unadorned gold band that gleamed in the evening sunlight. He looked down at the ground, and she saw that his hand was trembling.

"This was my mom's," he said. "Before she died, she gave it to me. She said she didn't want to be buried with it. She wanted me to have it, to keep until I grew up. Until I was ready to … "

Michelle tilted her head to see his eyes, but they were hidden behind the black mop of hair. "Yes?"

He looked at her, placing the ring in her hand. "Until I was ready to get married."

Michelle let out an involuntary gasp. Laman held her gaze, not blushing for once. She tried to think of the right thing to say, but the first words that came out of her mouth were, "You're only sixteen."

He did blush at that. "I'm almost seventeen. And after what we've been through, I feel a lot older."

Michelle touched her whitened hair, then laid her hand on the scarred cheeks she bore from Kareem's fiery death. "What would you do with a crazy old lady like me?"

"I wouldn't mind. I would take care of you, and him—"

"Her."

"Her." He gave Michelle an embarrassed smile. "Does she have a name?"

"I've been a little too busy to think about that."

"You and your names," he said, shaking his head. "Anyway, I wouldn't expect you to … to think of me as a *real* husband. But I'd be there if you needed me. I know my dad and Athan better than anyone, and I learned a lot about surviving on our way out west. I'd be willing to fight for you and … for her."

Michelle considered it. Being married to Laman—even if it was a marriage in name only—might not be the worst thing in the world. He was kind, and caring, and he'd more than proved his loyalty despite everything she'd done to push him away. She couldn't imagine herself ever being attracted to him, but that didn't matter; she couldn't imagine being attracted to anyone ever again. It was when she had that thought that she knew what her answer had to be. She placed the ring in his palm, folding his fingers over it.

"Thank you, Laman," she said. "Really. But it would never work out. I've spent my whole life depending on other people, and now I feel like I have to be free. And," she added, surprised by herself even as she said the words, "so does she."

Laman looked stunned, maybe from the shock of her rejection. "Your baby? How can *she* be free?"

"She can be free of me," Michelle said. "Free of a fate she had no part in making. Don't you see?" Her conviction strengthened as she spoke, though her heart broke at what she was about to propose. "Whether your dad and brother have been taken by the Skaldi or not, they'll be looking for her, and if she stays with me, they'll always be able to track her. Without me, she has a chance not only to survive, but to forget the past, to shed the burden of who she is. She can disappear and never be heard from again. Then she can truly be free, even if she can't be mine."

Laman squeezed the ring, and his eyes were bright. "Who will she go with?"

"Arachne," Michelle said instantly.

"She might have a tracker, too. I'd have to use the doc's tablet to check."

"But she's *Arachne*," Michelle said. "She's smarter than all of us put together, and besides, they won't be looking for her. She can take the truck, the one with the formula. She'll know how to hide, from Skaldi as well as from everyone else. The girls will help her."

She could see in his eyes that he didn't agree. "And you?"

"I'll find my own way."

"But then," he said, swallowing, "*I'll* never see you again."

"That's right," she said. "It would put all of us, including you, at too much risk if anyone knew where I was."

He opened his mouth as if to utter another objection, but he swallowed again without saying a thing. The way he looked at her, she knew what he'd been about to say. So she answered him, in words she hadn't known she had inside her until now.

"I think," she said, "that everyone has a secret love. Someone they can never have, but someone they want all the more strongly because of that. It doesn't mean they can't love anyone else. But it does mean they can never fully give their heart to another."

He was crying for real now. "I don't have anyone like that."

"Of course you do," she said. "You have me."

He cried even harder, and she held out a hand to draw him close while, with the other, she cradled her sleeping baby to her side. They lay down on the dune, his face pressed against her shoulder, and Michelle felt the tidal pull of the future washing over her. The baby's breaths and the boy's cries were the two rhythms that rocked her to sleep, but she knew that, when daylight came, she was bound to let them both go.

# Chapter 20

Arachne roused her at first light.

Laman was gone. He'd left the ring. It lay on the ground beside her, gleaming in the morning sun. She reached out to touch it, but didn't. She'd given up everything: her home, her name, her love. Soon, she'd give up her baby, too. She would have nothing that tied her to the past anymore.

She left the ring there, gold against the dusty red.

The baby was awake and fussing, making the little choked cries that Michelle had learned preceded full-throated screaming. Arachne went to wake the girls while Michelle nursed her daughter one last time. Her breasts felt swollen and tender; it was a relief to have some of the pressure slurped away. Even when the baby was finished and had fallen quickly asleep, Michelle felt full to overflowing. She wondered if she could express some of the milk, store it for Arachne to use later. But that would never work; there was no way to keep it cold. Of all the things she might miss, she knew she'd miss this the most. She could go without security, without good food, without sex; she'd had sex only twice in her life, and it had been wonderful both times, but it would never be as wonderful again, so what was there to miss? But the feeling of holding another human being against her, looking into her face—she still hadn't opened her eyes—while life flowed from her own body to the baby's … It was almost too much, and if anything made her second-guess her decision, this was it.

The sun stood above the eastern horizon and the day held a peculiar stillness when Michelle finished changing and bundling the baby, then packed the few supplies she could spare to help prepare her daughter for the long road ahead. The rest of the wipes, the cleaned bottle Aristodeme had nursed her with. *What will she do for diapers when she gets bigger?* she thought, and that thought was followed by another: *She doesn't even have any clothes.* But Arachne, she was sure, would find a way. Looking at her daughter sleeping peacefully in her baby burrito, Michelle tried to imagine the toddler, then the girl, then the woman she would become, but the future was closed to her, a gated barrier she couldn't see through. A place she'd never be able to go to play with her daughter, sing to her, hold her at night when a nightmare came. The life she'd borne inside her would become nothing but a dream, a hope for a time she would never see.

Michelle buried her face beside her daughter's, inhaled her sweet scent, and wept for everything she'd lost, everything she would never have. Each time she thought the tears might stop, another reminder of what she was giving up buffeted her, and they started again. Her tears were a single word, a word with no end, and that word was *never.* At seventeen, that was the one word she'd never thought her life could hold.

In time, her weeping subsided enough that she became aware of other sounds, Arachne and the twins loading up the truck. She gave her daughter one more squeeze, kissed her cheeks one more time. Then she stood to meet Arachne, who was coming toward her, wiping her hands on her black pants. The silver pistol with which the redoubtable sentry had defeated Udain and Athan Genn hung at her side.

"You okay?" she asked, but Michelle could only shake her head in answer.

"I drove Laman to the other truck," Arachne continued. "Gave him a few lessons along the way. As long as he drives slowly, he should be all right."

"That's good."

"Also, I keep meaning to tell you. I've got your bow and arrows in the back. You should take them, just in case. Before we go."

Michelle looked at her. "Laman told you what I decided to do?"

Arachne nodded.

"And you'll do it?"

"You don't even need to ask me that," Arachne said, her eyes sparkling. "This is Kareem's baby, and you're ... well, you're like a daughter to me. I'll take care of her. I'll die before I let any harm come to her."

They held each other for a long time before Michelle placed the sleeping baby in Arachne's arms. When they pulled away, she felt her heart break for good, and she could only be thankful that this meant she would never have to feel anything like it again.

"Here," Arachne said, wiping her own eyes. "Laman left this for you."

She handed Michelle a piece of paper, college-ruled and raggedly torn at the edge where it had been yanked from a spiral notebook. It was covered, front and back, with words written in blue ballpoint. His penmanship—not to mention his spelling and grammar—was as messy as everything about him, but at least deciphering his note gave her something else to think about. She tucked a strand of white hair behind her ear and read.

*Dear Diana,*

*I'm sorry I left without telling you goodby, but I thought it might be better that way. Their were so many things I wanted to say to you, and some of them might have been alright, but some of them might have been things you wouldn't want to hear, and I wasn't sure which were which. So I'll try to keep this short and sweet, just to say the most important things you have to know. Plus Ash is looking impatiant, so I better not take to much time or she might kill me.*

There was a smiley face after that, then the note continued.

*I want you to know, first, that I'm not going to take any stupid risks with my life. I'm going to lay low for a while, spend some time out here on my own learning how to live before I even think of going back to the base in Texas. If I do go back, I'll be careful and make sure I'm not walking into any kind of trap. Maybe my dad and Athan will show up eventualy—as theirselves I mean—and if they do, I can tell them some story to mislead them about you and Ash without making them suspitious. But if they never return, I guess that'll mean the Skaldi trials will shut down, at least at that lab, and maybe I can convince some of the people to come away with me. To start a new survival colony, one thats trying to defeat the Skaldi for good.*

*But even if my dad and Athan do come back, I'm dettermined not to stay with them forever. That would be taking the easy way out. Sooner or later, things would come to a head between my dad and I, and when they did, I'd have to face him. I can't allways be backing down, letting him and Athan have there way. So I just wanted you to know that you don't have to worry about me giving up any of your secrets, or telling them where you or your baby are at, because I'm done with being that guy. I'm going to be a man soon, and maybe I'm going to be a father myself one of these days, and I can't let someone else run my life. And I wanted to thank you for helping me to see that. I'll never forget you or the things you've done for me.*

*And the last thing I wanted to tell you is that, even though I understand why you made the desicion you did, and I'll never try to change your mind about any of it, I do hope I get to see you again someday. I actualy hope that all of us might be together again, me and you and Ash and the girls, and your baby to. Maybe, when I start my own survival colony, we could all be together like that. But I promise that if that happens, I won't let on that I know who you are, I'll just pretend your—what did you call yourself?—some crazy old lady who just happened to join up with us. But at the same time, if we do end up together again, I'll do my best to protect you, and everyone else, and not leave anyone behind. Because you know what I allways say, thats what a leader does.*

There was another smiley face, then an illegible scrawl that must have been his signature. After that, he'd written a final note:

*P.S. I know your real name is Michele. But I won't tell anyone that either.*

She smiled to herself as she folded the note and put it in her pocket. Leave it to Laman to get her name right *and* wrong at the same time.

Arachne held the baby in both hands, looking incrementally less awkward than the last time she'd tried it. "Anything important?"

"Not really. Something about starting his own colony."

Arachne laughed. "I wouldn't put it past him."

"Let's just hope he's fixed himself up by then."

"He's a late bloomer," Arachne said. "Give him ten, fifteen years, you might be surprised."

Michelle painted a smile on her face to keep the sadness from spilling out. "And what about your colony? Do you have a name for it?"

"I'm going to stick with Survival Colony Nine," Arachne said. "That's when she was born, by the way," she added, hoisting the baby as if she were a trophy to be shown off. "The ninth of December. I know dates don't matter much anymore, but I like to keep track. Oh, and I almost forgot."

She switched the baby to her shoulder, and Michelle saw that Arachne would soon become adept at the motions of motherhood—more adept, in time, than herself. The bitterness of that foreknowledge was in her mouth when Arachne reached inside her jacket and withdrew the collection jar.

"I think you should have this," she said. "For keeps."

Michelle stared at it, the green glass catching glints from the sun. She hesitated, wanted to accept it, but her hand wouldn't leave her side.

"Come on," Arachne coaxed. "It belongs to you, and it's much more than dead cells. It's *him*, and what you had together. It's memory and love and loss all rolled into one. You should take it, and if you find the mountains you were look-ing for, then you can do what you were planning to do."

Michelle reached out and took the jar, feeling its smooth and slightly cool surface against her skin. She tucked it into her own jacket, beside her heart.

"Thank you," she said softly.

"You're welcome," Arachne replied. "Take good care of him, you hear me?"

Michelle nodded. Every second they lingered, she be-came more and more aware that it would never be enough, that when the time came for them to part, these final seconds would be gone and their memory would only sharpen her be-reavement.

"Remember," she said. "She can't ever know I'm her mother. She can't even know my name."

Arachne placed a comforting hand on Michelle's shoul-der. "Speaking of names, what's hers?"

Michelle thought about it, but nothing immediate came to mind. She considered *Rosie*, but quickly decided she didn't want her daughter to bear that burden. Maybe this wasn't the time, or maybe she shouldn't be the one to give the baby a name. Maybe that would only make it harder to let her go.

"You name her," she told Arachne. "She's yours now."

Arachne looked taken aback. Then she smiled, as if she'd been hoping for this opportunity all along.

"Kareem told me a story once," she said. "About a girl who lived where he was from centuries before his time. May-be it was only a legend. He said that she led her people in bat-tle against impossible odds, but in the end, she won. I guess by never giving up." She held the baby out for Michelle to see. "Her name was Aleka."

Michelle tested the sound. It was a fitting name, she decided, for a child of sorrow who'd fought her way to freedom, only to face a life adrift on the western desert. She would need courage, and luck, and most of all, the strength to keep going even when it seemed the darkness was closing in all around her.

"Aleka," she whispered, and her baby opened her pale gray eyes for the first time, staring with a wordless query at her mother's face.

THE END

The Book of the Huntress, Volume Two ends here

The hunt concludes in *Scarred City* (Book of the
Huntress, Volume Three), due June 2021

# Sneak Peek

*Scarred City*
(Book of the Huntress, Volume Three)

Read on for a preview!

# Prologue

The Skaldi chieftain stood at a window high above the city, gazing westward over the desert.

For millennia, travelers heading in that direction would have arrived at one of the wonders of the western world: a great saltwater lake that stretched for miles across the arid landscape. But like the city that had taken its name, the lake had been mostly swallowed by desert in the past sixteen years, shriveling to a vestige of molten gold against the red-brown earth. Though its waters had always risen and fallen in response to cycles of rain and evaporation, now it was on the verge of vanishing entirely, leaving nothing but a shallow bowl as a reminder of the deceptive oasis whose promise had never been able to quench the wanderer's thirst.

The Skaldi turned from the unappealing vista to face the empty room. The creature had taken the form of a man, but it was not a man. The eyes that flicked restlessly this way and that saw everything their long-dead host would have seen: the shattered glass, dust-covered table and chairs, and scorched walls of this boardroom in one of the few remaining sky-scrapers of the scarred city. But they also perceived traces no human eyes could see—paths of organic molecules floating in the air, webs of movement emanating from living things far distant from the city. Human beings thought Skaldi detected prey by sense of smell, but they were wrong. It was in their nature to feel the presence of life energy and be drawn to it. From miles away, they tapped into this living force, an irresistible lure that alone could fill their empty bodies.

Today, the chieftain had no time to search for the vital energy it craved. The sickness had come upon it, as it did in every Skaldi's life cycle, and the creature ached with hunger so keen it could barely concentrate on the task at hand. If food did not come to it within weeks—possibly days—its body would simply disintegrate, melting into the common dust that covered this shell of a city.

Its eyes turned to the door as others of its kind shuffled in. There were ten of them, a core group their leader had assembled from the hundreds that still dwelled in the city, themselves a mere fraction of the swarm that had descended on this place months ago. Many of the original host had departed weeks earlier to search for food; many more had died the final death and faded into the general dust. Those that entered the boardroom wore the body of the last victim they had consumed, men and women and children they had found wandering the city and attacked without thought or remorse. Yet even those that had feasted on young humans bursting with vitality had turned listless and gray, with skin drawn tightly across their faces and eyes that bulged with the unbearable hunger inside them. None had reached their desiccated final state, but they maneuvered carefully around the husks of furniture lest an accidental bump or jostle cause parts of their bodies to flake into dust.

Once they had settled gingerly into their seats, the chieftain stepped forward, riveting their attention as it stood at the head of the boardroom table. The Skaldi shared no love, but they were capable of coordination, teamwork, collective decision-making. Insofar as their leader could read their minds, it judged that they were committed to a common purpose. The sickness had come upon all of them at once, and there was nothing here to feed it—nothing their own bodies could supply. If not for that fact, they might have turned on each other, but as it was, desperation united them.

"My kindred," the chieftain said, and the others bowed their heads.

"You know our situation," the thing at the head of the table continued. "The city is dead, its population decimated. A few survivors remain, but nowhere near the numbers we need to sustain ourselves. We require a new infusion of life, or we will pass into nothingness like the great majority of us that came before."

"Could this not have been foreseen?" one of the others spoke. It was tall and thin, a woman at one time; now it seemed a shadow thrown by chance sunlight against a wall. "Could the Skaldi not have anticipated that to feed so recklessly, so wantonly, was to doom ourselves to nonbeing?"

"What else could we have done?" another retorted. This one was shaped like a child, and spoke in the piping voice that had cried out in fear and delight when it was alive. "We are what we are, and must feed."

"Until nothing remains for us to feed upon," the woman-shape replied.

"Something remains," the chieftain said. "If we have the wisdom to obtain it."

The others looked at it, quivering at this mention of fresh food. The chieftain bore their gaze for a long moment, drawing out their hunger almost to the point of madness before continuing.

"There are human life forms beyond this city," it announced at last. "Small colonies that roam the great waste to our south."

"We know this already," the skeptical one said. "We cannot reach them."

"Then we draw them to us."

"And when we exhaust them in turn?"

The chieftain snarled, its chest scar opening. Instantly, the others responded in kind. Retaining the veneer of humanity had become increasingly difficult as their hunger deepened, but the headman chastised itself for losing control. Tamping down its anger, it forced its stolen face into a conciliatory expression. When it did so, the chest scar closed, and the others in the room relaxed.

"There is yet something we can do," the chieftain answered the skeptical one's question. "Something that may enable us to overcome what we have been. It will not come without struggle and sacrifice, but if we succeed, it will give us a chance to earn immortality rather than crumbling into worthless dust."

Its eyes wandered to the door. Turning, the others became aware of something outside the room, something they had never felt before. Even with their innate capacity to detect the life force of others, the thing beyond the door eluded them; they could sense its power, but could not grasp that power's nature or dimensions. They knew only that it was a power far greater than their own, and, for the first time in the succession of lives they had stolen and lost, they felt the cold grip of the thing their host bodies had called fear.

Their eyes returned to their leader's. It smiled, and as it did, the scar that ran down its chest opened to mimic its smile.

"Let us begin," it said.

# Acknowledgments

So, whom should I embarrass today?

Let's start with my wife and children, who've been with me on this journey for the past ten-plus years, giving me the time and encouragement I needed. My kids aren't kids anymore, and they're not as awed as they used to be that their dad is a writer, but from what I can tell, they're quietly proud that I've pursued my dream. If I've helped set an example for them, I'll consider this second career a success.

Christa Yelich-Koth has been my editor for several years, and I always count on her to catch the things I miss (which, pantser that I am, adds up to a lot). The various writing groups to which I belong—my friends in Pittsburgh, the extended YA community, and the folks who love and write speculative fiction—have provided so much support of such a varied nature, it's impossible to specify my debts to them. The same goes to my favorite bookseller, Riverstone Books, who have helped me to find and keep my audience.

Which brings me to you, my readers. It might be a cliché to say you're who I'm writing for, but that doesn't make it any less true. For your time, your enthusiasm, and your faith, I am truly humbled and thankful.

# About the Author

Joshua David Bellin has been writing novels since he was eight years old (though the first few were admittedly very short). A college teacher by day, he has published numerous works of fantasy and science fiction, including the post-apocalyptic Querry Genn Saga, the deep-space adventure *Freefall*, the fantasy-adventure Ecosystem Cycle, and the Book of the Huntress series. In his free time, Josh likes to read, watch movies, and take long nature hikes with his kids. Oh, yeah, and he likes monsters. Really scary monsters.

To find out more about Josh and his books, visit his website and sign up for his e-newsletter. He promises not to send it to you more than once a month!

joshuadavidbellin.blogspot.com

# Also by Joshua David Bellin

### The Ecosystem Cycle

Only those born with the psychic power known as the Sense can survive within the planetary Ecosystem. When Sarah, a seventeen-year-old Sensor, sets out from her village on a mission of vengeance, she discovers that the Ecosystem is far more perilous than she ever dreamed.

### The Survival Colony Novels

A desert world. An embattled remnant of humanity. A monstrous enemy that mimics the bodies of the living. And two teens who might hold the key to survival.

Available from online merchants and selected booksellers